DEGENERATES

DEGENERATES

THE BOHICA CHRONICLES™ BOOK TWO

C.J. FAWCETT   JONATHAN BRAZEE

MICHAEL ANDERLE

LMBPN Publishing
PMB 196, 2540 South Maryland Pkwy
Las Vegas, NV 89109

First US edition, July 2019
Version 1.02, August 2019
Print ISBN: 978-1-64202-387-9

DEGENERATES TEAM

Thanks to the JIT Readers

Dave Hicks
Diane L. Smith
James Caplan
Peter Manis
John Ashmore
Kelly O'Donnell
Jeff Eaton
Dorothy Lloyd
Paul Westman

If we've missed anyone, please let us know!

Editor
Skyhunter Editing Team

CHAPTER ONE

Harvesters Camp; the Sahara Desert; Container Alley - Thor

It had been five days since Thor had seen another living creature. He'd given up pacing and was weak from dehydration, heat exhaustion, and lack of food. The animal lay on Charles' cot. The smell of the large man had all but disappeared. In fact, all three of his humans' scents had gone—replaced by the smell of his own stench.

The door to the converted shipping container was locked from the outside. Thor had tried to open the door several times, pulling on the handle with his teeth, but he hadn't been able to manage it. He'd been forced to defecate in a back corner of the container.

His only way to track time was the difference in temperature—sweltering hot during the day and barely tolerable at night. Aside from the slim crack at the bottom of the door, there was no light. While he didn't need the light—his enhanced eyesight made darkness irrelevant—he now grew tired of the perpetual gloom and darkness.

He wanted to run free outside and to play fetch with the old rubber tire.

Thor wanted the men to come back. Either that, or he wanted to join the other animals he could hear at night. Sounds from the Zoo would drift to him. The call of that alien place echoed in his head and he knew it was where he belonged. It was where he'd come from, after all.

A week after it had last closed, the door to the container screeched open. A man was silhouetted in the blinding daylight. Thor could hardly raise his head to look.

"What the fuck have you been doing, you dumb fucking dog?" the man growled. He yanked a bandana hastily from his pocket and clamped it over his mouth. "You aren't worth whatever that idiot is paying me to take care of you."

Thor dragged himself off the bed and wagged his tail weakly. He was careful to remain out of his caretaker's reach as he remembered the last time he had kicked him in the ribs.

The man wasn't large. He was short and thin and smelled like sweat, alcohol, and tobacco.

"Stupid goddamn animal."

He grabbed the empty water dish, stepped out of the container, and slammed the door shut behind him. Thor slunk to the center of the space and waited on shaky legs. He wasn't sure why the human didn't sound happy with him.

When he returned, the animal smelled the fresh water and moved forward. He knocked against the man as he lowered the bowl to the ground. Water sloshed out, and some soaked through his pant leg and splashed on his shoes.

"You fucking mongrel!" He straightened and swung the metal bowl at Thor's head as he jerked to a standing position. It collided with the animal's jaw with enough force to rattle his teeth.

He backed away from him, his tail tucked between his hind legs.

"Not so tough, are you?" the bully sneered. He threw the heavy metal bowl at him.

The canine wasn't fast enough, and the bowl hit him on the shoulder, which made him yelp. The man laughed.

Thor growled. His hackles raised, but he didn't attack. While he'd been conditioned not to attack humans, this one wasn't as deserving as those who usually cared for him. He might be weak, but he wasn't completely depleted of energy. Something stirred in the pit of his stomach.

"I bet you're hungry, huh?" The man leaned forward and bared his teeth at him. "Well, that's too bad. You've been a bad dog, and bad dogs don't get any food."

He pulled a beer bottle from his pocket, drained it, and threw the bottle at Thor. The animal dodged and the bottle struck the metal wall and shattered. The man laughed.

Thor picked his way carefully around the shards of glass and hopped onto Charles' cot.

Instead of leaving, the bully stepped deeper into the container. He shut the door behind him and flipped the lights on at the same time.

"You think you can just get away with shitting in the corner, huh? Don't think so, you little fucker," he said and stepped menacingly toward him. "You have to be punished for that shit."

He looked around and finally noticed a small fire extinguisher propped in the corner. With a grim smile, he picked it up and swung it a few times. Thor eyed him warily.

"Come here, mongrel," he commanded.

The animal didn't move.

"I said," he yelled, "come here."

Thor still didn't move.

"Fucking piece of shit. That's it, you goddamn dog." He raised the fire extinguisher and fired it at him.

The rushing sound it made prompted the animal from the cot and he was immediately met by the blast of white chemicals. He yelped and tried to dodge the spray.

His attacker cackled and moved forward while he continued to spray him in short bursts. Any time the creature tried to dodge out of the way or escape to another part of the container, he cut him off.

Soon, Thor was backed into a corner. The man was less than five feet away and the fire extinguisher emptied. He frowned at it, shook it, and attempted to fire it again.

Thor relaxed, the chemicals dripping from his fur. He bared his teeth at his attacker, but nothing more than that.

The man shrugged, made to turn away, then swung around and brought the fire extinguisher up in an arc. He intended to hit the animal on the head with it, but Thor lunged upward in a purely instinctive reaction and bit down on his forearm.

He screamed as the teeth sank deep and reached the bone. Reflexively, he dropped the fire extinguisher and it hit Thor's shoulder, but his jaws retained their vise-like hold.

The man drew a long knife with his free hand. "Let go,

you stupid fucking animal!" he screamed and buried the blade deep in the animal's side.

Thor bit down harder in surprise and lurched backward. With a rip of tendon and crunch of bone, the bottom half of the arm severed as he tried to avoid the blade.

Blood gushed from the stub and he screamed in agony as he tried to slash at Thor again but missed. He scrambled backward and the animal bounded toward him.

Thor growled low and bared his teeth. The man's blood dripped from his jaws. He slunk forward and his eyes glowed red.

"Stay back, you dumb fucking mutt!" he yelled. He threw his knife but it missed completely and clattered uselessly to the side.

He slipped in the spilled water and sprawled painfully with a thud. His movements frantic, he attempted to stand but slipped in the water and his own blood with each attempt.

Finally, he managed to drag himself upward. He remembered the gun he had strapped to his ankle. With his remaining hand, he drew it from the holster and aimed the small handgun at the animal.

"This is what you get, you goddamn mutt."

Thor leapt at the same time that the man pulled the trigger. The round buried itself harmlessly into one of the cots, and he buried his teeth into his attacker's throat.

Hot blood gushed and filled his mouth. He held his jaws clamped tightly while the man struggled feebly before he gurgled his last breaths. The body twitched once and stilled and blood pooled around him before the animal finally released it.

He recognized that he'd killed a human being—something like Charles. While he knew it had been unavoidable, he also knew the big man wouldn't like what had happened. Something inside him clicked into place. His eyes glowed a deeper red. His mind reeled with the coppery taste of the man's blood in his mouth.

His stomach growled.

Thor paced the length of the container, then sat on Charles' cot. He stared at the body. His stomach growled again.

The animal knew instinctively he was about to cross a line that would change things. He didn't understand the different signals his body was giving him. On the one hand, he knew Charles and the other two wouldn't be happy with him. But he also knew the man was different than his humans.

He licked the dead man's blood from his jaws. The taste of it overwhelmed and excited him.

Finally, he slunk off the cot and began to eat.

CHAPTER TWO

Des Moines, Iowa

Charles Tillman sat at the bar in his family's kitchen while his mother checked the pot roast she had in the oven. The whole house smelled like garlic and roasting meat, and it transported him back to his childhood. He'd gone directly from the Marine Corps into the alien world of the Zoo, and he missed his mom's cooking.

"You aren't eating enough, Charlie-boy." She tsked from her position at the stove. The steam momentarily fogged her glasses when she lifted the lid on a pot. She took them off and wiped them on her apron.

"I'm eating just fine, Ma."

Yvette Tillman didn't look convinced.

He shrugged. "Really, Ma. They feed me well."

"They better! You boys put your lives on the line for God and country. The least they could do is give you a decent meal. A true shame."

Charles winced and tried to cover it up by ducking his

head. He didn't want his guilt to show. Yvette still didn't know he had been discharged.

He looked out the window and saw his sister's black Honda Accord fly into the driveway. Jackie slid out of the car and tossed her large sunglasses back into the vehicle. She kicked the door shut, which made him wince. The woman chewed through vehicles faster than Thor chewed through bully sticks.

Charles tapped on the window. She looked up and grinned—then flipped him the bird. He looked over his shoulder to make sure Yvette hadn't seen, but she was still leaning over her pots and pans. When he turned back to his sister, she laughed and shook her head.

Jackie soon entered the small kitchen. She gave Yvette a hug and a kiss on the cheek. Then she turned her attention to Charles. He rose from his seat and gave her a hug.

"Big brother!"

"Little sister."

She broke the hug and punched him in the shoulder. "You big jerk, you didn't tell me you would be home! I had to find out from Angela Winter from a Facebook message. Who even uses Facebook to message people anymore?"

"Apparently you," he said and grinned as he sat again.

Jackie sat beside him. "I'm serious. Why didn't you say anything?"

"It was last-minute," Charles said with a shrug, "and I wanted it to be a surprise."

She rolled her eyes. "You hate surprises."

"I hate being the surprisee. I love being the surpriser."

"Not real words."

"They are now."

"Children! Not even two minutes together and the two of you're already goin' at it. It's a Sunday. No fighting on Sunday," Yvette said.

"Yes, ma'am," Charles said.

"You got it, Ma. Besides, we weren't fighting. Just a minor disagreement amongst siblings. No bad feelings here."

"Good. Now make yourselves useful and set the table."

"How many places?" Charles asked.

"Four," Yvette answered. "Gammy is joining us."

Charles put out the plates while his sister arranged silverware.

"I'm sorry you had to learn I was back home from someone else. It really is only a short trip, and I didn't know you were going to be here."

"Yeah. Nice that it lined up like that."

"How'd Angela know I was back?"

She rolled her eyes. "Angela is a busybody who's always had a major crush on you. The psycho still lives in her parents' basement across the street."

"Jacqueline Marie Tillman, you be nice! Angela is a lovely girl," Yvette scolded. She put a dish of steaming potatoes on the table. "She can't be faulted for having a harmless crush on Charlie-boy."

Jackie waited until their mother was out of earshot to shove her phone toward him. "She really is a psycho. She sent me this." Curious, he looked at a picture of himself standing on his mom's porch, drinking coffee.

He grimaced. "Well, if she does decide to lose it, I think I can take her."

She grasped his wrist, pulled his sleeve up, and raised

an eyebrow at some of the fresh scars there. "What have you been doing, Charles?"

"Nothing." He pulled his sleeve down.

His sister glared at him but couldn't press him further as Yvette returned with their Gammy in tow.

He hugged his grandmother. When she pinched his cheek, he held his grimace back.

"My favorite grandson!"

"Gammy, you can't say stuff like that."

"Sure I can. I'm old. I can say whatever I want," Carol-Ann said and waved a hand dismissively. "Besides, your no-good cousin has been kicked off the good grandchild list."

Jackie rolled her eyes. "Here we go. You missed all the family gossip, Charles."

Carol-Ann smacked her on the back of the head. "Oh, hush, you."

"What did he do?" Charles asked.

Yvette brought the roast in and set it on the table. "Are you talking about Brandon again?"

"Yes."

"Mom, I told you not to talk about that anymore," she said.

The old lady ignored her daughter-in-law. "He got himself messed up in some shady dealings. He was thrown in jail!"

Charles nodded slowly.

"Why aren't you more scandalized?" Jackie asked.

He shrugged. "Is it really that much of a shock? Besides, it could happen to anyone."

The three women stared at him. He ignored them and carved the roast.

Charles was fixing one of the cabinets in the kitchen when Jackie entered. She leaned against the counter and folded her arms across her chest.

"I haven't seen Dad around much. Why has he been working so much? I thought he was going to retire?"

She raised an eyebrow and put a hand on her hip.

He checked the cabinet door to make sure it clicked shut silently. "What?"

"What's up with you, Charles?" she asked.

"I don't know what you're talking about."

"You've been weird."

"Weird?"

"Evasive."

"Evasive?"

"Stop repeating what I'm saying."

"Then start making sense."

Jackie sighed. "You haven't told us where you're stationed and what you've been doing."

"You know I can't disclose missions."

"You've always told us what you were up to before."

"Things change," Charles said. He climbed off the stool he'd been standing on and began to replace the tools he'd used. "Now, answer the question about Dad."

She cracked her neck. "I finally got it out of Mom. He's had to pick up extra shifts at the factory to pay all the bills.

Especially since Gammy's health isn't what it once was. Assisted living facilities are pricey."

"I wish someone would've told me that," he said.

"I've tried to help where I can, but I think you're in the same boat as I am. I know they don't pay lance corporals much. I looked it up. But don't worry. They understand."

He shook his head. "No. I can pay for all of Gammy's bills. And do Mom and Dad still not own the house? Is this where they want to stay, do you think, or would they want to move somewhere nicer?"

"What are you talking about, Charles?"

"I can help them out. I was recently...promoted. I got quite the pay raise. I'm not doing anything with it, and the least I can do is help out."

Jackie squinted at him with suspicion.

"What?"

"Nothing."

"If something's bothering you, you can tell me."

She opened her mouth but Yvette breezed into the kitchen.

"You fixed the cupboard, Charlie-boy?"

"Good as new," he said. "Ma, why didn't you tell me you and Dad needed more money?"

His mother frowned. "Because, Charles, it isn't the burden of the child."

He folded his arms and fixed her with a firm look. "Ma, let me help out. I was just promoted. I have more money now. I *want* to take care of all of you. Let me."

"We can't accept anything from you, Charles."

"Yes, you can," he said. "Listen, you've given so much to

me my whole life. I'm in a place where I can give back. Please let me."

"If Charles is Mr. Moneybags all of a sudden, let him help out. He's clearly not putting any of it to good use, Ma. I mean, look at the way he still dresses," Jackie said.

Yvette looked from one of her children to the other. Finally, she sighed. "I'll mention it to your father."

"He can finally retire—or at least cut way back. It really isn't that much trouble and I want to help out," Charles said.

Yvette merely smiled and patted him on the arm before she left the kitchen.

"Come on," Jackie said and tugged him toward the front door. "We're going."

"Going where?"

"Since you're so flush with cash, you're taking me to dinner," she said as she snatched up her keys and purse. "You're going to treat me to Nick's. Then we're going to have a good long chat."

They had barely sat at a table when Jackie looked at him with a set expression.

"All right, Charles, spill it," she said.

"There's nothing to spill, Jackie."

"Bullshit."

Charles flinched and looked around.

She rolled her eyes. "Oh, come on, Charles. Ma and Dad aren't here. You aren't going to get reprimanded for swearing."

"Still. This is a public place. There are families here," he said.

Jackie shrugged. "Don't really care. Tell me what's up."

"I got promoted."

"No, you didn't."

"What makes you say that?"

"You didn't announce anything. You didn't send any pictures of your pinning ceremony. And if you really did, I want to see proof. Badges or pins or whatever the hell you Boy Scouts get. Besides, I looked up what a corporal makes, too."

"I'm not in the Boy Scouts."

"You know what I mean."

They stared at each other but she caved first. She'd always been bad at staring contests and he had more patience than she did.

"Charles, just tell me this—are you in trouble? You aren't getting into anything…illegal, right?" she asked with a sigh. "I don't know if our family could handle the perfect child doing anything dastardly."

"I'm not doing anything dastardly," he said. "Not really."

"Okay. That's not an answer. That's the opposite of what I wanted to hear! You aren't like a drug dealer or something now, are you? I heard a cocaine ring just got busted at West Point."

"Those are Army jags. I'm not dealing drugs, Jackie!"

"Okay. Then tell me you really are still in the Marines and you really were promoted," Jackie said. "And don't lie to me."

Charles leaned back in his seat and rubbed a hand over his face. "Look, Jackie…"

"Ah-hah! I knew you were lying," she yelled.

"Keep it down," he protested and smiled apologetically at a family seated at the table next to them.

"So, you admit to lying," she said and looked smug.

"I'm not in the Marines anymore."

Her smile slowly faded. "I thought this would feel a little more satisfying, to be honest."

He shrugged.

"Tell me what happened."

Charles recounted the incident that caused his discharge from the Marines during the operation in Patagonia. He told her how the government had done the same to many of the soldiers and Marines who were involved— and some who weren't. It was all to show the Chilean government that they didn't take the riots lightly. The higher-ups hadn't cared that he wasn't involved. His career was a casualty no one batted an eye at.

"Wrong place, wrong time," he muttered when he'd finished.

Jackie pressed her lips together in displeasure for a moment. "Why didn't you say anything?"

He shrugged. "Didn't want to be a disappointment."

"What are you doing now?"

Charles looked down at his empty plate.

"Charles."

"I have a job."

"Okay. Doing what?"

"I helped start a company and we go on missions for people."

Jackie leaned across the table and lowered her voice. "You aren't an...assassin, are you?"

"What? No!"

"Just checking."

"I wouldn't do something like that."

She shrugged. "I wouldn't have thought you would lie about being kicked out of the military, but here we are."

"I didn't really mean to lie," he said with a sigh. "It was just an omission of the truth."

"So, whatever you're doing now pays well, huh?" Jackie asked.

"Yeah. It pays really well."

"And it isn't as a gun-for-hire," she said, "or a drug runner?"

"No."

She folded her arms on the table and studied him. "You'd tell me, wouldn't you, if you were in trouble?"

"What would you be able to do to help if I was?"

"I'm more than an Olympic volleyball player, you know," she said, irritated. "I *am* in law school, after all."

"You're only in the second year. You aren't close to being a lawyer yet. Then, you'd have to pass the bar to become a practicing attorney."

Jackie groaned. "Who asked you about the path to becoming a lawyer? I'm just saying, if you needed help, I know some people. I'm the clerk for a state judge. He's not huge but he'd have some pull."

Charles smiled at her. He seriously doubted a local judge would make any impact on the international Zoo, but he appreciated his sister's determination.

"So, would you?" she asked.

"Would I what?"

"Would you tell me if you were in trouble?"

He looked at his sister. "I'm not in trouble, Jackie. But if I was, you'd be the first to know."

She smiled. "I'll let you off the hook for the details…for now. But I will get my answers eventually." She clapped her hands together. "Since you're paying, I think we should get dessert."

"Of course, you do."

———

Charles wasn't only visiting his family in Iowa. He was there to recruit for the company—the BOHICA Warriors—he'd started with his two fellow ex-soldiers, Booker and Roo. He'd made phone calls to some of the friends he'd had in the service to drum up recruits, and one name kept coming up—Corporal Serenity Nguyen.

He called her and she said she'd give him an hour to convince her, so he borrowed his mom's minivan and drove to Davenport.

She'd suggested they meet at a dive bar she knew, and he parked in the lot with a few minutes to spare. He was getting out of the minivan when a black-and-chrome Harley Davidson Forty-Eight Special roared into the parking place next to him.

The rider was dressed in faded Levi's and a black leather jacket with a giant burning skull emblazoned on the back. She dismounted and glared at him.

"That's your ride?"

He grinned. "Good to see you, Corporal Nguyen."

"I'm almost embarrassed to walk in with you, Tillman. And come on. Call me Reen," she said and shook his hand.

Her grip was strong and sure, and she maintained eye contact. She patted her curly mohawk and jerked her head toward the entrance of the bar. "Let's get this over with."

Charles followed her in. The bar was mostly empty, but she drew the attention of the patrons. She was tall for a woman—five-ten—and her Vietnamese and African American heritage made for an exotic appearance. Topped off with swagger to rival John Wayne's, she gave even him a run for his money in animal magnetism.

They ordered their drinks—whiskey neat for her and a PBR for him—and sat in a corner booth at the back of the dimly-lit bar. Reen shrugged her leather jacket off to reveal the intricate weave of tribal tattoos across her shoulders and sternum. She took a swig of her drink.

"Nice ink," he said.

"Thanks."

He had known she had tattoos, but she seemed to have significantly more now. Especially in highly-visible places where he knew wouldn't be allowed in the military. "Those new?" he asked and indicated the sternum tattoo.

Reen shrugged. "Figured I wasn't in the Corps anymore, might as well get more."

"Yeah, I heard you were turned down for reenlistment," Charles said.

She raised her left eyebrow and the piercing there glinted in the bar light. "Heard you got discharged for participating in riots in Patagonia."

"I wasn't participating. Just happened to be around at the same time."

"Sure."

"It's okay. I guess it was just my time to be out of the Corps."

"You miss it?"

"Sometimes. Do you?"

"Don't know yet. Haven't been out long enough to answer that. But I busted my ass in the Corps, you know that. It was a pretty shitty way to end it all. All because of my ink. NCO's don't have tattoos, the first sergeant said. 'Not recommended for promotion.' Shit. I also think they were annoyed that a woman whipped their asses and put them to shame."

"What's your next move?"

Reen looked at him over her glass. "Haven't decided yet. Don't know if you remember or not, but I was an MP. I've been thinking about going into private security or law enforcement."

"I've been doing this job," Charles said. "It pays really well. It's dangerous, though. But a lot of action."

"This what you came to recruit me for? I'm going to need more details, Tillman."

He looked around the bar. No one seemed to pay attention to what they were doing but ever cautious, he leaned closer to her anyway. "It's merc work, essentially. Although I've started a company with a former SAS guy and a former Australian Army soldier. We're trying to expand our team and need highly skilled individuals."

"Mercenary work, huh?" she asked. "Don't know if I want to go around killing people."

"No killing people," he assured her.

She pursed her lips. "Somehow I don't believe that."

"No people. There is some killing, but it's more along the...animal variety."

"Animal variety?"

"Yes."

"Like lions and tigers and shit like that? I won't kill endangered animals."

"Who knew you were such an environmentalist?"

Reen shrugged.

"No endangered species," Charles said. "Promise."

"What's it pay?"

"There are obviously no guarantees in work like this. But we've managed to make a name for ourselves and pull in the pay pretty steadily. It averages out to between twenty and fifty a mission."

She swished a sip of whiskey in her mouth and swallowed. "Between twenty and fifty?" she asked, incredulous.

He nodded.

"And I won't have to kill people."

"No."

"Lodging?"

"Included if you come and work for us."

"And there are three of you?"

"Yes."

"You vouch for the other two?"

"They're good guys," Charles said. "Roo might give you some crap, but you could whip him."

Reen grinned.

"Where is it?"

Charles pursed his lips but said nothing.

"Tillman..."

"It's in Africa."

"Get more specific. Africa is a continent."

"Specifically, it's in the Sahara Desert."

She wrinkled her nose for a second and tossed the rest of her drink back. "I'm out. I don't do deserts." She stood from the table.

Charles lunged after her. "Wait! Wait. It's not really in a desert."

Reen turned on the heel of her combat boot and looked back at him. "What do you mean, it's not really in a desert?"

"Sit back down, please. I'll explain."

Clearly irritated, she sat again and waited with a not-amused expression.

"It's called the Zoo," he said, his voice low.

"The Zoo?"

"Yes."

"Wait." She leaned over the table toward him. "Wait. Is that that alien shit that people have been whispering about?"

He nodded. "Remember when there was word a few years back about the ACZ?"

"Sure."

"That's what it is."

"You're not really making this very appealing."

"It's not all the insane depravation crap those rumors talked about. It's not a vacation, but you could handle it."

"And it pays well?"

Charles nodded again.

Reen looked around the bar. She ran her finger along the rim of her empty glass and finally looked at him.

"The Corps sent one of my sergeants there when I was a PFC. Word is that the shit was hot. He sure wasn't drawing fifty K, though, not as a sergeant. Word also was that he got out and joined Franklin Security, or one of the contractors. Now, it makes some sense," she said, her gaze piercing as if she tried to read his soul.

He sat motionless and returned her gaze. She was sizing him up. They'd been stationed in Oki together, and they'd shared a few drinks at the E-club with the brothers, but it wasn't often and she didn't really know him that well. She remembered that he had a reputation as a good Marine, capable and strong. And she knew he was a good guy—his reputation preceded him always in that regard.

"Ah, fuck it," she said. "I need to get out of this shitty town. Might as well try my hand at mercenary shit."

Charles grinned. "I'm glad to have you on the team. You're going to be a great asset."

"Yeah, yeah. When do we leave?"

"When are you available to leave?"

Reen considered this, then shrugged. "Got a few loose ends to tie up. Shouldn't take me long." She stood again and put her jacket on.

"How does the end of the week work for you?" he asked as he followed her out of the bar.

She mounted her Harley again. "Works fine for me. Perfect really. Had a relationship I was getting tired of anyway. This is a great reason to break it off."

She saluted him and roared away.

He slid behind the wheel of his parents' minivan and started on his way home, buzzing with the success of recruiting a Marine of Reen's caliber.

CHAPTER THREE

Perth, Australia

Walker "Roo" Demopoulis surveyed the party he'd put together. He'd returned to Australia and promptly bought a house with a big yard and a great view of the Swan River. Now, the yard was filled with his immediate and extended family. The alcohol flowed steadily and a whole lamb roasted on a spit over the open firepit he'd had set up for this occasion. There was no party quite like a Greek-Australian party.

He was showing off.

"Dad!" A young girl's high-pitched giggle-scream filled the room.

Roo turned and captured his daughter in a giant hug. "You made it," he said, held her close, and kissed the crown of her head. He pulled back and held her at arm's length. "Let me look at'cha. You've gotten so tall, Cassie!"

Cassie laughed and smiled in response. She twirled one of her strawberry blonde braids and shoved him away. "I'm going to go find Brian and play. See ya, Dad."

He straightened and watched her run off.

"Amazing the things you miss, isn't it?"

Slowly, he turned toward the speaker—Brittany Abbi, Cassie's mother and his ex-wife. She tossed her long blonde hair over her shoulder and smiled at him.

Roo hugged her before she could protest. "It's so good to see you."

She patted him on the shoulder and laughed. "Cassie was very excited that you were back home."

"How have you been?"

"Oh, good," she said. She turned and looked over the yard and the view. "You've got a beautiful place. Looks like you've really been doing well."

"All in a day's work, honey."

"Craig and I broke up." She turned back to him.

He stared at her. Brittany had always been—and probably always would be—the one woman who struck him speechless.

Theirs was a brief and unhappy—on her part—marriage that resulted in Cassie, who was the light of each of their lives. He was still in love with her and he dreamed they'd get back together and be a proper family. In fact, he had hoped she would arrive at his barbecue and see how well he was doing. He thought that would be the tipping point that would make her realize she'd been wrong to leave him.

"I bought this for us, you know," Roo said and dared to take Brittany's hand.

She pulled it away from him and linked her fingers. "It's beautiful." She took a couple of steps away from him.

"Craig and I just had differences we couldn't quite overcome. He could be a real dick sometimes."

"Did he hurt you?" He almost growled the question.

Brittany laughed him off. "Of course not! You know I don't tolerate that sort of behavior. No. It just didn't work out. Sometimes, things just don't work out." She sighed and looked at him. "Thank you for inviting me. I'm going to go say hello to some of your family."

She sauntered off and left him staring after her.

"You look like a right bogan drooling after that bitch," someone said.

Roo turned, his teeth bared. "Fuck off."

The man held his hands up, one holding a sweating beer bottle. "Hey, mate, just trying to help you out. She's totally playing you. You know that, right? She sees this house, figures you're in the money. Wants it, wants more child support."

He wanted to argue. But, while he wanted to think Brittany might want to get back together, he knew her and she could be after a bigger slice of the pie.

"Sorry," he said. "It's just complicated."

"Always is with the pussy."

Roo studied his new companion. Mick Bennelong had the dark skin and distinct features that pegged him as Aboriginal. The two men had been in the Australian Army together and this was the man he intended to recruit. He'd known the best way to draw Mick out from retirement was with the temptation of free beer and food. It had clearly worked.

"It's been a long time," he said and shook Mick's beer-free hand.

The man shrugged. "It's been a minute. What have you been up to? Clearly, it's been treating you well, whatever it is."

Roo clapped him on the shoulder and steered him into the heart of the party. "I'd like to talk to you about that, actually."

He tensed and sidled away from him. "You sound like a used car salesman."

"Nothing shady going on here."

Mick didn't look convinced.

"Look," he said, "I have something I want to talk to you about. That's sort of why I invited you to this piss up."

"And here I was thinkin' we were just good mates."

"We are. Which is why I wanted to talk to you. But it'll have to be after this. So, don't just shoot through."

Mick emptied his beer and Roo handed him another. "Why the hell not?" he said with a shrug.

He grinned and elbowed the Aboriginal in the ribs. "Great. Now, I've got an ex to win back."

"Whatever you say, bunj," Mick said and wandered off in the direction of the buffet table.

Roo worked his way through the crowd, always headed in Brittany's direction, but she seemed to stay two steps ahead of him.

"Walker, darling, this is so wonderful!" his mother exclaimed and squeezed him tightly.

"Hey, Mum, you like it?"

She wiped her eyes. "I love it. How thoughtful of you to invite us all. And what a wonderful view. Whose house is it?"

"It's mine."

She blinked at him. "Yours?"

Roo's father walked up to them at that moment. His mom turned to him. "Did you hear that, Greg?"

"Hear what, Annabel?"

"This place belongs to Walker."

"You're shitting me."

His wife smacked him on the back of the head. "Language!"

"We're all adults here," Greg said. One of Walker's nieces ran past at that moment.

"Where did you get the money to get a place like this? Are you letting?"

"No, I'm not letting, Mum," Roo said. He shrugged. "I bought it outright."

"What have you been doing, son?" his father asked, his eyes narrowed.

"Yes, what exactly has you gone from us for so long making enough money to buy extravagant houses like this one."

Roo grinned at his parents. "I've been keeping myself busy," he said, "and out of trouble. You don't have to worry about that."

"You sure you're staying out of trouble? Myrna's son started making loads of cash, but it turned out he was dealing drugs. You aren't doing anything like that, are you, Walker?" Annabel asked.

"No, Mum. I'm not dealing drugs. Myrna's son is a real wombat. You know I'm better than that."

"Of course I know that! I just need to ask."

"So, where have you been exactly, son? What's been keeping you away from your family?" Greg asked.

"I can't exactly tell you," Roo said. "I can tell you that I've been in Africa, but I'm not really authorized to say. It's some real James Bond shit." That earned him a smack on the head like his father.

"Really, the pair of you," his mother said. "I'm going to go check on the lamb."

When she was out of earshot, Greg turned and studied his son. "You really are staying out of trouble, son?"

"Yes, Dad. I'm staying out of trouble. I've started a company with a few other ex-soldiers. We're doing very well for ourselves."

"I can see that. Just don't get ahead of yourself."

Roo laughed. "I'm not getting ahead of myself."

"Tell you what, your mother sure is happy you've bounced back so nicely from being kicked out of the Army. That Myrna bitch she's always gabbing with was really high-and-mighty about it, bragging on her perfect son. Well, now the son of a bitch is in prison and Myrna's eating her own shit."

"Don't look too happy about it, Dad."

Greg merely grinned.

"I can't stay around for long," Roo said. He watched Cassie swing on the swing set he'd had installed for her. "I've got to be getting back. I'd hoped you and Mom wouldn't mind watching the house. You can stay here, of course. You don't have to worry about paying for anything. I'd just rather you watch it. I'm not going to let it out and don't want it to be empty. The staff will be around to clean it, so all you'd have to do is relax. Eventually, you can pick out a house of your own nearby. Or farther away, if that's what you wanted."

"Are you being serious, Walker?"

"Serious as a fucking coronary."

Greg pursed his lips. "What you're doing is dangerous, isn't it?"

Roo didn't answer.

"What about Cassie?"

"What do you mean? I'm doing this all for her. So she can have a better life. So she doesn't have to worry about anything."

"That's money, son. What about time? What about having a father around?"

"I'm doing my best. Maybe someday soon, I'll be able to retire, but for now, we'll just have to be apart. She understands. She's a smart kid, despite who her parents are. She gets it."

Greg nodded. "As long as you know what you're doing."

"I do," he said. Then he changed the subject. "So, what do you say about watching the house?"

"I'm sure your mother could be easily persuaded."

Roo left his father to go find Cassie.

"Have you been good while I've been away?" he asked.

Cassie nodded.

"How's your mom been?"

"She's been good. She and Craig broke up. Which I think is fine. I never liked Craig."

"No?"

"No. He talked to me like I was some kid."

He laughed. "You are a kid."

She put her hands on her hips and tipped her chin in a mirror of something he had seen her mother do on many occasions. "I'm twelve, Dad. I'm not a little kid."

Roo ruffled her hair. "Of course not, Cas."

Cassie smiled at him. From across the yard, Annabel called her name.

"Go on to your grandma," he said.

She scrunched her nose. "Do I have to? She's going to make me eat the sheep's eyeball. That's so disgusting, Dad."

"Oh, come on. It's good for you!"

"There's no way that's true. It's too gross to be good for you."

"It's good luck."

"I don't believe in luck," Cassie declared.

Roo folded his arms. "Oh, you don't, huh?"

She shook her head.

"That's a real shame. You know why?"

"Why?"

"You're a Demopoulis. We're the luckiest bastards there are. But you've got to soak it up quick while you're still young. That's the only way to make sure you stay lucky."

"Really?"

"Strewth."

"Fine. I'll go eat an eyeball, but I'm not going to enjoy it."

"No one said you had to enjoy it, Cas. Now go on before your greedy little cousin gets it first."

Cassie ran off in the direction of her grandmother.

"You're so good with her," Brittany said as she materialized at his side.

He put his arm around her, and she let him. "She's a good kid."

"Yes, she is."

"I wasn't lying to her, you know."

"About what?"

"About Demopoulises being lucky."

"Is that so?"

"Yeah."

"You think you're lucky, Walker?"

"I think I'm about to get lucky, Brit," Roo said. He leaned in for a kiss but was met with her palm. He frowned.

"Not now, Walker. I just broke up with Craig. I'm not in a good place for this. It's always so complicated with you. I think it's better if we just focus on Cassie," she said. "For now."

"For now?" he asked, hopeful.

She smiled and walked away from him again.

"So," Mick said, "what's this big thing you're trying to get me to help you with?"

The two men sat in front of the giant 4K Ultra television watching a rugby match—the Wallabies vs. the All Blacks in a pre-World Cup warm-up test.

"You make it sound like a favor. I'm offering you a job," Roo said.

"What makes you think I want a job, mate?"

He shrugged. "Man's gotta work."

"I like having free time."

"Sure. Okay. But what if I said you could make a shit ton of cash and then be able to retire and do anything in luxury?"

Mick shrugged and drank more of his beer.

"It's some pretty badass shit, Mick. I think you'd like it. I definitely think you'd be good at it," Roo said.

"I mean, good on you for making something, but I like going with the flow."

"Ah, bullshit. The flow's for weak-ass men and pussies. Why go with the flow when you can conquer the whole goddamn thing?"

The man sighed. "Fine. I'll humor you. What exactly is this job?"

"Picture this," he said and held his hands apart. "Aliens."

Mick sputtered on his beer as he laughed. "Bugger off. Aliens?"

Roo nodded.

"You've lost your touch with reality there, bunj."

"I haven't."

"Aliens?"

"Yeah. Aliens."

His companion sighed. "You doing something in space? I don't like space. It freaks me the fuck out. Too much darkness, not enough oxygen. If we were meant to be in space, we'd be able to fly."

"It's not in space. It's in Africa."

"There are aliens in Africa?"

"Yes. Well, sort of."

"It's a yes or no question, mate."

"Yes. Remember that alien missile a while ago?" Roo asked.

Mick thought for a few moments, then nodded slowly. "Sure. I remember some bullshit about a probe or some fucking nonsense the governments of the world were freaking out about."

"Well, it's out in the Sahara now. Things aren't all lined up like they'd wanted originally."

"Of course it fucking isn't," Mick interrupted. "Hey, wait. Wasn't Frank involved with this in the beginning?"

"Frank?"

"Yeah. Frank Petrone. He was shipped over there in the beginning. Didn't you know Frank?"

"No. But anyway, I'm trying to make a point here."

Mick took a gulp of beer and held his hands up. "Right. Continue with the spiel."

"They took some of the stuff in it—the goop, they call it—and created a test project in the Sahara to see what it would do. Then things got a little out of control and the scientists realized they couldn't control alien shit like they thought they could. The alien goop reacted with the preexisting environment and took on a mind of its own. All those scientist wankers may have fucked up in the beginning, but they're still trying. They're still trying to study it. They're just too pussy to do it themselves, which is where we step in. Our job is to go into the Zoo and bring out things for them to study."

"Things?"

"Yeah."

"Like, alien things?"

"Yes."

Mick was quiet for a while. He watched the All Blacks dominating the Wallabies. When there was a commercial break, he turned to his companion.

"How much exactly does this pay?"

Roo shrugged. "Upward of twenty a mission."

"You're shitting me," he said and jackknifed off the couch.

He shook his head.

"How dangerous, exactly, is this job?"

"It's pretty fucking dangerous. Think of it as a special alien playground where everything wants to kill you."

"You're really good at this convincing me to join you shit, you know that?"

Roo gave him a two-finger salute. "Look, hell yes, it's dangerous. But danger's never scared you away, if I remember right. Besides, I've already been in and out a bunch of times and I'm still in one piece."

Mick shrugged. "And it really pays that well?"

"How do you think I bought this house?"

"Yeah," he said. "You know what? Why the hell not? What have I got to lose?"

"I like to think of it as what do you have to gain? The answer to that is a fuck-ton."

"Dad, why do you have to go so soon? You just got back," Cassie said. Her bottom lip trembled and tears threatened to spill down her face.

Roo crouched in front of her and held her shoulders. "I know. I'm sorry I couldn't be here longer, but I've got work to do. You understand that, right, Cas?"

She nodded and sniffled.

He wiped away a tear that escaped. "Hey, it's going to be okay. Where's my brave, strong girl?"

Cassie threw her arms around his neck and he held her close.

"You'll be careful won't you, Dad?"

"I'm always careful."

He glanced at Brittany, who stood and talked quietly to Mick. They were at Perth Airport and although Roo simply itched to get back to the Zoo, he felt reluctant to walk away from his daughter. Leaving Cassie behind was never easy. He hated how much she grew in the times between his visits home.

"I'm going to have a better phone this time around," he said. "We can call more. How's that sound?"

"That sounds good," Cassie agreed.

"See? It's going to be all right."

She nodded and her bottom lip stopped trembling and she smiled at him.

"Secret handshake?" Roo asked.

Cassie nodded and they performed their secret daddy-daughter handshake they'd invented when she was seven. It was a complicated series of high fives and handshakes and elbow bumps that always made her laugh.

He patted the top of her head. "You be good, kid."

"I will, Dad."

"I love you."

"I love you too."

Roo gave her mother a hug, and she let him. "I'll be back again soon," he whispered to her. "Just know I'm doing this all for the both of you."

Brittany smiled at him.

Mick hiked his rucksack up higher on his shoulder.

"Not to break up this delightful domestic moment, but we've gotta jet. Our flight's boarding soon."

He nodded and followed the other man through the airport. He looked over his shoulder and waved at Cassie before the crowd of travelers separated them completely.

"You going to be okay?" his companion asked. "Need me to get you a tampon or something?"

Roo elbowed him. "Fuck you."

Mick laughed. "Just playin'. She's a good kid."

"I know."

"This is your moment of truth, buddy."

"What?"

"I'm here to see if your alien thing is just bullshit or if you've really hit the motherload."

He laughed. "Well, you've still got quite a ways to go before that moment, but it'll all be worth it. Trust me."

CHAPTER FOUR

Falmouth, England

Eustace Percival Coddington—Booker to his teammates—sat alone at the top of Pendennis Point and ate a liver and onion pasty. No one else was around. It was a gray day and drizzling, but he didn't mind.

He'd been in Falmouth for a few days and simply wandered aimlessly, mainly because he no longer knew anyone who lived there. No one he wanted to see, anyway. He'd merely killed time while he waited to meet Benjamin Whitehall in London. The idea had been that being in Falmouth again would maybe bring up happy memories, but he only revisited the foul ones from before, much to his disgust.

With his coat pulled tighter around him, he continued to stare into the distance. He had no idea why he was in England. When the others had suggested they each go home and recruit, he'd agreed because they'd seemed so eager. Charles and Roo had families they wanted to visit and check on. Booker had none of that.

He stood and stretched and glanced around again. A woman made her way up the trail toward him, her head lowered into the wind that seemed to have picked up a little. Curious, he watched her approach.

She stopped when she was about twenty feet from him, her arms pressed against her middle, and her dark brown hair refused to stay out of her face. "Eustace?"

Booker didn't reply.

"Eustace, is that you?" The woman took another tentative step toward him.

"Joanna," he said flatly.

She smiled at him and moved closer, still cautious. "I thought I saw you in town. Figured this would be the best place to find you. And here you are."

"Here I am."

"Eustace, how have you been?" she asked and moved to within arm's length. "It's been a long time."

Booker stepped back when it looked like she would reach out. "Not long enough. What are you doing here?"

Her smile faltered but she fixed it back in place again. "What do you mean? I live here."

"You know what I mean. Why are you here talking to me?"

Joanna did frown then. "I don't see why you're so upset. Can't I come see my long-lost brother?"

"I'm not long-lost. I'm long-left, remember?"

"Oh, come on, Eustace. Water under the bridge."

He responded with a mirthless laugh. "The old man sent you, didn't he?"

She made no reply.

Booker shook his head. "Unbelievable. Of course, he did. You still doing his bidding?"

"I don't see why you have to be so bleddy cruel to him. He never did anything to earn your censure," Joanna said. She folded her arms across her chest and scowled at him.

"Never did anything? That's rich, Joanna. So, he never locked me in the chicken coop when I didn't complete my chores the way he wanted? He never whipped me with his belt if I didn't move fast enough for him?" His laugh was entirely mirthless. "Let me guess, you also don't think he took his fists to me when he'd had too much to drink."

"Stop," she protested, "just stop talking. If you're going to be like this then I'm not going to invite you back for supper."

"Good. Brilliant, actually! I don't want any part of whatever toxic circle jerk you had going. I'm done with it all. You hear me, Joanna? I sat here and wondered why I came back, and now I actually regret it."

"You ungrateful fucker."

"Ungrateful? Sure, Joanna. No. You know what, I am bleddy grateful. I'm grateful that son of a bitch treated me the way he did so I left when I did. I'm glad I was homeless for a spell until I found the SAS. They were more family then you ever were." Booker started walking away from her.

"Don't walk away from me!" Joanna yelled after him. "You bleddy waste. Da wanted me to come get you, and I thought it was a bad idea. But he insisted. I guess I was right!"

He turned back to her. "Fuck you, Joanna. Run on back home to Da. Cry to him. Maybe he'd give a shit. I don't."

His spine rigid, he marched to the parking lot where he'd left his rental. She yelled at him the entire time but the wind snatched most of her words away. He rolled his shoulders—a habit he'd picked up from Charles—got in his Range Rover, and drove to London.

The tube screamed to a stop and Booker stepped out. He glanced at the sign that told him he was in Piccadilly and wove through the crowd toward the way out. Thanks to his unwelcome clifftop visitor, he was early, but he didn't mind. Benjamin thought punctuality meant fifteen minutes ahead of time.

He made his way to the pub they'd chosen for their meeting and found the man already seated at a table in the back.

Benjamin stood and grinned. He shook the newcomer's hand vigorously. "Booker! It's been too long."

"How've you been keeping yourself?"

"Can't complain. I swear I'm busier now that I'm out than I was before. The wife's been putting me to work."

"Yeah?"

"Hope you don't mind, but I already ordered for the both of us," he said. He pushed a pint glass toward Booker. "Three Hammers cider for you. I remember how you love that wimpy cider bullshit."

"It's not wimpy. It's bleddy delicious."

The man shrugged. "How have you been?"

"I've been really good," he responded. "I've been

working this job. Setting myself up real nice for the rest of my life."

Benjamin raised an eyebrow.

"I started my own company with two other career men. American and Australian blokes."

"That's great, Booker."

"I think so. It's down in Africa. You remember all that buzz of aliens a few years back?"

"Sure. Some shit about a missile or probe we intercepted?"

"That's it. The work involves that."

"So, you're a mercenary now?"

Booker shrugged. "It pays well." He paused to take a few sips of the cider.

When he made to continue, his companion held his hand up. "Look, I'm going to stop you there, Booker. I feel like I know what's coming next, and before you waste your breath and time explaining how much money you make and how relatively easy it all is because of our training level and backgrounds—I'm going to tell you no."

"No?" he asked with a frown.

"Nope. I'm good with my retirement here. I've got my wife and daughters to think about. We're happy where we are. I loved being in the SAS, but I'm ready to be home now. New chapter and all that."

"You don't even want to know what the job entails? Or how much you can make?"

"Not interested, Booker," Benjamin said firmly. "I'm sure it's a great gig and I'm sure you're making loads, but it's not for me."

"You sure?"

"Positive."

"Damn. I really thought you'd be into it."

Benjamin shook his head. "Might've been a few years ago. But things change. I wish you all the luck, of course."

Booker nodded.

The other man's phone rang, and he glanced at the screen. "Look, it's really good seeing you, Booker. I've got to go. Thanks for the job recommendation. I'll keep an ear to the ground to see if anyone else may be interested in your work."

He stood and the two men shook hands. "I'll be seeing you, Booker."

"Be seeing you."

A little disgruntled by the rejection, he sat at the table and finished his drink alone. He wondered if the other two had any luck with recruitment. Probably. He imagined Charles could convince anyone to join him. Roo probably had friends who were just as restless and money-hungry as he was. Booker was a good negotiator but selling a job to someone was apparently not his strong suit.

"Can I get anything else for you?" The waitress came over. She was a pretty brunette with brown eyes and a tired smile.

He looked at her and her smile brightened a little. "Sure," he said, "I'll take another cider. Also, your name."

"I'm Lucy, and I'll be right back with your drink."

"'Also, your name?' What the fuck kind of line is that, Booker?" he muttered after she'd left.

Lucy soon returned with a full pint glass and a small basket of chips.

"Thanks. I didn't order any chips, though," Booker said.

She shrugged and winked. "I won't tell if you won't." She sashayed off.

He looked down and saw that she'd written her number on the napkin of the basket. While he ate one of the chips slowly, he looked at Lucy as she bussed a table. She smiled at him.

"Maybe tonight won't be that big of a bust after all."

Booker had just left Lucy's flat early the next morning when his phone rang. He answered without looking at caller ID. "Hello?"

"Booker, it's Benjamin."

"Oh, hey. You reconsider?"

"No. But I do have a name for you."

"Oh really?"

"Yeah. You remember Lester Bight?"

He stepped around a horde of tourists trying to take photos beside a red telephone booth and rolled his eyes. "Lester? Isn't ringing any bells."

"Shorter, balding. He was a bit of an asshole," the other man said. "People called him The Blight when he wasn't paying attention."

"Ah, okay. Yeah, I remember The Blight. That's your big recommendation?"

"Look, I know he probably isn't the kind of fellow you'd want long-term, but if you really need a position filled, he'd do the job. He might be a complete tool, but he was capable and could follow orders on mission."

"He's available?"

"Probably. He was just court-martialed, actually. Word is he's now in trouble with the civilian police too. He's probably looking for a ticket out."

"Again, you aren't making this seem like the best option, Benjamin."

"I know. I just didn't want to leave you with nothing. I'll text you his info. The Blight would be better than nothing."

"I'll think on it. Thanks for telling me, Benjamin."

"No problem, Booker. It was good to see you. Don't be a stranger. I know Elizabeth and the girls would like to see you."

"Can't. I'm leaving here soon. Maybe next time."

"Sure, Booker. Next time."

Booker hung up and stared at Lester Bight's information. He vaguely remembered the man from the SAS. Admittedly, he had been an asshole but he was efficient and knowledgeable on a mission. And he really didn't want to return without a recruit. He couldn't be the one who failed in that.

Despite his misgivings, he called Lester and arranged for a time to meet within the hour. He had his flight already booked and was leaving that afternoon. It might be worth it to give the man a chance, but his window of opportunity would be limited.

Lester Bight slunk into the café as Booker finished his breakfast. He wore a dirty hoodie and ripped jeans. His hair—what was left of it—looked like it hadn't been washed in a while. The man's gaze darted around the small pub and it was obvious that he noted the exits and other patrons. In all honesty, he looked a little the worse for wear, but perhaps it would be best to keep an open mind.

"Booker, long time no see," Lester said. They shook hands.

"Hey, Lester, how you been? Thanks for meeting me."

"Sure. Wasn't doing much."

"Listen, this has to be quick. I only got your name this morning and that's why I didn't contact you before this. I'm leaving this afternoon and was wondering if you wanted to come work for my company."

"What sort of company?"

"Mercenaries, after a fashion."

The man pursed his lips. "Mercs, huh?"

"We really just need highly skilled soldier types for the sort of work we do."

"What kind of work?"

"You ever hear about that alien zone down in Africa? It's called the Zoo now, but you've probably heard it mentioned as something else. The SAS sent some men down there a while back."

"Sure. Here and there. Don't know much about it."

"That's what my company does. We run missions in the Zoo. We get assignments and fill them. Mostly it's asset retrieval."

"Sounds easy enough."

"It is, although you have to understand that it's dangerous. We need weapons experts and men who can follow orders under pressure."

"I can do that. How much does it pay?"

"Depends. But you'd be making a decent chunk of change."

"You said this was in Africa?"

"Yes."

"You know if they have extradition there?"

"Um, no. I don't know if they do or not."

Lester nodded. "When do you leave?"

"This afternoon."

"All right, count me in," he said.

"You…uh, you don't want to know more?" Booker asked.

He shook his head fervently. "Nope. Don't need to know anymore. Whatever I need to know I'll figure it out. I won't lie to you Booker, I need to get away from here, and pretty fast. So this job has come at a perfect time."

"All right then. Meet me at Gatwick at sixteen hundred, and we can be on our way."

"Brilliant." Lester stood and shook his hand again. "I'll be there." He slunk out of the café.

Booker sat and finished his coffee. He was happy he'd secured the man as a recruit. Maybe. He could only hope it turned out all right.

CHAPTER FIVE

Frankfurt Airport

Charles and Reen were the first to arrive at the Frankfurt airport. He snagged a table at the bar they had designated as a meeting place while she went to freshen up.

Roo and Mick soon arrived.

"Charles, you son of a bitch, how are you?" The shorter Australian walked up to him and punched him in the arm.

Charles grinned. "Roo."

"This here is Mick Bennelong," he said and gestured to the Aboriginal.

Mick gave him an easy smile and shook his hand.

Roo made a big show of looking around. "No recruit for you, eh, Yankee?"

He smirked and pointed. Both men turned to look. Reen sauntered toward the bar, a look of bored disinterest on her face.

"Holy fucking shit," Roo muttered.

Charles elbowed him in the ribs. "Keep it in your pants, buddy."

"This just got a whole lot more interesting," Mick said.

"Guys, this is Reen. Reen, this is Roo and Mick."

She shook both their hands. "Hey."

"You ex-military?" Roo asked.

Reen nodded. "Corporal in the Marine Corps."

They all sat at the table. There were two empty chairs.

"When's Booker supposed to be here?" Roo asked.

"Right now," the man in question said and strolled up to their table.

Another round of introductions happened. Then, they all settled and a waitress soon came to take their orders.

"You got any cider?" Booker asked.

She smiled at him. "Sorry, no. I've got an IPA."

He grimaced. "No, that's okay. I'll take a stout."

"You like cider?" Mick asked.

Roo laughed. "Hell yeah, he does. We keep telling him it's a pussy drink—no offense to the present company," he added hurriedly and nodded to Reen.

She grinned. "None taken. No one's ever referred to me as a pussy."

Lester laughed. "Watch out for this one, she's got a mouth on her!"

Reen gave him a fierce look that squashed his laughter cold, her mouth a grim line and her eyes promising pain. He looked away quickly.

The waitress returned with their drinks. Roo noticed that when she put Reen's whiskey tumbler down, their hands lingered. He felt a little disappointed.

Booker raised his pint glass.

Charles heaved a sigh. "You going to start making speeches now, Booker?"

The Brit grinned. "Let's call it an exception this once, then Roo can corner the market on toasts."

"Fuck you," Roo said.

Booker brandished his still-raised glass. "Here's to Germany, the place we always seem to meet."

His old teammates raised their glasses.

"And here's to new beginnings with new comrades," Charles added.

The other three raised their glasses as well. Lester looked unimpressed, Reen looked mildly annoyed, and Mick seemed as happy as could be.

"And to making a shit-ton of money," Roo finished. "Now, everyone, drink while the beer's still cold." He chugged half the contents of his pint glass.

Reen looked at him, impressed. "Who knew you had that in you, ginger?"

"You'll find, Reen, that we lads from down under can handle our liquor."

"Is that so?" she asked and laughed.

Mick joined in. "Hell yeah. We Aussies could drink an Irishman under the table."

"Never heard of that being a thing before," she said.

Booker rolled his eyes. "It's not."

"Don't listen to the wanker. He's just jealous 'cause he's a lightweight," Roo said with an obscene gesture for good measure.

"You seeing anyone, Reen?" Mick asked.

"Nah. Ditched my boyfriend before I came on this trip," Reen answered. "What about you?"

Roo perked up at that. Maybe he'd misread the little touchy-feely thing going on between her and the waitress.

"Free agent, baby."

Charles cleared his throat. Roo repeated the offensive hand response.

"When's the next flight, Booker?" Roo asked.

"About two hours, which you could have read on the itinerary I sent you. Besides, you have a ticket."

He shrugged. "Why look at some paper when I can just ask you?"

"Is this the kind of lazy-ass people you work with, Charles?" Reen asked.

"Hey!" Roo said. "I'll have you know I work very hard. But, if I don't have to, I could compete—and win—any wombat competition hands-down."

"Yeah, that isn't doing anything to change her mind, bunj," Mick said.

"What's a 'bunj?'" Lester asked.

"Y'know. Mate. Buddy. Pal. Bunj," Mick said. "It's a real word."

"Sure it is," Lester said.

"You've gotta expand your horizons, mate." Roo grinned. "Mick likes to keep people on their guard. I've asked him if all Aboriginals do it but he refuses to answer."

"That's not true," Mick protested. "I'm one of a fucking kind."

"It's good to see you chose someone with the same level of maturity as you, Roo," Booker said.

The two Aussies fist-bumped over the table.

The waitress returned and all of them ordered food and another round of drinks. Booker and Lester were the only two who hadn't traveled for an extended period of time, so they were the most awake. They let the lulls in the conversation wash over them and didn't hold them against their new companions.

"So, what exactly are these missions like?" Lester asked.

The Brit glanced around to gauge how close the other patrons were. "Most are your typical asset acquisition. We're given an objective, go into the Zoo, and bring that objective back."

"Well, that was vague," Reen said.

"Can't give away all our secrets, sweetheart," Roo said.

She glared at him. "Yeah, don't call me that."

"Or what?" he asked, his grin a little challenging.

"You strike me as the kind of man who'd like to stay in pretty close touch with your balls. Call me that again and you can say goodbye to them."

Roo whistled. "Big talk."

"Don't worry," Charles said, "her bite is worse than her bark."

"Um, Charles, hate to break it to you, but that's not how the saying goes," the Aussie responded.

Charles shrugged. "I know what I said."

"Back to the matter at hand," Mick interjected. "Walker said this was pretty dangerous."

"Yeah, it is dangerous. Think of it this way—you're going into a place where literally everything is trying to kill you," Booker said.

"Everything?" Lester asked.

"Everything," he confirmed.

"Even the plants try to eat you," Roo added.

"Seriously?" Mick looked skeptical.

The three nodded.

"It's a good thing I've never cared much for plants," Reen said with a shrug.

Lester laughed. "I like a woman who's no-nonsense."

She grimaced. "Okay, boys. Let's get one thing straight. I'm not going to expect different or special treatment because I just happen to be a woman. Don't try to give it to me either. Let's not flirt with the subject. Get your laughs out now, because when we're on mission I won't tolerate all this 'but you're a woman' bullshit. Got it?" She stared at each of the men except Charles in turn. He sat beside her with his arms folded over his broad chest and his own challenging glare leveled at the others.

She leaned back, satisfied. "Glad we got that out of the way."

"Right. Any more questions?" Booker asked.

The three newcomers blinked at him.

"Hell yes, I've got questions," Mick said.

"How exactly do I get paid?" Lester asked.

"Will you actually tell us anything here?" Reen asked at the same time.

"Lester, we'll pay you with a digital transfer," Booker said. "And as for the other question, that all depends."

"On what?" Mick asked.

"On what information we're willing to divulge in a public place," he explained.

She rolled her eyes. "So, that's basically nothing, right?"

He shrugged.

The six sat in silence and continued to drink. They watched the other travelers stroll past them. It all seemed like such a domestic scene.

"Oh," Charles said, "anyone allergic to dogs?"

"No," Mick said. Reen shook her head.

Lester gave a one shoulder shrug. "Not allergic, but not exactly a big fan. Why?"

The American frowned slightly at Lester and the others gave him strange looks. Lester merely shrugged again.

"I've got a dog," Charles said. "He sometimes goes on missions. He's a real asset. He also lives at the base with us."

"What kind of dog?" Mick asked.

"He's a mutt," Charles said. "I rescued him from being abandoned and left for dead in the Zoo when he was a puppy."

"Is that the kind of human filth we have to look forward to working with?" Reen asked.

"No. We don't necessarily work with other people," Booker said. "Operating your own company has its perks. Picking who you get to work with is one of them."

An announcement crackled to life above them. The Brit stood and stretched.

"That's us."

"Next stop the Zoo," Roo said.

CHAPTER SIX

Harvesters Camp; The Zoo; The Sahara Desert

"Just as goddamn hot as I remember," Roo said and glared at the surrounding desert.

"You make it sound like it's been years. We were only gone two weeks," Charles muttered.

At the main entry into the French Quarter, they were stopped by a guard. Booker, Charles, and Roo showed their IDs and said the other three were new recruits. The guard looked at their dog tag-like IDs and waved them past. Booker drove the SUV down the bulldozed path into the camp.

"This is it?" Reen asked, unimpressed by the sprawl of cobbled-together buildings.

"What were you expecting? Bells and whistles?" Roo asked.

She shrugged. "I do like all the bells and whistles."

"We have to get you three registered," Booker said. "Normally, the fee is pretty high, but we'll pay your way since you'll be working for us. Consider it a sponsorship."

"Hey, Booker, let me out here," Charles said.

Booker stopped the vehicle. "Where are you going?"

"Don't think you really need me for registration," he explained. "I'm going to go check on Thor. You have all the paperwork side handled. I'll meet you at the Wateringhole when you're all registered."

He slid out of the SUV and watched it drive toward the registration building before he strode across the camp toward the converted shipping container they lived in. They'd negotiated with Prince Akachukwu, the man they used to work for, and had rented the container next to theirs for their employees. Booker said they'd eventually get their own housing, but renting would work for now.

Charles reached the shipping container and flung the door open. He was instantly overwhelmed by two things at once—the distinct odor of shit and the animal himself.

Thor launched himself out of the container, barreled into his chest, and knocked him over. He barked and yelped happily and his tail wagged so hard his whole body shook. His big purple tongue slobbered and licked him all over,.

"Hey, Thor. You miss me? Did you miss me?" He wrestled the animal into a headlock and scratched his long black-and-tan fur. "Were you a good boy?"

A happy bark seemed to indicate the affirmative.

"Man, you've gotten huge!" Charles struggled out from under the adolescent dog. Thor now came up to his waist and had to weigh at least a hundred pounds.

He brushed himself off and moved back to the container. When he took a step inside, he immediately staggered out and gasped for air. The stench was horrible

—a mixture of feces and rotting flesh. Instinctively, he gagged.

Once he'd recovered a little, he looked cautiously into the container but couldn't see much of anything. "What the heck is going on here?" He looked at Thor, who sat and wagged while he stared at him with bright eyes. "Stay."

Charles stepped inside again and held his breath. He flipped the lights on and surveyed the scene. "That mother-fucker. I'm going to kill Bronson for this. And if he thinks he's getting paid, he's got another think coming."

The shipping container was wrecked. Fragments of bone and old, unidentifiable liquids were everywhere. Bedding and other various items were strewn about. Thor had run out of room in the back corner and had to defecate all over the container. Some of the men's things were chewed but mostly, they were intact and simply flung everywhere.

He toed the empty fire extinguisher out of the way. "Unbelievable. I'm so sorry, Thor. There's no way this is your fault. He was supposed to take care of you."

The animal whined from outside.

Charles stumbled out of the container again when the smell overwhelmed him. He closed the door firmly and retrieved his phone to call Booker.

The Brit picked up on the second ring. "Yeah?"

"Hey, we need to get a different place for the night," he said. "That asshole Bronson didn't take care of Thor, and the container needs to be cleaned."

"Must be really bad if you're swearing about it," he commented.

The American grunted.

"Okay. Sure. Not ideal, but we'll find something," Booker said.

He hung up and looked at Thor. "Stay. I'll be right back with some food and water."

The dog obeyed and sat in front of the container until Charles returned. He lunged for the water jug and lapped enthusiastically.

"Woah, slow down, Thor," he said and pulled back on the animal's collar. "I know you're thirsty, but you'll make yourself sick guzzling it all down that fast."

He tied Thor to a stake outside the container. He trusted that he would stay in one place, but he would be in the container cleaning and thought it would be better for him to be able to move around some.

Charles tied a damp bandana around his nose, but it barely helped with the rotting stench. He started putting trash into the bag he'd brought, cleaning up the bits of debris that littered the container. He picked up a sliver of bone and threw it away without giving it much thought.

Thor sat just inside the container door and watched him clean the mess.

"How'd this happen, Thor? Huh?"

His tail thumped on the ground in response and his ears swiveled to pick up the sounds the man made.

He found another bone that had been chewed clean. It had the indentations of Thor's teeth on it and he held it toward the animal. "Man, you must've been really hungry. You sure cleaned this up good."

Thor lunged toward the long bone and Charles chuckled, willing to play tug-of-war with the dog. Then, he looked more closely at it. "That's odd," he said. "Drop it." The animal released his end of the bone.

He lifted it for closer inspection. His eyes widened after a moment and he dropped it. Thor reached for it. "Don't touch that!" he said. "Holy shit. That's a femur. A...a...a *human* femur!"

Charles spun in a slow circle and looked at the chaos of the container again. He saw more bone fragments and his stomach lurched and roiled. Slowly, he moved to the container door, shut it, and locked the two of them inside.

He turned and saw Thor gnawing on another bone fragment. "Hey, drop it."

The dog seemed reluctant but he released the curved fragment.

When his stomach heaved involuntarily, he spun and puked into the trash bag.

"Sweet Jesus, Thor, that's a skull," he said and rubbed a hand over his face. "Oh, Thor, you killed him, didn't you?"

Thor sat and wagged his tail.

"Fuck," Charles muttered. He thumped his palms against his forehead and grasped his hair. When he looked at the dog, his tail wagged harder. "Shit." He wiped away a few tears. He knew what he had to do despite every fiber in his body screaming, "No!"

His breathing grew ragged as he walked to the back of the container and unlocked the gun safe. He retrieved his shotgun, loaded it, and turned the safety off before he walked toward Thor.

The animal yipped happily and his tail thudded rapidly against the floor of the container.

Charles raised the shotgun, then propped it against the

wall. He squatted in front of Thor and ran his fingers through the dog's fur. He pulled him closer to his chest in a hug that he tried to struggle out of. "I'm sorry, bud, I have to do this," he said and gritted his teeth.

After a long moment, he stood again and wiped savagely at the tears that streamed freely down his cheeks. He picked the shotgun up and aimed it again. His hands shook and he tightened his grip to try to steady them. "Fuck, I don't want to do this to you. You're such a good dog."

Thor rolled over and begged for a belly rub.

"Good boy. Just sit there, okay? I'll make this fast. I promise, buddy."

He cocked his head to the side and stared at the man and the gun.

"Shit." He lowered the shotgun and flipped the safety on. "There's no way you did this without being provoked. I have to know before I do this."

Charles looked around the container and located the security camera they'd had installed before they'd left. Roo had made fun of Booker and called him paranoid and a skitzo, but the Brit had insisted it was a good idea. He was glad now that he hadn't added his protest to the Aussie's.

He pulled up the video feed. "Whatever's on here, buddy, it doesn't change what has to happen. You *killed* someone. There's no coming back from that, Thor. The entire camp would riot if they knew. I know it doesn't seem fair, but that's how it has to be. I just need to see this first."

While part of him dreaded what he would find, he rewound through the previous days and skipped a large portion which only showed Thor pacing and sleeping in the dark container. Then, he saw the altercation with Bronson. He watched Thor kill him and eat him.

Charles kicked one of the nearby cots, upended it, and careened the bed into the opposite wall. Thor jumped and scrambled to the opposite side of the container, his tail tucked between his legs.

"Shit, sorry," he said. "This is so unfair."

He slumped and sat with his back against the wall. Thor approached him cautiously, then crawled halfway into his lap. He ran his fingers through the dog's fur. He scratched behind his ears, then his fingers moved across the top of his head. His eyes widened.

When he'd left, the animal had only one horn growing on the top of his head. Now, he had two.

"No, no, no, no," he muttered. He looked closer and saw the two perfect horns twisting from the top of the animal's head. The truth was unavoidable. He'd seen horns like those before—on animals in the Zoo.

Charles closed his eyes. "I guess it makes sense. There were all those times your eyes looked like they were glowing. I thought it was just the light, but I guess I was in denial. Shit, you're from the Zoo."

Thor wagged his tail.

He sat on the floor of the container and stroked the dog until the animal dozed off. No other choice existed. He knew he needed to put Thor down—he'd killed a person, and he was also from the Zoo. Charles knew that if word of what had happened got out there would be hell to pay. There was no way they'd let Thor live, and the BOHICA Warriors would be through.

For a moment, he considered trying to smuggle Thor away and take him home to Des Moines. Maybe he could get a small place out in the countryside where they could be alone. But that was his heart speaking, he knew, not his brain. He didn't care if Thor was from the Zoo, but others would. He couldn't get him out of the country, and there was no way in hell he could get him into the US. It was bad enough with one horn, but with two? And as big as he'd gotten?

Charles knew his duty, and duty was one thing the Marines had taught him. But for the moment, he simplu sat there, slowly petting Thor.

After about half an hour, he nudged the animal out of his lap and drew himself to his full height. He looked at Thor. "When people find out what you are and what you've done, there's no stopping them from killing you. You have to understand, I don't want to do this, but it's better me than someone else."

Charles put the muzzle of the shotgun to Thor's head, right between the two horns. He wagged his tail and bit at the shotgun like they would play tug-of-war as they usually did. His finger tightened on the trigger, but he hesitated again.

In the distance, a faint howling issued from the direction of the Zoo, not out in the Sahara. The animal's ears perked up and he attempted a howl of his own.

"Hush," he said and looked around at the still messy container. "I can't do this here. Come on."

He put Thor on a leash and walked across the sand toward the gates that would lead him into the Zoo. It was already dark so not many men were walking around, but when they were halfway to the gate, someone stopped them.

"Would you look at that. If it isn't the BOHICA dream team," the man said. He crouched to pet Thor. "Haven't seen you for a while. You either, Thor."

Charles grimaced. "Yeah," he said, his voice tight.

"Hey, man, you okay? You don't look so good."

He shrugged. "Jet lag."

"Ah, you just got back today?"

Charles nodded.

"America, right?"

He nodded again. "Look, I can't really talk right now. Sorry, I've got some things I need to do before I can hit the hay."

"Oh yeah, of course. Sorry. Don't let me keep you," the man said. "Bye bye, Thor."

Charles walked on.

The guard who was on duty grinned when he saw them. "Hey, long time no see! When'd you get back?"

"Just got back today. Listen, I need to go out into the Zoo. Just for a minute."

The guard frowned. "You going on mission already?"

"No. No. Just...wanting to re-acclimate myself is all. Get back in the mindset and all that."

"Really?"

He simply waited in silence.

The guard shrugged. "Oh, what the hell. I suppose there've been weirder reasons for going into the Zoo." He pressed the code into the keypad and the personnel gate slid open. "Just be careful. You don't want to get yourself killed the first day back."

Charles nodded and walked through.

When he'd made it through the three sets of walls and was finally in the Zoo, he paused. He stood on the burned-clear track of sand and looked around. Thor wagged his tail beside him and vibrated with energy.

He looked at the Zoo animal at his side. "I guess it makes sense why you loved it in here so much."

His throat constricted and he took a deep breath of humid Zoo air and moved toward the line of the jungle that loomed ahead of them in the darkness. The plants moved toward him, leaning and retreating like the whole jungle breathed in and out.

He led Thor into the trees for several hundred meters until he was sure they were out of sight of the guards who patrolled the top of the fence.

There were more howls in the distance, although closer and more distinct now. The animal's ears perked up and he threw his head back and gave an answering howl.

Charles' blood ran cold.

Thor looked at him again and his eyes glowed a faint, deep red.

His teeth gritted, he raised his shotgun and pressed it to Thor's temple.

The Zoo creature blinked back at him and wagged his tail.

He unclipped the leash and undid the parachute cord collar. Then, he put the shotgun back to his head.

With no more reason for delay, he wrapped his finger around the trigger and started to apply pressure. "Fuck! Fuck, I can't do it."

Charles lowered the shotgun and ran his fingers through his short hair. "Shit, why is this so hard?"

Thor wagged his tail and sat and watched him. He sat beside the animal, who put his head on his shoulder.

"Don't do that, buddy," he said, but he didn't try to remove his head.

He couldn't help that he was crying. In that moment, he was glad that Roo wasn't there to see his breakdown. Thor licked the tears cautiously from his face. He shoved him away.

"Don't. Don't you're already making this hard. Don't make it harder."

The animal looked at him and his eyes glowed red—the red of the Zoo. With a rush of relief, Charles realized he'd been looking at this wrong. Thor was of the Zoo and he belonged there, not as a pet of humans. He needed to be with his own kind.

Being abandoned might kill him just as certainly as if Charles had pulled the trigger. There was that orca that had been born in captivity, the one all the people wanted freed. It was released into the wild where it died. It didn't know how to survive on its own. But in the Zoo, Thor had a chance.

He pulled the animal's head in close and said, "I know you don't understand this at all, Thor. I know you aren't going to get it, but it has to happen this way."

Charles dragged himself to his feet. He slung the shotgun over his shoulder.

"Now, go on! Git! Get out of here!" he yelled. He flung his arms in Thor's direction.

The creature stood and looked at him in confusion and his tail wagged slowly.

"Go on!" he yelled and stamped his foot.

Thor thought he was trying to play. He crouched low and sprang up again, barking happily.

"No! No, you dumb mutt, get out of here! Go on!"

Charles threw the leash into the jungle. Thor lunged after it. He watched him for a moment, then turned to go, but the slight delay was enough and he ran back almost immediately with the leash in his mouth. Expectantly, he dropped it at his feet and his tail wagged vigorously.

"I can't play anymore, okay?" he yelled. Thor took a step back, clearly confused. "You can't stay with me. They won't let you, and they'll kill you. You need to be out here. I don't know if you can survive here or if you can find your own kind. But at least you've got a fighting chance out here. With me, you've got no chance."

He looked at the animal. His bulk blurred through the tears and emphasized the dog-like shape. More than anything, he wanted to walk back to the camp with him but knew he couldn't. Even if they covered up the fact that he had killed a man, he didn't think they would be able to hide the fact that Thor was a Zoo animal for much longer. He already had twin horns coming in. Who knew what would be next?

Charles rubbed his hand over his face and wiped his tears angrily.

"I'm not angry at you, Thor. I'm angry at this situation. It's not your fault you just weren't born a dog."

Thor's tail wagged again.

"Sit," he said.

He sat.

"Good. Now, stay."

The animal panted happily and Charles thought his canines looked longer than they had before.

He began to walk away. When he looked over his shoulder, Thor watched him attentively. "Stay," he repeated. He walked farther into the jungle and left the animal waiting behind him.

Once he was confident Thor could no longer see him, he ran all the way back to the gate. Although he listened for any sign of pursuit, all he heard was the sound of his own footsteps.

CHAPTER SEVEN

The Zoo - Thor

Thor watched the man's retreating back and wagged his tail. He was glad the men were back. He assumed Charles was accompanied by the other two, although he would've been happy with only the large man. He was his favorite.

The jungle around him smelled so good and he wanted to run through it until he couldn't run anymore. The man had told him to stay, though. So, he'd stay where he was.

He couldn't see him anymore, but that didn't worry him. Charles would come back. He always did.

Thor waited, and waited, and waited. The temperature dropped around him, but still the human didn't return.

Night closed over the Zoo, and he sat and continued to wait. It wasn't until the sun made its first appearance over the eastern sky that he gave up. Maybe Charles had gotten lost and was looking for him. If that was the case, he would find him and they'd go back to the container together and play fetch with the old rubber tire.

He followed the faint trail of Charles' scent all the way back to the edge of the jungle.

Thor paused before his paws could sink fully into the sand. He could see the gate from where he stood but an unpleasant sound assaulted his ears and made his hair stand on end.

He bared his teeth but couldn't find anything to attack. He slunk forward, determined to reach Charles. He couldn't see him but he could still smell him.

The animal crawled forward, his belly low on the sand. When he brushed against the gate, he leapt back as an electric jolt coursed through him. He yelped and retreated into the jungle again.

Thor repeated the process twice more before giving up.

In the distance, he could hear howling. He replied to it, although his own howl was weak and didn't sound exactly like the others. He wanted to find those who were like him. He knew they were out there, but the man had commanded him to stay and he'd already disobeyed.

Despondent, he plodded back to the place where he had been told to stay. He dropped prone, put his head on his front paws, and waited, staring at the place where the man had disappeared.

CHAPTER EIGHT

The Harvesters Camp

Charles worked on cleaning the container. He collected all the fragments of Bronson's remains, careful to gather all the splinters of bone and any other fleshy chunks he could find. He tied them tightly in a bag and marched across the camp to where he knew he could find an incinerator.

He reached the warehouse where Booker generally got their assignments from Franco, a dispatcher for a third-tier shadow company. The structure was a glorified, nondescript pole barn. Two guards slouched outside the personnel door.

"Evening, gents." He strode up to them, a wide, friendly smile plastered on his face.

They nodded warily at him. Thankfully, they'd seen him around when he'd occasionally accompanied Booker to get jobs.

"The incinerator up and running?" he asked.

The guards exchanged a look.

"Maybe it is, and maybe it isn't," the man on the right said.

Charles nodded slowly. "What'll it take for it to be running?"

The two looked at each other again. "It certainly needs some extra fuel if you're wanting to use it," the man on the left said. He rubbed his thumb and two fingers together.

The American dug into his pocket for his wallet, careful not to jostle the bag too much. While he didn't think anything would fall out—he'd double-bagged it—he felt he couldn't be too careful.

He handed the guard on the right three hundred dollars. The man counted the money and divided it with his partner. He indicated with his head that he could go ahead and use the incinerator.

"Wait," the guard said before he could walk past. "This isn't anything illegal is it?"

Charles raised an eyebrow. "I feel like it's a little late to have a crisis of conscience unless you want to hand the money back. Besides, if it was illegal, would you care?"

The two men exchanged hurried glances again, then the one who had stopped him shrugged. "Right. Go on ahead. Make it quick."

He nodded and approached the incinerator, opened the door, and shoved the bag inside. Once he'd closed the door firmly, he pressed the button to heat it again. Smoke plumed out the top. He watched it for the moment as the last traces of Bronson floated into the night sky.

Charles turned on his heel and made his way back to the converted container.

Working systematically, he scrubbed the entire place

with bleach. He scoured obsessively and went through four sponges before he finally gave up. By that point, he was drenched with sweat and smelled like chemicals. He looked at the spotless interior, satisfied that no one else would be able to tell what had taken place there. With that need in mind, he'd destroyed the memory card in the camera and the camera itself and had deleted it off the digital feed Booker had set up. The evidence might have been gone, but Charles would always know what had happened. He tried not to think about Thor in the Zoo. Was he still alive? He hadn't been able to pull the trigger himself, but had the Zoo done what he couldn't?

His chore complete, he changed his clothes, threw out the ones he'd had on, and made his way reluctantly to the Wateringhole where the others were waiting.

He walked in and located the group at a table in the back. Charles stopped at the bar and threw back a shot of whiskey, then two more. He ordered a double and made his way to the table. Reen was telling the story of how she'd been demoted from lance corporal to private.

"We were all on shore leave in Barrio Barretto, Subic Bay," she said. "Beautiful place. Beautiful people. I love the Philippines. Anyway, we were on liberty at the same time as some Navy guys were. You've got to watch out for those fuckers. They like to party, but none of them knows how to handle their liquor." She paused to take a sip and smirked at her rapt audience.

"I was out at a bar, minding my own goddamn business, when this asshole Navy lieutenant saunters in and starts hitting on the chick I was trying to pick up."

"Typical," Roo muttered.

Booker stifled a laugh and his teammate gave him the moutza, palm forward, all five fingers splayed.

"Some people just don't have manners," Mick said.

She grinned. "I told him, 'Look, buddy, I was here first. Find your own.'" The woman leaned back in her chair and knocked back the rest of her whiskey. She put the cup on the table and ran her finger along the rim of it, making the glass tumbler sing.

"What'd he say to that?" Lester asked. He tried to sound bored but failed.

"Don't know," Reen said with a shrug.

"You don't know?" Mick asked. "I'm confused."

"I didn't catch what he was saying because his mouth got a little obstructed by my fist."

The men laughed.

"They demoted you for that?" Roo asked. "What fucking wombats."

"Nah. It's just I didn't stop there. I beat the shit out of that fucker. There was a huge brawl and I got demoted for it. At least I didn't get kicked out."

"I thought Charles said you were a corporal?" Roo asked.

"Oh, I retired a corporal. After I was busted down two pay grades to private, I worked my way back up and then some. Made it in record time, too."

Charles tried to participate in the conversation, but his mind was still reeling.

Booker nudged him. "Hey, you're looking a little peaked. What's wrong? Where's Thor?"

"I need to talk to you," he muttered through his teeth and finished with a hiss.

The Brit frowned. "Can it wait?"

He shook his head. Abruptly, he stood from the table, grabbed the man by the arm, and hauled him upward. He jerked his head at Roo, then stormed out of the bar with his two teammates in tow.

"What the hell's the matter? Where's the fucking fire?" the Aussie asked. "I was enjoying myself in there."

"Thor killed someone," Charles said bluntly.

The two men stared at him.

"You're going to have to repeat yourself, Charles, because I'm pretty sure you just said Thor killed someone," Booker said.

He nodded.

"Holy fuck. For real?" Roo asked.

Once again, he simply nodded.

"Are you sure?" the Brit asked. "I mean, are you sure it was him and not another person?"

"I'm sure," Charles said. "I saw the footage." He lowered his voice. "Thor killed Bronson, the man I hired to take care of him while we were gone. He didn't take care of him at all. In fact, he abused him. It was self-defense. Bronson stabbed Thor and he attacked." He rubbed his eyes wearily. "Then he ate him."

"Fuckin' a," Roo muttered.

"It has to be reported, Charles," Booker said. "We can't just pretend this didn't happen. It has to be reported, and Thor has to be put down."

"I know. I know. I've already handled Thor."

"You've 'handled' Thor? What does that mean?"

"I've already handled it. I know he can't be around

people anymore. He's a danger, even if he was forced into it." He sighed. "Even if he's just a puppy."

"Jesus H. Christ, I can't believe this happened," the Brit said. "We have to report it."

"You keep fucking saying that, Booker. I think we get the bloody point." Roo glowered at his teammate.

Charles stared at the other two. "We can't."

"What?" Booker asked.

"We can't report it," he said.

Booker's glare was obdurate. "The fuck we can't. We bleddy *have* to, Charles."

"No," Roo said, slowly. "I think Charles is right. We can't report this."

The man gaped at them.

"Look," Charles said, "I like following the rules as much as the next guy, but we can't report this. Our company is just starting out. We can't afford to make any mistakes. And now we have employees. We dragged others out here and told them this was the way they'd be able to make a decent living."

"Reporting it would be throwing that all down the fucking drain," Roo reminded him.

"But we have to! A man *died*. More than that, he was fucking *killed* by a pet of ours! No one's going to give a shit that Thor was just a puppy or that he was forced into it. It only matters that Bronson was human and Thor isn't."

Charles shook his head. "You think I don't fucking know that? Of course I'm aware that this is a bad situation. But we just can't do it, Booker."

"Besides," Roo added, "Bronson was a motherfucking

asswipe. Nobody liked the wanker. He won't be fucking missed. Just another Zoo casualty."

The American winced but his companions didn't notice.

"We've worked too hard to get where we are now. We are just getting started and it's only up from here!" Roo said. "We can't shoot ourselves in the foot with this. So, the world is down one more asshole, who gives a shit? Sometimes, you have to look out for yourself."

"I just don't think it's right."

"It isn't right, Booker," Charles said. "It's not. But it's what has to happen. Let's be realistic here. We aren't earning an honest living to begin with. We're glorified mercenaries. No one cares if we live or die except our families. No one cares. We're just numbers. Bodies going into the Zoo and bodies coming out. Bronson is just one more body."

"We've worked too fucking hard for this, Booker. Now's not the time to get fucking squeamish."

Booker stared at his teammates. He looked into the night sky and counted some of the stars.

"Fine," he said. "Fine. We won't report it."

Charles heaved a sigh of relief. Roo smiled.

The Brit leveled a finger at them. "We won't report it, but I don't like it. This is going to come back and bite us in the ass, I just know it."

"We'll figure it out if we have to," Roo said. "For now, Charles here looks like he needs to get pissed. He's had a rough day."

CHAPTER NINE

The Harvesters Camp

"You can't be fucking serious. You want us to wear these?" Reen asked. She held up a bright red t-shirt. Lester and Mick held identical garments. BOHICA was stitched on the left breast above the name of the person. The word *trainee* was emblazoned across the back in all capital letters.

"Serious as a heart attack," Charles said and grinned. He shrugged into his own t-shirt. It was Army green and only had his name and BOHICA on it.

Roo and Booker also wore green shirts.

"We're professionals," Booker said. "We have to present a united front."

Roo looked at the shirt he had on. "You know, I'm glad we went with the green. Way better than that ugly-ass puke yellow color you wanted, Booker."

His teammate merely gave him the finger.

Mick, whose normal laid-back attitude was a little shaken by the shirts, frowned and raised an eyebrow.

"Hold up. Please tell me you weren't thinking about *Star Trek* when you made these."

Booker shrugged. "It makes sense. Space and aliens and all that shit."

"We aren't in space, though!" Reen protested.

"No, but this is a sort of final frontier," he retorted.

Roo groaned. "You're such a goddamn nerd."

Charles laughed. "You're one to talk, Roo. You suggested we make the new recruits' shirts red."

The Aussie turned as red as his hair and the shirts the three held. "I did not."

"Real mature comeback. And you did. I seem to remember a conversation where you thought it would be funny if greenhorns wore red shirts."

Mick shook his head. "Nope. Now I really don't want to wear this." He held the shirt away from himself as if it would explode or get him killed simply by holding it.

"Oh, come on. It's just a joke from some shitty old TV show," Roo said.

"A shitty old TV show you watched religiously, if I remember correctly," the Aboriginal said.

He held up both middle fingers. "Don't make me regret recruiting you."

Mick held his hands up and laughed. "All right, I'll wear the damn shirt."

"Don't listen to him," Roo said to Reen.

She grinned. "Once a Trekkie, always a Trekkie."

"So we have the uniform. What's next?" Lester asked.

"Next, we equip you," Booker said.

"You guys get to meet Dan," Charles said. "He's a real treat."

"Who's Dan?" Reen asked.

"The asshole we get all our gear from. He charges insane prices, but his shit's reliable," Roo answered. "And, despite the fact that he'd overcharge his own mother for oxygen, he's about as honest as a man in his position could be."

Dan stood behind his table, his back to the gleaming racks of equipment. He had ammunition, fuel, explosives, sample containers, and weaponry of all kinds. They knew that if they ever needed anything, he probably had it, and if he didn't have it, he probably had a way to procure it. All for a price, of course.

"Ah, the prodigals return! How was the vacation?" Dan asked and grinned. "I see you were successful in roping more people into your company."

"It was good, but we're ready to be back in the Zoo. We just need to equip our new hires," Booker said.

"Great." The supplier sounded enthusiastic.

Roo could've sworn his eyes turned into dollar signs.

"What'll your poison be?"

"We need three sets of armor," Booker said. "Plus three SIGs. And they each get a weapon of their choosing."

"How generous of you," Roo said and rolled his eyes.

"Just don't get carried away," Charles said. "The Zoo is a close-combat zone. You need maximum efficiency in a short range."

"I'll take an M4...uh, is that a 92?" Reen asked and her eyes gleamed as only a gun nut's could when she saw a new toy. She stroked the barrel suggestively as a lover would, which made Roo gulp. "I'll take that, thank you very much. And nix the SIG. I want a

Beretta." She shrugged at Booker. "I can use anything that goes bang, but I figure it's best to go with what I know best."

"Fine. But know that this is the only time this is going to happen," Booker said.

"Don't listen to that twat. He likes to pretend he's hot shit, but you can wear him down," Roo said and leaned closer to her.

She tilted away from him. "Whatever you say, Roo."

"I can still hear you, you know," Booker said.

Roo gestured dismissively.

"You got any M5s?" Lester asked.

Dan nodded. "I've got whatever the hell you want."

"I'd like an F88C," Mick said.

"All right. I'll go wrestle these up for you folks and you can pay me and be on your way." Dan disappeared into the stacks to retrieve the weapons and armor.

"I feel like a kid on Christmas morning," the Aboriginal said.

Roo grinned at him. "It's pretty great, right?"

"Don't get too caught up. Remember, we have to pay for it all," Charles said.

The supplier returned with the items while Roo was off to the side with the recruits explaining the workings of a new landmine. "Hey, Charles, how's the fleabag?"

The American winced.

Booker stepped in front of Charles. "Thor had a bit of an...accident. Nothing to concern yourself with. What's the damage here, Dan?"

Dan looked from Charles to Booker and back again. He pursed his lips but decided to drop it. "Whatever," he said.

"For you three? A special price. It's all yours for an even hundred."

"Seventy-five," Booker countered.

The supplier raised an eyebrow. "Do you think I'm running a charity? No fucking way. One hundred is the absolute lowest I will go. Sorry, Booker. That's a steal, and if you leave the deal on the table too long, it'll only go up."

"Fine," he said after a short moment. Dan grinned and Booker paid him begrudgingly.

"Is that guy for real?" Reen asked after they'd left.

Booker shrugged. "I'd say you get used to it, but then I'd be lying."

"We make more than enough to make up for it, but it still is a pain in the ass," Roo said.

"Jesus, you'd think he was selling gold-plated shit for those prices," Mick muttered.

"So, we have our equipment. What happens now, boss?" she asked and looked at the Brit.

The newcomers had been told that the three men owned the company equally. Despite this, it had become clear that Booker, as the highest ranking, often defaulted into the leadership role.

"Now, we drill and train."

Within half an hour, they were set up in the alley behind the converted container where they stood in two lines in the sand. The newcomers and the original team regarded one another with calculating gazes.

"We'll run you through some immediate action drills," Charles said. "Get you used to working as a cohesive unit. Luckily, the three of you have the proper backgrounds for this so it shouldn't take too long for you to work together."

Twenty minutes later, the six were out in the noon Sahara sun. Charles, Roo, and Booker spent the afternoon yelling commands to the rookies as they sweated.

"There's movement at your six," Charles snapped.

Lester swung, his weapon at the ready.

"Something at two o'clock," Booker called.

Reen adjusted her position. The three shuffled to maintain their formation.

The others at the Harvesters Camp strolled through or stopped to stare at BOHICA's new recruits. They made fun of the training, just like they'd made fun of Booker, Roo and Charles when they'd first started drilling.

"Just ignore the wankers," Roo said loudly. "They won't be laughing when they're dead." That cleared the area of gawkers for a while.

"This is bullshit," Lester said after two hours of it. "I thought we were going to get right into it. I'm ready to be paid. None of this shuffling back and forth while being mocked shit. I've already done that. I did my time for queen and country. Now, it's my bloody turn."

Charles folded his arms over his chest and scowled. "You don't really have a choice, tough guy. You aren't working for yourself. You work for us."

Lester immediately squared up to him, but the large American easily had three inches on him and didn't back down.

"Look," Booker said. "I know it's a bit of a pain, but it'll be worth it in the long run. Trust us. The casualty rate for the Zoo is extremely high. The three of us are an exception to the groups that go in and don't come out. Statistically speaking, one in four gets either badly maimed or killed.

We've been in plenty of times, but we still drill and train. You can't be complacent with an environment that's constantly evolving like the Zoo is. You've got to stay vigilant and sharp. Complacency will get you killed."

Mick and Reen nodded. Lester still didn't look convinced.

"Fucking run through it again," Roo growled. "Reen, you've got point."

She took the role and called the commands. The three shuffled forward and back, always with their weapons at the ready.

The three original teammates stepped aside to watch.

"What do you think?" Charles asked.

"I think that Lester is a real asshole," Roo said.

Booker winced. "I'll be honest, he wasn't my first choice."

"No shit," his teammate muttered.

"He might not have the most winning personality, but the man is supposed to be bleddy good under fire. We get him out in the Zoo and I'm sure he'll pull through."

"'Supposed to be?' Let's hope you're right," Charles said. "We can't afford any more mistakes right now."

"I'll drum up a mission soon and we'll get to really see what they can handle."

"We starting them on flora?" Roo asked.

Booker nodded. "What else? It would be bleddy stupid to start with fauna."

The Aussie shrugged. "Don't know...out of the pan and into the fire and all that."

"Flora's the way to go," Charles said. "Then, we can give them a bigger challenge. Uh, make sure you've got a

picture of a Pita flower. With a big 'Do Not Touch' plastered across it. I know some teams harvest the flowers, but
we've steered clear of them for now. The animals apparently only go crazy when you pull the whole plant, but for
now, I'm not willing to take a chance."

"Probably a good idea," Roo said. "But someday…"

CHAPTER TEN

Harvesters Camp

"When are we done with this sitting around bullshit?" Lester asked. He sat in the shade of the converted container, flipped a pocketknife in the air, and caught it by the handle in endless sequence.

Roo glanced at him from where he watched Charles and Reen—or more specifically Reen's ass—as they sparred. "This is the worst part of the job if you ask me," he said. "It's a whole lot of waiting between missions. You've only been here a few days. We wanted to give you lot the chance to adjust. Plus, we wanted to run you through some drills."

"That's not really an answer, Aussie."

"We'll be leaving soon," Charles said and halted the sparring. Sweat poured off him. He had managed to keep Reen at bay, but he wasn't sure if he'd be able to fend her attacks off for much longer. "In fact, Booker should be wrangling us up a job right about now. He'll be back any minute."

The American sat in the shade beside Lester and guzzled water. Reen leaned against the wall next to him. They passed the canteen between them. Roo glared at how they shared casually like husband and wife. Or maybe as two Marines. Jarheads always took that brotherhood thing too far. They both ignored him.

"Hey," Lester said and kicked Charles lightly in the thigh, "where's the fleabag you were telling us about?"

The American bolted from the ground and stepped forward to force the man back in his chair until it tipped. "You shut the fuck up."

Reen and Roo leapt forward and dragged him away from Lester, who held his hands up.

"Jesus, man, it was an honest bloody question!"

Mick, who attempted to play cat's cradle by himself, glanced up at the action but didn't move from his place.

"Walk it off, Charles!" Roo snapped and shoved his teammate aside.

He strode away while he muttered and gripped his short hair. They watched him go in silence.

"What happened to the dog, Roo?" Reen asked finally.

Roo sighed. "There was an...incident while we were away."

Mick grimaced. "Yikes. The thing didn't make it?"

"Yeah. Something like that," he confirmed.

"Something like that?" Lester asked. "What does that mean?"

"It just means the dog isn't around anymore. End of discussion," Roo snapped. "And it's obviously a sore subject for the big guy, so don't fucking mention it or you assholes will have me to deal with."

Reen rolled her eyes. "Real scary threat. I think it's bad enough to have Charles to deal with."

He glared at her. "I could whip your ass, you know."

She gave a surprised laughed. "Sure."

"No, really, I could."

"Whatever you say, big guy."

Booker walked up to the small group. "Good news! I got us a job." He looked around. "Where did Charles go?"

"Someone mentioned the dog," Roo said and scowled at Lester, who simply shook his head.

"Okay. Well, we need to get him back. Work is the best way to process this. We've got to head out," the Brit said.

"What's the big job?" Mick asked as he shoved the parachute cord he was using into his pocket and stretched.

"Flora collecting."

"Wait. Flora collecting?" Lester asked. "We're glorified gardeners? I thought you said this was merc work."

"It is," Booker said. "Most flowers don't try to eat you when you collect them. They don't trigger blood lust in any animal and plant around it when they are pulled up," he added by way of explanation.

"It's not a stroll into your granny's rose garden." Roo's tone was belligerent. "These plants have bigger fucking defenses besides thorns."

Charles returned at that moment, his shoulders tense, but he showed no other sign of his outburst.

"You good?" Booker asked.

He nodded.

"All right, let's gear up. Time for the red shirts' first time in the Zoo."

"I'd really prefer it if you didn't fucking say that about us," Mick said.

Booker laughed. "You superstitious?"

"Hell, yes."

"What is with you Australians? I didn't realize you were all so prone to flights of fancy."

"Flights of fancy?" Roo asked.

"Yeah. You know, superstitions and all that other third-eye shit."

"We aren't fucking fortune tellers and palm readers," the Aussie protested.

"Actually," Mick said, "I've been known to read tarot cards on occasion."

"And I wouldn't say heaps of Australians are like this. You just happen to have a semi-psychic and a bit of a superstitious one in your gang."

"Semi-psychic?" Reen scoffed.

Roo puffed his chest out. "Yeah. My whole family has a bit of intuition and luck to us."

She rolled her eyes. "Great. Well, let's get this freak show on the road then."

Booker led the group into the three walls that separated the camp from the Zoo. Roo was in the center of the line and Charles brought up the rear.

"What the bloody hell are they trying to keep out?" Lester asked as he stared at the flamethrower-wielding guards who stalked along the top of the wall they'd just walked through. He looked at the machine guns pointed into the space between the walls they traversed. Large chunks of cement forced them to wind around like a maze.

"They're not trying to keep anything out," Booker said over his shoulder, "they're trying to keep everything in."

The Brit led them across the marked path on the other side of the second wall. "Just stay on the path," he said as if the many warning signs posted everywhere weren't enough.

"What happens if you step off the path?" Mick asked.

Roo shrugged. "Nothing good."

They entered the last wall and Booker paused halfway through. He turned to the new recruits in the dimly lit walkway. "This is a flora gathering job. It's pretty routine, but that isn't an invitation to slouch through this. The Zoo is a dangerous place and following orders is imperative."

"Got it," Mick said. "We're on the highway to the danger zone."

Roo snickered. Reen and Lester grimaced.

Booker frowned. "This isn't funny. I'm serious as the fucking grave about this."

"All right, Booker. I think they get the point. Let's get on with it," Charles interjected.

Their leader made sure the door they'd just walked through was firmly shut, then he pressed a button on the wall and the door leading into the Zoo slid open.

The three newbies looked around at the short stretch of scarred sand. They studied the creeping plants that attempted to make their way across the burned strip to the wall and the churned earth that held the tell-tale signs of old firefights.

The jungle that was the Zoo rose ahead of them, a

massive wall of vibrant green that moved faintly like the whole thing was a monster breathing quietly.

Mick looked around. "I'll be honest here, mates, I was expecting something a little more...well, more."

"Yeah," Charles said and shouldered his way up to Booker, "it's a little underwhelming at first. But trust me, it'll get weird real fast."

"This'll be a quick mission," Booker said. "We're only going ten klicks in, north-northwest. We'll need to bring back five pitcher plant blossoms. I'll give better instructions when we get there. There's a known plant not that far in. At least there was two days ago."

"Two days ago? Wouldn't it still be there?" Reen asked.

"Not always with the Zoo. It likes to rearrange itself. Maps are shit here. Unless you have the freshest map there is, it's not going to help you out much. GPS is out of the question. The plants and other alien shit fucks with the signals. It's all azimuths and guesswork, and if you've waited too long, well, you're shit out of luck," he explained.

"Wait, pitcher plants? Like the house plant? Why do we have to go through all this work for some of those?" Mick asked. "Hell, my granny's got heaps of the things at her place."

"These aren't your average, domesticated pitcher plant. They're just called that because of the shape of the blossom. The name is the only similarity between the two. This is a Zoo pitcher plant," Booker said.

"What's the big difference, then?" the Aboriginal asked.

"This pitcher plant can kill you," he replied calmly. "Move out."

He set a steady pace with Charles beside him. The

others fell into pairs behind them—Roo and Lester followed by Reen and Mick. The formation couldn't stay tight due to the dense undergrowth, but they held a relatively straight line behind the leaders.

They marched for two klicks, their weapons at the ready as the jungle closed in around them. Thick vines with small, pearl-white flowers wove an intricate netting over the ground. Vines twisted and moved, silent as snakes in the jungle canopy.

A humming sound providing the only warning of the incoming danger.

"Here it comes!" Roo yelled and readjusting his Czech VZ .58.

A locust burst from between the trees, followed rapidly by three more. Their blade-like legs sliced through the air and mandibles snapped.

Lester's rounds pierced the closest insect's wings and grounded it. It scuttled forward and Reen finished it with her M492.

"Wait for the mouths to be open," Charles said. His Remington thundered and the slug plowed through an oncoming locust that immediately exploded in a splatter of emerald green blood.

The others followed his lead. Reen's deadly aim and quick reflexes caused the demise of at least five creatures. Lester proved himself to be a fast draw, and Mick didn't slouch either. He dispatched several of the mutants cleanly and made sure the fallen stayed fallen.

The wave of attackers was over almost as soon as it began. They stood and surveyed the mangled carcasses.

"Well," Mick said, "that wasn't so bad."

"Yeah, if you like giant bugs. These things smell like shit," Reen said.

"Keep moving," Booker instructed. "You'll be seeing a lot of these, and trust me, the novelty wears off fast."

They marched on and the only things that disturbed them were the plants. Vines occasionally attempted to trip them as they walked past.

"Do you feel that?" Lester asked after they'd marched for another klick.

"Feel what?" Roo asked.

"Something's watching us."

Booker halted the column and they peered into the dense underbrush. There were a few indistinct rustles, but nothing appeared.

"Whatever it is, it's staying hidden. It'll be a problem when it chooses to be a problem. Move out," he ordered.

They'd traveled several more klicks when a giant Komodo-dragon-like creature, although bright blue, crossed their paths. The enormous lizard turned and hissed. Lester's finger tightened on the trigger, but the mutant rushed into the underbrush and was soon out of sight.

"Does that normally happen?" Reen asked.

Roo shrugged. "Eh. Not really, but then again, nothing in here acts like you expect it to."

"So, what exactly does the objective look like?" Mick asked.

"You said we were looking for some flowers?" Lester asked. "What about those?" He pointed to a small clump of vibrant blue flowers that blossomed from a dark green plant with diamond-shaped leaves. The blooms glowed and he stepped forward and reached toward one of them. Charles lunged forward, grasped his wrist, and bent it back. He hauled the man away from the plant.

"What the fuck, man?" Lester yelled. Charles released him and the Englishman shoved him away. "What the hell do you think you're doing, manhandling me like that? Don't fucking touch me."

"Both of you need to calm down," Booker said. "But also, remember what that plant looks like and don't touch it. Ever."

"What's so special about the flower?" Reen asked, seemingly unimpressed by the plant.

"That's a Pita plant. They are some of the most dangerous things in the Zoo."

"It's a flower," Mick said.

"You attempt to pull that plant out, and the whole Zoo goes berserk," Charles said. "There are teams who harvest only the petals but the whole jungle protects these plants. Even picking the flowers carries risk which we're not prepared to mess with right now. When anyone who tries to take a plant dies, it makes us wonder how much more there is that we don't know."

Lester scowled at him. "You could've just said, man. You didn't need to assault me."

He merely shrugged unapologetically.

"I bet they're valuable," Reen said.

"Oh, sure," Roo confirmed. "They're one of the most valuable things in the whole place. But the wankers aren't worth the lives you might or might not lose harvesting them."

"I'm glad we got to point them out to you, but it is a

little strange to see one so far from the center of the Zoo," Booker said and frowned at the small shrub.

"Why?" Mick asked.

"They're usually only in the center. There must be a lot of goop here," he explained.

"Goop?" Reen asked.

"Yeah, the alien stuff that this all sprang from. It's found in high concentrations in Pita plants. That's why they're so valuable. Everything in here has some goop in it, but the Pita is the best source."

A few howls sounded in the distance. "Keep moving," Booker said.

The group made it to the objective without incident after that and the pitcher plant was surprisingly easy to find. It had wound itself around a particularly large tree. The bright orange-and-red-spotted flowers were the same shape as a beaker and no more than five inches long. Two purple pistils coiled from the center of each bloom.

"We need five of these," Booker said. "They need to be cut three inches below the bloom. Whatever you do, do *not* tip the flower over or get whatever's inside on yourself. Not if you want to avoid breaking out in boils and losing your limbs." He clapped his hands and rubbed them together. "Okay. Who's first?"

The three newbies exchanged dubious looks.

He passed each of them a collection container. "Hop to it, then."

Charles and Roo walked around the large tree in opposite directions, their weapons at the ready. Reen, Mick, and Lester began to harvest the blooms needed. It was more difficult than they'd thought it would be as the stems were woody and tough. They couldn't exert too much force or the clear liquid each bloom was half-full of threatened to spill over. After Charles had made it all the way around the tree he glanced up, then nudged Booker with his elbow. He indicated upward with a jerk of his chin.

The heavy vines draped above their heads in the tree's branches slowly unfurled. Some of them were tipped with jawless mouths like a lamprey's. Multiple rows of teeth all led to two larger teeth that met almost like a beak and a rasping, flickering tongue.

"Let's hurry this up," Booker commanded sharply.

Charles ejected the slugs he'd loaded into the Remington and quickly re-loaded with buckshot. He sighted and his finger tightened on the trigger, but he waited, wary and watchful.

"This is the last one," Reen said and snapped the lid shut on the collection container. She stepped back from the tree in the same moment that a creeper dropped the remaining distance.

Charles fired and the buckshot severed some of the vines and struck others. Roo sprayed the top of the tree with rounds as the other vines writhed and reacted.

Booker calmly gathered the full collection containers and put the specimens in his rucksack. "Ready?" he asked.

"You really weren't kidding about the plants in this place," Mick said and stared at the vegetation that still strained toward them.

"Did you think we were?" Booker asked.

"I might've thought you were shooting the breeze or something." He shrugged.

They marched back toward the gate and followed more

or less the same path. The three newcomers discovered that the terrain of the Zoo changed quickly enough that tracks were unreliable. The path they'd made previously was already vanishing and in a few more hours, it would be completely gone.

Lester looked constantly over his shoulder. Roo, who brought up the rear with Reen, glared at him. After the third time the man looked, the Aussie snapped.

"Hey, man, what the fuck?"

"What?"

"Why do you keep looking over your shoulder?"

"Just watching."

"Just watching? What the hell do you think we're doing back here, huh? Do you not trust us to watch your six?"

The team halted and stared at the two men who squared off against one another.

"We don't have time for this," Booker said. "We've got to keep moving."

"It's not that I don't trust you. I just feel like something's watching."

"Something's always watching in here," Charles grumbled.

"I gathered that. I just feel like something is following us, you know?" he said. Then, he held his hands up. "Look. I wasn't trying to rock the boat or anything. Let's just keep going."

They marched on in silence and the newcomer didn't look over his shoulder this time.

They passed the Pita plant again on their way back.

"Remind me again why we're passing by this giant payday?" Lester asked.

"Because," Roo said, "the whole place goes berserk. We aren't outfitted to deal with that right now."

The other man rolled his eyes. "We've handled everything just fine."

"You haven't seen anything yet. There are bigger and badder bastards out there than the asswipes we've fought off so far."

"Oh, I see. You're just a pussy."

The other man was on him in a second with a guttural snarl. He grasped the front of Lester's armor and pulled him closer to eye level. "Listen, you fucking cocksucker. I'm not a motherfucking pussy. When I say there's shit you don't want to see, there is shit you do not want to see. You got that, asshole?"

Charles grabbed his teammate's shoulder and dragged him away from the other man.

"Sorry, man. It was just a joke."

Roo bared his teeth and gave him the finger.

Booker pinched the bridge of his nose. "For fuck's sake, all of you have lost your minds. Quit acting like a bunch of toddlers and man the fuck up. We aren't running a bleddy circus show. We're professionals. Fucking act like it."

Charles strode to Booker. "We've gotta pull people closer together. We have to work as a unit, none of this infighting bullshit," the Brit muttered.

He grunted. Of course, he felt a little guilty about his earlier outburst, but he chose not to bring it up again. He glanced around at the dense underbrush.

"I do think something is watching us," he said.

Booker nodded. "Yeah. I felt it too. There isn't anything

abnormal about that, though. We always feel like we're being watched."

Charles shrugged.

They traveled on in silence again and everyone was now clearly on edge.

"There definitely is something out there," Charles said in a low voice. He thought he saw a flash of black amongst the vibrant green.

"Nothing much we can do about it, I guess," Booker stated calmly.

He studied his teammate for a moment. The bigger man looked grim, and although he didn't normally go around smiling, there was definitely a heaviness about him. Booker knew the loss of Thor weighed heavily on him.

"You good, Charles?" he asked.

The man set his jaw and nodded.

They made it out of the Zoo without another incident. Booker took the samples they'd collected to Franco to get paid. The other two led Reen, Mick, and Lester back to the container to drop their gear.

CHAPTER ELEVEN

The Zoo – Thor

Charles hadn't returned, but still, Thor waited.

After two days, he had been forced to find something to eat and drink. He'd encountered a few smaller six-legged rat-like animals he'd caught. They scurried across his path and he pounced on them and killed the smaller animals easily. He drank the water that pooled in the leaves from the humidity. It wasn't enough and certainly didn't compare to the steady meals the man had provided. He was still weak from the stab injury in his side, but it was healing fast. The air of the Zoo and the alien genes interwoven in his DNA helped him recover quickly. The wound was barely a scratch now, and it didn't bother him much.

It had been a few days since Charles had disappeared and left him alone. Thor thought of giving up and moving deeper into the Zoo to find something more substantial to eat when he smelled him.

He perked up, sniffed the air, and smelled Charles. His tail wagged and he scrambled through the underbrush, following the scent. He could also smell Booker and Roo, although it was faint.

The smell of his humans grew stronger and stronger as he crashed through the jungle and ignored all the other animals and plants as he ran.

Thor skidded to a stop when he heard gunfire. He'd never gotten used to that sound and it bothered him still. Cautiously, he crept forward.

A swarm of locusts was attacking Charles, Booker, and Roo. He bared his teeth, his muscles coiled and ready to spring. Caution clicked in and he stopped when he noticed three other humans there too—strangers.

Thor whimpered quietly. The last stranger had attacked him, then he'd attacked the man and killed him. New people weren't to be trusted. He hunkered down to wait and watch.

Thereafter, he shadowed the group from a distance. He was often out of sight but could smell them strongly. While he wanted to go to Charles, he worried about the strangers and about how the man would react if he found out he hadn't stayed as instructed.

The animal watched intently when Roo and Lester seemed ready to fight. His hackles rose. The other two strangers didn't bother him as much as this newcomer did.

He followed them again as they headed back to the wall.

A six-legged panther crept forward toward the group of humans. He stared at the cat and it stared back, then slunk away and disappeared into the jungle again.

Thor kept pace easily with the humans. He got as close as he dared but still remained hidden. He could sense that

Charles was upset. It worried him and he wanted to go and comfort the big man.

He had almost made up his mind to run to him when the group broke free of the jungle and began the march across the sand to the wall. The animal shrank back and watched, hidden in the foliage.

The door shut firmly behind the humans and separated them from him again and he whined.

Howls sounded from deeper inside the Zoo. Thor looked in the direction. His tail wagged a few times, then stopped. He wanted to investigate. It was getting harder to resist plunging deeper into the jungle, but now that he'd seen Charles, his determination was renewed.

He returned to his place, lay down, and waited.

CHAPTER TWELVE

The Wateringhole

Booker found the others at the bar. He strolled in and nodded to the off-mission men he recognized.

The BOHICA group was gathered at a long table near the back. He was late to the game, so he had to sit with his back to the rest of the room along with Mick and Lester. It made him uncomfortable, but he was across from Charles and he knew the big man had his back.

"So, boss man, what'd we get?" Mick asked.

"Comes out to fifteen K each," Booker said.

Lester gave a low whistle. Mick raised his pint glass and downed the contents without waiting for anyone to toast him. Reen merely smiled.

"You weren't kidding about the paydays," Lester said.

Booker raised an eyebrow. "Of course I wasn't kidding."

The other man shrugged. "It just all seemed too good to be true."

"To celebrate your first trip into the Zoo," Roo said, "the next round's on me."

He was ordering more drinks at the bar when Shira del Mora walked in. The Israeli woman made a beeline for the him.

"Well, if it isn't Walker Demopoulis. Heard you boys've been making quite the name for yourselves with your little company," she said and leaned a hip against the bar.

He nodded to her. "Shira."

She turned around and looked at the bar, then focused on the team's table. "Who's the chick?"

"That's Reen."

"Reen, huh?"

"Yeah."

"She's pretty."

He grunted and tried harder to get the bartender's attention.

Shira walked her fingers up Roo's arm. "You haven't stopped by in a while." She pouted at him and batted her eyelashes.

"I'm sure you've managed just fine without me," he said and shrugged her off.

She straightened and scowled. "Fuck you."

"Oops. What happened to your cutesy act?" he asked.

"I was just trying to help you out, you ungrateful bastard." She hissed her irritation, the sound brittle.

"Don't really need your help, sweetheart."

Her laugh was mirthless. "Sure you don't. Well, just wait until your little baby company is looking for jobs and can't secure any. Then you'll come crawling back to me and the Lampton Company. You'll see, asshole."

"Don't need you. Or Lampton. We're doing just fine on

our own," Roo said. "Besides, I can get a mediocre wristy anywhere."

Reen walked toward them and he grinned at her. Shira seethed, her hands in fists while she ground her teeth.

"You'll regret this, fucker," she warned, then she turned on her heel and left.

The other woman leaned against the bar in the space Shira had vacated. She watched her walk out the door with her ever-present bodyguard, Ishmael.

Roo took the opportunity to study her. She was the exact opposite of Shira, who was a corporate shark. The bitch was cold and heartless and did all her killing from the sidelines, sending others to do her dirty work. Reen was capable and seemed like the kind of woman to just do shit herself.

"I was sent over here to make sure you didn't burn too many bridges, but looks like I was a little late," Reen said. "Who was that? She's hot."

He blinked a few times but recovered quickly. "That she-devil you just avoided meeting is Shira del Mora. Mouthpiece of the Lampton Company. Mouthpiece of a few other things too."

She laughed. "She seems like a bitch."

"That's 'cause she is a bitch."

"You slept with her, didn't you?"

"Hell yes, I slept with her. But that's beside the point. Was she a good rut? Sure. But she's a psycho bitch." He shook his head with disgust. "Besides, I only fucked her to get us back in her good graces. She blackballed us after our first mission, and we had to fight to get jobs again."

"Right, and you were that good of a lay that she changed her mind about you guys, huh?"

"Hell yes, I was. It worked like a charm. She was dick-matized. We started getting jobs after she eased up." He shrugged. "The plan worked, and I wasn't feeling it anymore."

"Use her and lose her."

"Well, when you put it that way you make me sound like a dick."

"You made yourself sound like a dick."

"Look, I was making a sacrifice for the bigger cause."

"I'm sure it was a real hardship."

"She may be a total bitch, but she should probably be with someone who's into it too."

"So, now that you've rejected her advances, you think she'll blackball the company again? Is it going to be a problem?"

"Nah, shouldn't be. We're doing just fine without getting handouts from Lampton."

Reen nodded, then changed the subject. "Who was Mr. Tall, Dark, and Deadly?"

"Shira's lapdog? That's Ishmael."

"Interesting." She turned and glanced at him from the corner of her eye. "Guess there isn't a lack of tail here, huh?"

Roo shrugged. "Guess that depends on which way you swing."

The corner of her mouth twitched upward although she didn't make eye contact.

A drunk stumbled up to the bar beside her. He grinned at her and she gave him a bored stare back. He looked over his shoulder at his group of friends who stood around a pool table, laughing, and gave them a thumbs up. She rolled her eyes. Roo glared.

"Haven't seen you before," the man slurred and listed toward her.

Reen poked him in the shoulder and pushed him out of her personal space. "Interesting fact."

"Play pool with me," he said.

"As exciting as that sounds, I'm going to pass," she said.

"Damn. Come on, babe. It'll be a good time. I can give you a few pointers," he said and wiggled his eyebrows.

She smirked. "Yeah. That's a definite no. Now, run on back to your little friends." She finger-waved at the group of men who leered from the pool table.

Reen turned back to Roo.

"Hey, come on now. I wasn't done talking to you." The drunk reached out and caught hold of her shoulder.

Roo stood so fast he upset his bar stool, but he wasn't as fast as Reen.

She drove her elbow into the drunk's nose to the satisfying sound of the crunch of cartilage, then whirled and the palm of her right hand connected with the man's shoulder. The force of the blow hurled him back onto the bar. Blood gushed from his broken nose and the angle made him sputter when it seeped into his mouth.

His friends made to move forward and help, but she dug her fingers into the pressure point in the man's shoulder and he yelled a protest. "Your friend is an asshole. I'm sure the rest of you don't want to find out what I do to assholes, do you?" The men hesitated and stared at the tall woman who held their friend pinned with one hand.

She grinned when they remained where they were. "Didn't think so. I think it's best if you go about your business, and I'll go about mine. Don't forget to take your trash out." She released the man from her grip. He whimpered, clutched his shoulder and nose, and slumped against the bar.

Reen walked back to the table and completely ignored the confused men.

"Holy shit. That has to be either the sexiest or most terrifying thing I've ever seen," Roo muttered.

He followed her back to the group. Her mixed signals confused him, but she'd said that she'd just broken up with her boyfriend before she left for the Zoo. Maybe he had a chance.

A flash of guilt swept over him. He would still try to get back together with Brittany for Cassie's sake. Plus, a part of him would always be in love with her.

But could he be criticized for his attraction to this woman? She was five-ten of sexy warrior woman and he didn't think he should be blamed if he found her attractive. It was only natural.

Reen took her place next to Charles. The other guys at the table congratulated her on putting the man in his place.

The American stared straight ahead.

She elbowed him. "Hey."

He blinked, then turned and looked at her.

"You good, Tillman?"

Charles nodded.

Reen raised an eyebrow. "I'm calling bullshit." She stood, then held her hand out for him.

He eyed her hand suspiciously but didn't take it.

She made an exasperated face, grabbed his hand, and hauled him from his chair. "Come on. Let's get you out of this funk."

"I'm not in a funk."

"Bullshit again, Tillman."

She led him over to a dart board and passed him the red-tipped darts. "Since I'm being generous and trying to cheer you up, you throw first."

"I'm fine."

He threw the dart and it landed outside the rings. He grimaced. His other three darts didn't land any closer to the bullseye.

"Sure, you are," Reen said. Her dart buried itself in the bullseye.

"I'm fine," he reiterated and yanked his darts from the board.

"It's okay if you aren't."

Charles didn't say anything. He rolled his shoulders and threw his darts. All four hit the center.

"See, I'm fine."

She shook her head. "Whatever you say, Charles."

CHAPTER THIRTEEN

The Harvesters Camp

Booker stood outside Franco's building with the other team leaders. It was early still and wasn't too hot yet. Although the others no longer treated him like a sideshow, he still stood apart from them. This was by choice. He didn't feel the need to spend time creating and maintaining relationships he didn't see would help their company. He was friendly with all of them but otherwise, he maintained his distance from the other team leaders.

The door to the warehouse opened and a few dispatchers stepped out. A man Booker didn't recognize exited with Franco. He looked like a scientist who did most of his work in a lab and wore khaki cargo pants, brand-new hiking boots, and a khaki button-down shirt. The Brit grimaced inwardly. The idiot was a khaki disaster.

Franco and his companion stood off to the side. The stranger talked animatedly and the dispatcher nodded. He looked pointedly at Booker and two other team leaders.

The three men he'd singled out let the other announced

flora and fauna jobs pass to others. Booker was interested in the job Franco and the stranger had. It would be something big, he knew. He was glad the dispatcher had selected him. It meant BOHICA was doing its job and rising through the ranks of low-level companies.

Soon, all the jobs were allocated and the other dispatchers filed back into the building. Franco stepped forward.

"Gentlemen, this is Dr. Richard Leishman," he said.

Richard nodded eagerly at the three leaders.

"He has a special assignment," the dispatcher continued, "and he came to me to select the team for the job. It's a fauna mission, after a fashion. A harvesting mission involving the locusts."

The team leader on Booker's right shifted nervously. He was from a newer company and had established himself just before BOHICA had come along. Booker noted the eager caution that surrounded the other man. He obviously wanted to prove himself, but the Brit had it on good authority that his team wasn't as well-equipped as BOHICA.

"So, what's the job?" the last team leader asked.

"I'll let Dr. Leishman here explain it."

Richard pushed his thick-rimmed glasses up the bridge of his nose. "Well, as I'm sure you're all aware, locust cuticles have one of the highest fracture toughness of any biological material," he started.

Booker blinked and the other team leaders shifted restlessly.

"My company managed to get their hands on a cuticle from one of the Zoo locusts, and we tested it. Our results showed that the fracture toughness of cuticle in locust hind legs is 4.12 MPa m$^{1/2}$ and decreases with desiccation of the cuticle. Stiffness and strength of the tibia cuticle were measured using buckling and cantilever bending and increased with desiccation. A combination of the cuticle's high toughness with a relatively low stiffness of 3.05 GPa results in a work of fracture of 5.56 kJ m^{-2}, which is amongst the highest of any biological material, giving the insect leg an exceptional ability to tolerate defects such as cracks and damage." He had to stop to take a breath, and Booker hoped he was finished.

He tried his best to look interested in the scientist's long-winded spiel, but he was confused and bored. The man had lost his attention after the first statistic. He could listen to stats of weapons or game consoles for hours, but he couldn't care less about the nitty gritty of insect armor. When he looked at the other team leaders, they wore the same glassy-eyed look he was sure he had. He didn't need the particulars of *why* a company needed the locusts. He merely wanted to know how much it would pay and if he got the job. The other team leaders attempted, at least, to maintain interest in the long-winded speech.

Richard pushed his glasses up his nose again and gave a delighted chuckle. He evidently had no clue that he'd long since lost the interest of his audience. Not that he had it in the first place. "Interestingly, the insect cuticle achieves these unique properties without using reinforcement by a mineral phase," he continued, "which is often found in other biological composite materials. These findings thus might inspire the development of new biomimetic composite materials." He finally looked at his bored audience and seemed to register their lack of interest. "Oh."

Franco patted him on the shoulder. "Very nicely done, Dr. Leishman. Now, gents, it's forty K up front. Then by the sample after. Who's interested?"

All three team leaders were, of course, interested.

"When do you need them by?" Booker asked.

"It's not exactly time sensitive since they're so durable," the scientist answered.

"Before I assign the job," Franco said, "there is a catch."

Booker raised an eyebrow. It had seemed like an easy enough mission—too easy. Especially for the price tag.

"Well, what's the catch?" another team leader asked.

"I go with you," Richard said.

The Brit's dreams of an easy job evaporated. The other two team leaders shifted beside him.

Richard frowned. "You were all so interested before."

"I think I'll pass," one man said and walked off.

Franco looked at the two remaining men.

Booker considered the risk and reward of the mission. Then, he shook his head. "Sorry. I just don't know if we want to babysit a civilian in there. No offense, sir."

"Offense taken! I'm not useless," he protested.

"No?" The other remaining man stepped in. "You ever been in a firefight? You ever stared down a slobbering monster and stood your ground because the lives of your team members relied upon it? No? Didn't think so." He walked away.

Franco and Richard looked at Booker, desperation in both their gazes.

"I just don't know," he repeated. "I'm saying no, but I can run it past the rest of my team."

Franco nodded vigorously. "Round up the troops and take a vote but bring me the answer within the hour. Or this mission will go to someone else."

"Sure," he said. He left the dispatcher to deal with the scientist, who obviously didn't understand the team leaders' reluctance.

He returned to the container and the others and told them about the mission.

"What did you say?" Charles asked.

"I said no," Booker said, "but I also said I'd run it past you and be back within the hour with a definite no."

"Why would it be a definite no?" Lester asked.

"Because I don't want some scientist's life on our hands. It's too risky. Especially with a fauna job. It puts him in danger as well as us. No. I don't think it's worth the risk."

"Even for the payday?" Lester asked.

"In the end, Lester, lives are more important than money."

"I think we should do it," Roo said.

Everyone turned to look at him. Lester seemed equally as surprised as the others that Roo had sided with him.

"What?" the Aussie asked defensively.

"You agree with Lester?" Mick seemed nonplussed.

"Hell yes, I do."

"Why do you think we should take it?" Booker asked.

Roo shrugged. "Look. Would it be a pain in the ass to have some wombat nerd tag along? Sure. But he has to know the risks, right? I mean, he's supposed to be smart. A doctor. He's taking his life in his own goddamn hands going into the Zoo. The fucker should know that. It's obviously something he's willing to risk, so who are we to stop him from coming along?"

"We'd need to make sure we get paid and it's not contingent on him coming back alive—or in one piece," Charles said.

"You think we should take it too, Charles?" Booker asked.

He shrugged.

"I do see what you guys are saying," Reen said and looked up from cleaning her fingernails with her Bowie knife. "It would be an extra risk to have an untrained man along, but it's completely doable. I've run missions with civilian tagalongs before."

"This could be a huge payday," Roo said. "I say we take the money. And the scientist. If he loses, he loses. We all die sometime."

"We obviously wouldn't hang him out to dry," Charles said. "But he has to know that we aren't equipped for complete protection of him. He needs to be able to pull his own weight if he comes."

Booker sighed. "All right. I'll go tell them we'll take the job."

Franco and Richard were involved in a heated discussion when he returned. The scientist looked upset that no one wanted to take his job and the dispatcher obviously tried to calm him.

He noticed Booker before his companion did. "Booker! So, what's your answer?" he asked hurriedly.

"I need a few more details."

"What details?" the scientist asked.

"Have you ever been in a combat zone before?" He asked the question even though he already knew the answer.

"Uh…no, not unless you count my paintball league," the man said with a laugh.

Booker stared at him. His smile slipped.

"No, I haven't been in a combat zone."

"Have you ever fired a rifle before?"

"Yes."

"A real one?"

"Yes!"

"Here's the important bit," he said. He glanced at Franco and the man grimaced. "Is our payment contingent on you coming back?"

Richard stared in shock. "What?"

"If you don't make it back, or if you don't make it back whole, does my company still get paid?"

"You're serious?" he sputtered.

Booker scowled. "I am bleddy serious. It's not just some walk through St. James' Park we're talking about here. You are going into an alien war zone where everything is actively trying to kill you. My team will do our best to keep you safe, but there are no guarantees. Anything can happen, and I need to know—before I put you and my team in danger—that we will be paid for our troubles."

"I would prefer to come back in one piece, obviously," Richard said, "but your payment doesn't hinge on it, Mr…"

"Booker. Just Booker," he said and held his hand out.

The scientist gave him a surprisingly firm handshake.

"We'll take the job, Dr. Leishman."

"Excellent! And please, call me Richard."

"All right then, Richard. Here are the details of where my team is set up. I expect you in an hour for a briefing and to prep for the mission."

"Oh! We're leaving now?"

"No. We're leaving in a few hours. Is that a problem?"

"No. No problem. I just wasn't expecting things to happen this fast," he said and looked a little pale.

He raised an eyebrow. "Things are going to happen a lot faster than this, so you better get used to it. See you in an hour."

Dr. Richard Leishman arrived looking like he'd stepped off a safari TV set. They stared at him in his khaki ensemble, complete with beige pith helmet and green bandana tied around his neck. A .44 Magnum nestled awkwardly in a holster at his hip. His pack hung loose and low on his back and sagged in such a way that the others knew it wasn't full.

"You can't be fucking serious," Roo muttered. "This is not going to go well."

"Booker said it's okay to lose the wanker, right?" Lester grumbled.

Charles frowned at them both. "Shut up."

Richard stopped awkwardly in front of the line of BOHICA personnel. He removed his pith helmet and began turning it in small circles as he held it in front of him.

Booker introduced the team. "Everyone, this is Dr. Richard Leishman."

"Please, call me Richard," he said hurriedly. "Also, I want to apologize because I'm terrible with names."

Roo smirked. "There's only six of us," he muttered. Charles elbowed him in the ribs and his teammate scowled in response.

The American stepped forward and smiled. "That's all right. You'll get it. I see you brought your own handgun," he said and indicated the .44 Mag.

"Hand cannon," Reen muttered.

Richard didn't hear her. He smiled and patted the gun. "Figured I could show you guys I'm not going to be completely useless."

"Right. You shoot it before?"

"I can shoot a gun," he retorted, a little indignant.

Charles gave him a placating smile. "Sure. I don't doubt that, but do you know how to shoot the weapon you currently have on you?"

"Of course I can!"

"Don't mean any offense, man," he said. "Just doing my due diligence."

Richard looked the team in front of him and his gaze stopped on Reen. She gave him a half-smile. He looked away quickly and a blush spread across his face.

"What a nerd," Mick whispered to her, loud enough that the man could hear.

She elbowed him and winked at the man, which made him blush harder.

"We're going to run through a few drills and then we'll be ready to enter the Zoo. Okay?" Booker asked.

The scientist nodded. "Yes, I'm fine with that."

"I wasn't asking if you were fine with it. Just telling you

how it's going to go. You may be bankrolling this mission and we may be working for you, but when we get out there in the Zoo you have to follow orders to the letter. Understood?"

He nodded again.

They ran through a few immediate action drills and made sure the civilian remained in the center of the group. His reaction times weren't as fast as theirs, but he did all right for a scientist. He proved that he could listen to orders, at least in a drill setting. Charles and Reen, who had the most experience running ops with civilians, were in charge of him.

After almost two hours of drills, his khaki outfit was soaked through with sweat, but he didn't complain. That earned him some respect from the team.

"I think that's as good as it'll get," Roo said. "Just follow our lead and our orders and you'll be fine, Dick."

"My name's Richard."

"I think I'm just going to call you Dick."

Before he could protest further, Roo walked off with Lester to prepare the gear. He turned and gave Charles a helpless look.

The American shrugged. "Do you have any gear that you're taking in with you?" he asked.

"Yes. If you tell me what gate we're leaving out of, I'll have it delivered."

"You got anything else to wear?" Reen asked.

"Uh, no? Is this not okay?"

Reen and Charles exchanged a look. Booker walked out of the container at that moment holding a flak vest.

"This is for you," he said.

"Do I need it?"

"Yes," Reen, Charles, and Booker answered at the same time. He took the vest and Charles helped him put it on.

They arrived at the gate at the same time Franco delivered Richard's forty kgs' worth of equipment and supplies. Booker grimaced and began dividing the gear out between the team. He avoided giving Reen any.

She stepped forward, glowered at him, and put some sample containers and other instruments into her pack.

"You ready for this?" Mick turned to the scientist as the first door slid open.

The man laughed. "I'm actually getting kind of nervous."

He clapped him on the back. "Eh, nothing to be nervous about, gubba. What's the worst that could happen?"

"Death? Dismemberment? Loss of a limb?"

"Right," Mick said. Then, he shrugged. "So what? I mean, this would be a way more interesting story than if you just died in your sleep like some average wombat, you know? At least you're out here experiencing life."

"I guess," Richard said, although he didn't seem thrilled by the encouragement.

They walked in single-file line through the three walls and into the Zoo. Richard walked between Charles and Reen in the center of the line. Roo brought up the rear with Lester immediately ahead of him. Booker and Mick led the group.

"So, where do we find the mutated locusts?" the scientist asked and pushed his glasses up his nose. They were fogging from the sudden humidity and heat of the jungle.

"A little deeper, and usually, we don't 'find' them anywhere. Usually, they find us," Charles explained.

The civilian jumped at any little sound as they marched into the interior. When he didn't grab for his .44—which Charles had to keep commanding him to keep holstered—he ogled the foliage.

"Incredible," he muttered while he walked. He looked at the canopy of leaves and the ever-moving vines that snaked their way through the treetops. Once, he stumbled and Charles reached out and hauled him to his feet by the flak vest. "Do you see that?" he asked excitedly. He pointed to a large, glossy-leafed plant with a bright red flower sprouting from the center.

The big man shrugged.

"I've never seen a bromeliad so large!" He stepped out of the line and leaned closer to the plant. "Although I guess it's not quite your average bromeliad, is it? Absolutely incredible." He hadn't noticed that the leaves curled toward him. "Look at how tough it is. And the number of trichomes!" He fumbled in one of his pockets and brought out a small pair of silver scissors. Blissfully unaware of any danger, he snipped the end of one of the leaves at the same moment that the plant tried to close on him and Roo yanked him back.

Richard gaped at the now completely closed plant.

"Look, Dick, we weren't kidding when we said every-thing in here wants to kill you. Now it's great that you want to do your little scientist thing, and that is what you're here for, but if you want to keep collecting plant samples, ask first. Got it?"

He nodded, still wide-eyed. Roo shook his head.

"They don't normally do that in the lab," he said with a weak laugh.

"Oh, no?" The Aussie gave him a patronizing grin. "Well, they do here."

The scientist retrieved a small, silvery sample bag from another of his pockets and placed the leaf tip inside. He sealed it shut and returned it to his pocket.

"Just be glad that one didn't have teeth," Roo said.

"Teeth?"

He grinned and pushed Richard back toward the line.

Reen patted him on the shoulder. "It's okay, Doc. Usually, plants don't try to eat you. Just be more careful next time, yeah? We'll cover you if you want to get a sample."

"It's...uh, it's Richard."

"Right. Let's just keep moving, Doc, okay?"

The man simply nodded.

They made it another klick into the jungle when Booker held a hand up to stop them. He peered into the foliage that surrounded them. They were in a particularly dark and cool patch.

The Brit motioned Mick to the left. The man stepped to the side and scanned the surrounding plants.

"What is it? What's happening?" Richard asked.

Charles held a finger to his lips and looked into the thick underbrush. He stepped forward while Reen stepped back so they were on either side of the scientist, who drew his .44 and held it in a shaking hand. The American raised an eyebrow at Reen over the scientist's head.

Roo and Lester turned their backs toward Richard,

Reen, and Charles. Booker and Mick moved closer and soon, Richard was surrounded by them.

A strange keening cry came from the jungle off to the group's left. An answering cry echoed on the right.

"Anybody got eyes?" Booker asked.

"Nada," Mick said and focused his attention in the direction of the first cry.

"Movement!" Lester said and he fired. A large panther-like animal launched from the trees. The man's first barrage grounded it, but a second was soon there to take its place.

The six-legged cats penned them in on all sides. Antlers curved back from their shovel-shaped heads and they bared their three rows of teeth.

"Jesus," Richard squeaked.

"My side," Mick said as another panther tried to leap at the group with its gleaming claws extended. He fired and felled the beast.

It was like the fall of the second companion triggered something in the other animals. They surged forward as one. The jungle exploded with the sound of the screaming cats and the barrage of weapons' fire. They were forced to step away from Richard, which left more room around him.

A panther leapt toward the scientist, and he fired. The .44 Mag thundered but the round careened past the animal. As soon as he pulled the trigger, Booker shot the panther, punctured its lung, and dropped it at the man's feet. The civilian scrambled away from the black blood that seeped from the corpse and bumped into Charles.

"Easy there, Richard," the American muttered as he calmly eliminated another attacker.

The gunfire died when no more felines attacked from the jungle. Whether they had run off or had all died, they didn't know, but the assault ceased.

Charles slung his Remington over his shoulder and took the gun from Richard. He flipped the safety on and handed it back to the scientist. "Nice job."

"They have six legs," the man said and stared at one of the bodies, "and antlers."

"Yeah," he said.

"Keep moving," Booker commanded.

The trees grew taller around them. The branches weren't as low-hanging, which allowed more than enough room for the large locusts to fly beneath the canopy.

"When do you think we'll see a locust?" Richard asked.

Roo was about to answer when four of the mutants burst through the vegetation and rocketed toward the humans. They approached at a rapid speed with their mandibles snapping, and their blade-like legs sliced dangerously through the air. Booker, Lester, and Reen annihilated them easily. A shower of emerald blood erupted as the giant insects were blown apart.

"What are you doing?" the scientist yelled. He stared at the mutilated bodies. "Those were the first locusts we've seen. We needed those specimens." He ripped his backpack off, dug through it, and retrieved a pair of rubber gloves.

"Who has a sample container?" he asked as he poked at the bodies in search of anything salvageable.

Reen handed him a container.

Roo, Booker, and Charles looked at the specimen

container and then at each other. It was high-end and they hadn't seen one quite like it before. Richard managed to salvage two leg sections. He sealed them in the synthetic receptacle. A hissing noise emitted when he shut it and a small green light turned on at the top.

"I've never seen a containment chamber like that before," Roo said.

"Ah, yes. My lab developed them for this purpose. It's environment-regulating so the specimens are in peak condition for longer. Though the material itself is resistant to decay, degradation is still a possibility," he explained. Roo nodded and turned away, but the man wasn't done talking even if he was done listening. "It's interesting, really. It's not just environmental regulation these chambers perform, but they're also pressurized. Through the tests we ran it was discovered that keeping a specimen at two-point-three-two psi preserved the integrity for a longer period of time. Which is, as I'm sure you know, the same pressure that human blood maintains. It's really very fascinating. It's something we'll be testing further with more specimens."

Reen patted him on the shoulder. "That's nice, Doc."

He looked at the others, shrugged off their zoned expressions, and turned his attention to the remaining locusts. "Well, I guess it's all right." He took a few deep breaths, then pulled out a small tablet and began calculating on it. "We need to set up a trap."

"A trap?" Roo asked.

"Yes. We'll string a mist net across two trees. I brought the nets," he said and once again rummaged in his pack.

"I hate to break it to you, Richard, but these things

aren't predictable. They most likely won't show up in this spot for the rest of our time in the Zoo."

The scientist shook his head. "If my calculations are correct—which I'm eighty-five percent sure they are—then there will be a swarm within hours."

Roo, Charles, and Booker looked at each other and laughed.

"A swarm, mate? Don't think so," Roo said.

"Sorry, but like we told you, they're not predictable," Booker reiterated.

Charles grinned. "Yeah, these things aren't going to cooperate with your supposed data."

"Don't worry," the man said, "I believe in my calculations. You men have your guns and your know-how, but this is *my* area of expertise."

They exchanged a look and the American shrugged. "You're the boss."

"Where do you want the net hung?" Booker asked.

They selected two trees that were about five meters apart. Roo opened the large roll of dark gray netting the scientist had brought. He'd called it a mist net, but it looked fairly substantial and not like mist at all. The netting was as thick as parachute cord.

Charles and Mick climbed the trees. The Aboriginal secured his side first, then threw the roll to the other man, who secured it.

Richard insisted it be hung three meters up.

The two men dropped to the ground and looked at the net. It virtually disappeared against the dark green background of the Zoo.

While the duo had put the trap in place, Lester and

Reen cleared away trailing vines and other plants to create a large enough space for all seven to lay in wait.

Mick cut the vines back for the third time since they'd begun their wait. Richard slowly stretched out the leg that had been ensnared. The plants weren't overly aggressive, but they constantly tried to wind themselves around the humans.

They'd waited for almost four hours and Booker didn't like how late it had become. They'd either have to return to the Harvesters Camp or stay in the Zoo. He didn't want to have to worry about the scientist overnight. They'd get the forty thousand dollars and whatever measly amount for the two fractured legs and call it good enough that he hadn't died on their watch.

A buzzing hum started in the distance and gradually grew louder until it was a drone. The team tensed and readied themselves seconds before a swarm of locusts hurtled through the trees. Many collided with the net, where they struggled in an effort to free themselves. The mesh vibrated between the trees and began to glow a faint blue. The small spines on the insects' legs snagged on the strands and trapped the giant creatures effectively.

The other mutants didn't stop to aid their trapped fellows and soon, the entire swarm had flown overhead and left eleven caught in the net. They struggled point-lessly and their red eyes glowed in anger. Despite the savage attacks at the restraint by the snapping mandibles, it didn't break.

The team stepped forward cautiously and approached the suspended locusts.

"Holy shit," Booker said, "they did swarm."

"I told you they would!" Richard said triumphantly. "My calculations are rarely incorrect. I'm glad. It took less time than I was anticipating."

"That's a fucking first. How did you do that?" Roo asked.

The man opened his mouth to explain, but the Aussie held his hand up. "You know what? Never mind. I won't be able to understand your science shit anyway. Just answer me this—how are we getting them down?"

"Don't worry, that net was specially designed for this exact purpose. We just need to untie it and bring it down. It's imperative that it be laid locust-side down. We can secure it to the ground and have easy access to the cuticles that way." The scientist smiled broadly and practically buzzed with excitement.

Mick and Charles climbed up the tree once again and untied the net. They lowered it carefully and the other team members stepped forward to lay it down as Richard directed them. Soon, eleven pairs of locust hind legs were safely tucked in sample containers.

They looked at the de-legged insects as they struggled beneath the mesh. Emerald green blood was everywhere, and it began to smell.

"What do we do with them?" Roo asked.

Charles shrugged. "Without their hind legs, they're mostly harmless. They can't really get anywhere. It seems a waste of time and ammo to kill them all. I think we can safely leave them here."

"You need the net back?" Booker asked.

Richard nodded. "It would be better to have it."

The American rolled the net quickly. The insects twitched and flopped on the ground but couldn't seem to manage without their hind legs.

"It's kind of sad," Mick said as he watched them. "You sure we can't just kill them?"

Booker shook his head. "We've got to be moving. It's going to be dark soon and I'd rather not have to stay the night in the Zoo right now."

They headed back. The scientist couldn't stop talking but the others ignored his near-constant stream of data about the locusts. Booker had given up trying to keep the man quiet. In all fairness, Richard had tried, but after thirty seconds, he burst with words again.

He had insisted on carrying the samples in his pack, so what little supplies were in his rucksack were divided amongst the others. Once again, he walked in the center of the group and they moved in an oblong oval shape.

The jungle around them grew steadily darker, but the foliage began to thin out. The trees were not as tall, and the brilliant oranges and pinks of the sunset showed in glimpses through the canopy.

The relative silence was shattered by ferocious howls and giant orange-and-black striped creatures stepped from the jungle around them. They launched into an assault from all sides. Richard stood helpless in the middle, where he grasped his gun tightly and clutched the pack with the samples to his chest. He watched, wide-eyed, as the team systematically killed the beasts as they attacked.

Each of the alien animals had six glowing yellow eyes

and long claws. Saliva dripped from their jaws. The humans were slowly forced back by the size and numbers of the saber tooth tiger-like creatures.

Reen seemed to have the worst of it. Two of the animals closed in on her and took turns to lunge at her, which forced her to divide her attention between them. Their hides were tough and the rounds she fired didn't do as much damage as they should have. She emptied the clip on her M492, pulled her Beretta swiftly, and continued to fire.

Roo, who fended off a vicious attack of his own, noticed that she was about to be overwhelmed. The animal he fought opened its mouth to roar and he shot it calmly through the back of the throat. He stepped in and helped the woman to dispatch the two monsters ranged against her.

His movement opened a gap in the protective ring they'd formed around Richard. A monster leapt through the opening and almost reached the scientist, but Charles tackled him out of the way at the last second. When the two men jarred with the impact, the .44 Mag went off. By some miracle, the round plowed through the roof of the animal's mouth and into its brain. Charles would never figure out how it had happened. The gun had gone off when the man fell. He hadn't aimed at all and actually had his eyes closed but had still managed to kill it.

The others were able to eliminate the rest of their adversaries.

Charles stood up and pulled Richard up after him. "You okay, man?" he asked.

"I think so," the scientist said, his voice shaky.

He grinned. "Nice shot!" He held up his hand for a high five.

The man stared at the hand as if confused.

Mick stepped up and lifted Richard's hand to give Charles a high five.

"How's about we get you home, eh?" Booker asked.

He nodded. "I need to get these back to the lab."

They marched back toward the gate. Mick walked beside Richard and his particular brand of dark humor distracted the scientist.

Charles brought up the rear and constantly scanned the foliage. He wasn't sure they were quite prepared for another attack. While he didn't doubt they would survive, it would be a struggle.

They began to catch glimpses of the wall through the jungle. Richard began his steady stream of scientific information again.

The American heard a rustle off to the right. He looked toward it, his gun raised, but he didn't sound an alarm in case it was the wind.

Two glowing red eyes blinked back at him from the darkness.

His finger tightened on the trigger, but he hesitated. There was something strangely familiar about them.

Suddenly, the animal moved and stepped forward. He almost fired but then recognized the creature.

Thor stood in the underbrush. He looked slightly larger than he remembered, his two thick horns bigger and twisted more prominently between his ears. They had begun to curve slightly backward like an Ibex's.

Charles stared at him and his heart raced. Thor had

survived. Not only that, he looked...great! Huge, in fact. He looked around to see if any of the others had noticed their erstwhile pet. No one was looking—in fact, they were out of sight.

Thor's tail wagged slowly once, twice, then stopped. He cocked his head to the side and watched the man while he gave a small whimper.

Charles wanted nothing more than to call Thor over. But to what end? He still couldn't take him back, and from the looks of him, he was thriving out here where he belonged. He grimaced and his stomach churned as he waved a hand at Thor. "Go on," he said quietly and struggled to keep his voice steady.

Thor sat and looked at him.

"Please, get out of here. We can't let anyone see you." Charles took a step toward the animal.

Thor's tail thumped happily, and he started to stand, but the man retreated a few steps. He moved cautiously forward.

"No," Charles said. "Stay."

With a puzzled whine, Thor stopped and looked expectantly at him.

"You have to stay here. You can't come back with me, boy. They'll kill you if you do. Stay!" He turned his back on Thor and jogged to catch up with the others. Despite the almost overwhelming temptation, he was afraid to look back—afraid that Thor was following...and afraid that he wouldn't be.

CHAPTER FOURTEEN

The Harvesters Camp

On the other side of the gate, Reen rounded on Roo.
She slammed the heel of her palm into the center of his
chest and forced the muscular man back. With surprising
strength, she pinned him to the rough concrete of the wall.

"What the fuck?" he sputtered and put his hands up.

"What the fuck were you thinking?" she hissed.

"What?"

"I don't need the fucking princess treatment, asshole.
You fucked up. You leaving your position put Richard—
and by extension, Charles and everyone else—in danger.
You wanting to play goddamn hero almost got someone
fucking killed."

Richard went pale when he heard her words. He actually seemed even paler than when Charles had tackled him
out of the way.

Roo opened his mouth to defend himself, but she
shoved away from him and pushed him into the wall again.

"And you." She hissed with fury when she turned on Booker.

He held his hands up but didn't back away.

Reen stepped forward to literally get in his face, which wasn't hard since they were the same height. "What the fuck were you doing not giving me anything to carry? Is it really just because I have a fucking vagina? Huh? You think I'm too weak to pitch in on something like that, asshole?"

"It wasn't my intention to make you feel that way," he said calmly.

Charles moved to intervene, but she pointed her finger at him, still snarling in Booker's face. "Don't you dare, Charles. Stay right the fuck there."

He stopped.

She poked the Brit in the chest and forced him to take a step back. "You think I'm too fucking weak, is that it? Is there something in your caveman brain that says I can't possibly physically exert myself in that way? Newsflash, you stupid asshole. I can take any of you out. I told you not to give me special fucking treatment, but what did you do?"

He grimaced and took another step back when she jammed her finger into his chest again. "I'm sorry, okay? I didn't mean any harm."

"Oh, so you're sorry now, huh?"

"It won't happen again."

"It better fucking not. And maybe to make sure it doesn't happen again, I should challenge you to a bench press competition if you think I'm too fucking weak to carry a few extra kilos."

Booker shook his head. "Not necessary. I'm not trying

to prove anything here. Believe me, the mistake has been made, I've learned from it, and it won't happen again. You have my word."

Reen took a step away from him. She folded her arms over her chest, her eyes narrowed and nostrils flared.

Lester started to laugh. "Oh, my God, that was good. You two should see your faces!"

She leveled her scowl at him and his amusement faltered.

Mick stepped toward her. "I'm sure you've worked up quite the appetite after that. Let's get something to eat."

"Fine," she said, turned, and stalked off toward the container with him. Roo gave them the evil eye as they went.

Richard cleared his throat. "Well...um, this has been an exciting time, gentlemen. I need to get the samples back to the lab, and you probably want to get paid."

Booker nodded. "Yes. Sorry about that."

The scientist shrugged.

"We'll help you take your equipment back," the Brit said.

They followed him through the camp to Franco's.

"How'd it go?" the dispatcher asked from where he leaned against the warehouse and smoked a cigarette.

"We got it!" Richard said.

Franco smiled. "And you made it back in one piece, I see. Enough excitement for you?"

He nodded fervently.

"Thank you, Booker, for escorting me into the Zoo and assisting with the harvesting. You and your company did an exceptional job."

"Of course."

After Roo and Lester dropped the equipment off, they wandered off to stow their gear in the container and then go to the bar. Charles remained with Booker.

Richard pulled his tablet out again and made some calculations. "You've already received the forty grand. Then we got the first two more fragmented pieces, but the net managed to catch eleven for a total of twenty-four leg segments. I'd say ten each for the damaged two segments, and let's call it a nice sixteen for the whole ones." He muttered through his calculations while they watched him, a little slack-jawed.

He verified the electronic pay number Booker had set up for BOHICA and transferred the money. Even though he'd listened to Richard's calculations, the Brit still almost choked that the total for the job was just over four hundred thousand dollars. The scientist was unfazed by the large sum for the day trip into the Zoo.

"Thanks again, Booker. I'll be sure to remember the BOHICA Warriors for any future needs my company might have."

Booker shook his hand. "It was our pleasure. Any time. I mean that. *Any* time."

For a job he hadn't wanted to take, this one had paid huge dividends.

Richard and Franco disappeared inside the warehouse. The scientist talked about everything that had happened and all the experiments he was going to run on the locust cuticles.

After the door shut, Booker turned to his teammate.

"Holy shit, Charles, look how much he paid us for that." He showed him the number.

Charles whistled. "Fudge. For real?"

He nodded.

The two men glanced at the guards who stood on either side of the door and began to walk away from the warehouse.

"I'll set aside a hundred thousand of that, just in case. Always good to have an umbrella fund. But that still comes out to about fifty-six K a piece."

Charles grinned but immediately began to laugh.

"What got into you?" Booker asked and narrowed his eyes at him.

"You should've seen your face when Reen challenged you to a bench press competition."

He frowned. "I really didn't mean to single her out like that. I guess it was just an automatic reaction."

"Yeah, that's something I definitely wouldn't do again. She isn't kidding when she says she'll whip your butt. It's also a good thing you didn't decide to take her up on the bench press competition."

"Why?"

Charles laughed again. "Seriously, Booker? She'd wipe the floor with you. You don't have the best upper body strength."

"I'm not weak."

"I didn't say you were weak. She's just stronger than you. Though I admit, it would've been entertaining."

Booker gestured rudely and Charles continued to laugh.

CHAPTER FIFTEEN

Harvesters Camp

Several days after the locust mission, Booker returned from Franco's with some interesting news.

"A Russian team went out in the Zoo, packing for bear, and apparently, the whole lot of them was slaughtered," he announced.

Roo and Charles leaned forward with interest.

"I'm sorry, but we're happy about people being slaughtered? I know this is a pretty competitive environment, but I don't think we should be excited that some soldiers lost their lives," Mick said.

His countryman waved him off. "Oh, for fuck's sake, Mick. You going to pretend you have a strong moral compass now?"

The Aboriginal shrugged.

"We aren't excited that people died," Charles said. "I'm assuming Booker is telling us this because there was something significant left behind."

Booker nodded. "Rumor has it there's a specialized

armored vehicle. Something that was created for deep penetration into the Zoo. It's real high-end shit. And the Russians want it back."

Roo frowned. "I mean, why wouldn't we just keep it for ourselves?"

"Can you do that?" Reen asked.

"Sure. There's a salvage rule. Sort of finders keepers," Charles said.

"Is there a reward?" Lester asked.

The rest looked at him and he shrugged. "It sounds like whatever they lost, it was probably pretty expensive. I'm sure they'd pay a pretty penny to get it back."

"Good point," Roo said. "We should go get it."

"You want to go to the heart of the Zoo and take back a specialized vehicle?" the Brit asked.

He nodded.

"It seems really risky," Booker said.

Roo pulled Booker and Charles to the side. "Look, this could be big for us. Imagine the pay day if we decided to return it to the Russians. Even if we kept it for ourselves, imagine what a great asset that would be."

"I don't know if we're ready as a team yet," the American hedged.

"I'd have to agree with Charles."

The Aussie shook his head. "All right, bogans, here's the deal. We can do this now or hear about someone else doing what we are more than capable of accomplishing. Are we the most cohesive team yet? No. But we sure as shit are better than most other teams in this section. Besides, this is the perfect opportunity to try to expand beyond the

French Quarter. We have no idea what the other quarters are doing. This is our chance to get an in."

"I do see what Roo is saying, Booker. Besides, if word has gotten out that the Russians are seeking help to recover their vehicle, then it must be really important."

Booker groaned. "Fine. Okay. We'll do it."

"Yes," Roo said and pumped a fist in the air.

"I've got a bad feeling about this," the Brit said.

His teammate clapped him on the shoulder. "I've got a great fucking feeling about this. Have my feelings ever led us astray?"

The two men didn't answer.

Booker used some of the funds he'd set aside for a rainy day to purchase full body armor for the team and extra supplies and ammunition. He also purchased a few billy-club-like electrified batons. Dan described them as cattle prods on steroids.

While he was buying supplies, Charles and Roo argued over whether or not to take the mule they'd salvaged previously. The American had the vehicle working like it was new and it hadn't had any hiccups lately.

"They were lost almost in the heart of the Zoo. Not to mention, we'll have to take whatever shit we find back to the Russian Quarter. That's a fuck ton of walking I sure as shit don't feel like doing."

"Firstly, it would be a pain to drive the mule that far into the Zoo. Secondly, if there really is a vehicle there, then I don't see why we couldn't just drive it back out. If that happened, we'd most likely have to leave the mule behind and we don't want to do that."

Mick strolled up to Charles and Roo. "So, I did some poking around like you asked."

They looked at him expectantly.

"Right. So, turns out the Russians were pretty deep. There were conflicting reports, but it sounds like they were near Chinese territory, or in the heart of the Zoo by the biodomes. One guy said the vehicle was rumored to be about sixty klicks away from us here in the French Quarter."

"Great work, Mick."

He shrugged.

"Deep for them, but not so impossible for us to reach," Roo said.

"I don't like that they were in Chinese territory," Charles said. "I don't think we've ever passed into another quarter in the Zoo before."

Roo looked toward the sky. "Jesus H Christ, don't be a scaredy-ass, Charles. Grow a pair."

His teammate scowled. "I'm not scared. Just pointing out it might be more than the Zoo we're contending with."

"You think the Chinese would attack us?"

He shrugged.

"I would," Lester said.

They looked at him and he shrugged. "It's an opportunity to see what the competition is working with. Not to mention you'd get a sweet armored vehicle out of the deal. And, from what you've told me, if you killed anyone, all the evidence would be swallowed up by the Zoo itself. It's a no-brainer really. I bet everyone will be after what the Russians left behind."

"Well, we better get started, then, shouldn't we?" Booker said as he walked up to the group.

"You got the goods?" Roo asked.

"You know, Aussie, it's insulting that you'd even ask me that. What do you think I was doing? Getting my nails done?"

The Aussie shrugged. "Wouldn't be the first time."

"Fuck you."

The energy as they entered the Zoo was different than any other mission they'd run so far. They were all excited by the possibility of the Zoo-specific vehicle. Also, none of them had ever seen the center of the jungle and were curious to find out what ground zero looked like. Their new kit added to their feeling of excitement.

Dan had shown Booker newer versions of body armor, but those were all out of their budget, even considering the big locust payday. Instead, he'd purchased older-generation armor instead. It still allowed for better movement than any other he had used in the military. The material was thinner than expected and looked almost like spandex, which Roo didn't appreciate. It resembled interlocking scales with reinforced sections on the torso, thighs, and shins.

The helmets had been downgraded when they'd been given to Dan to sell, so they were essentially only visors, but that was better protection than they'd had before.

Booker spray painted the names of the team members onto the back of each helmet. It'd been a rushed job and the bright white paint dripped from some of the letters before it had dried.

Charles brought up the rear as Booker set off at a steady clip toward the heart of the Zoo. He looked around. He hadn't been able to stop thinking about Thor after he'd seen him and hadn't told either of his two friends that the animal was still alive. When he'd told them he'd "taken care of it," he knew they assumed he'd put him down. He could feel Thor watching and keeping pace and didn't mind. In fact, he liked having the dog-like animal near. Zoo animal or not, he had still been his pet and he'd loved him.

Ten klicks into the jungle, he could no longer feel Thor keeping pace with them. It worried him. He could tell that he still behaved like a domesticated animal, but he was a wild animal, and what would happen when he finally gave in to the Zoo? He tried not to think about it.

The night was uneventful and the next day, they headed even deeper into the jungle. They'd made it thirty klicks on the first day, and Booker hoped they'd make it to the vehicle by the end of the day or early the next morning.

The Zoo around them had changed. The foliage was thicker and more aggressive. Vines reached out and tried to gain purchase on the armor and packs they carried. The colors seemed over-saturated and almost everything glowed. The closer they got to the biodomes at the center of the Zoo, the brighter everything seemed to gleam. The trees still resembled regular earth trees, but the rest of the plants had evolved completely. The team were now surrounded by strange colors and textures. They tried to avoid confrontation with the plants, knowing they were outnumbered, and they also tried not to draw attention to their expedition.

The foliage wasn't the only thing that had turned unfamiliar. The air was alive with the calls of unseen animals, the sounds unlike anything they'd heard before.

They walked past one tree and Charles stared at the small flock of birds perched there. These had the wings and talons of falcons but the beak of a parrot. The disproportioned avians stared at them as they walked beneath the tree. One of them opened its mouth and shrieked, but they didn't attack.

He looked back at the trail they had created as a long furry tail wound around Reen's middle and yanked her toward the canopy. Charles lunged forward and managed to grab her legs. Whatever had taken hold had no intention to let her go, and he left the ground as well. She struggled to free her arms.

Roo grabbed his teammate and pulled.

"Stop fucking pulling!" the woman yelled. "Playing tug-of-war with me isn't going to solve this!"

Mick, Booker, and Lester stared into the canopy in an effort to identify what had captured her.

"Any fucking time now!" Roo grunted.

More tails snaked from the canopy and tried to snag the others.

"Ah, fuck it," Lester said and opened fire.

The man-sized body of a monkey-like creature plummet out of the tree and landed with a wet crunch.

The canopy came alive with screams and howls. The mutants pushed out of hiding, their lips pulled back to reveal mouths full of yellowed fangs.

Reen managed to free her left arm. "Charles, let go."

"You'll be pulled up!"

"Just let me go. It'll be okay."

Another monkey fell when Booker and Mick added their firepower to Lester's.

Charles looked at Roo. "I'm going to let her go."

"You can't fucking do that!"

He looked at Reen again. She nodded.

"Three...two...one." He released his grip on her legs. She launched three feet higher in the air and the sudden weight loss momentarily threw off the equilibrium of the animal that held her. The moment gave her time to draw her knife from the sheath at her ankle. She hacked through the tail that held her and dropped on top of Charles, then drew her Beretta and fired once. The now tailless monkey fell from the canopy at her feet.

"Fuck you." She growled, thrust the blade into its chest and dragged it out again, and kicked the still-twitching body away.

They looked up into the canopy but no longer saw any movement. They'd managed to kill fifteen of the large monsters.

"Everyone okay?" Booker asked.

They all nodded.

"Let's keep moving."

They marched for another klick before he slowed their

pace. He knew they had to be near the Chinese Quarter—or, at the very least, would reach Wall One at any moment.

As they walked, they began to notice giant spider webs woven among the leaves of the trees.

"Nope. If there's a Shelob-looking motherfucker in here, I'm out," Mick said.

"What, you afraid of spiders?" Roo asked.

"I think it's perfectly rational to be afraid of giant spiders," his countryman retorted. "Don't be a koona about it."

"Whatever that is, I'm not sure it's a spider," Reen said and pointed.

A six-legged animal hung suspended in a web off to their right. The body portion of it looked to be about eight feet across. The legs were plated and had strange round joints that made it look almost mechanical.

As they looked at it, the mutant began to glow.

"Well, that can't be good," Lester muttered.

Mick stepped forward, pulled the trigger, and simply continued to fire. He yelled as he moved forward. The creature didn't have a chance to even defend itself as his rounds shredded it.

Finally, he stopped firing, turned to the others, and shrugged. "Fear conquered. Let's move on, shall we?"

They pressed forward, although they didn't cover ground as rapidly as before. The thick foliage forced them to take their time in an effort not to upset the plants. Still, their earlier progress meant they'd traveled far enough to soon reach the crumbling remains of Wall One.

The cement of the barrier was being ripped apart by the vines. Words had been spray painted on it, but they were too faded or covered to be able to tell what they might have read.

"Let's follow the curve of this toward the Russian Quarter," Booker said. "Hopefully, the vehicle isn't far from it."

They followed along the wall and caught glimpses of the jungle on the other side through the large sections that were missing. Pita flowers were abundant, the brilliant blue flowers easy to identify against the green. The whole jungle seemed to glow blue.

A chunk of the wall had been blown outward from the center and they decided it would be easier to climb over it than to walk around. Booker also hoped that the top would give them a better vantage point to see if they could locate the Russian vehicle.

"When do we reach the Russian's territory?" Reen asked while they climbed.

"We're probably in the Chinese Quarter. We have to walk through a bit to get to the Russian Quarter, but we've got to be close." Booker said. "It's not like they have an exact line of demarcation. There's no way you'd be able to track that perfectly, not with the way the Zoo moves."

The higher elevation didn't add an advantage at all. The vehicle they looked for was nowhere in sight.

"What do you think that is?" Charles asked and pointed.

They all looked a little ahead and off to the right where there was movement in the foliage, but they couldn't see what created it.

"It's either one giant something or a bunch of smaller somethings," Booker said.

"I don't know which I'd prefer," the American said.

"Well, I guess we'll find out what it is." The Brit began to make his way down the wall.

When they'd clambered down to the jungle floor, they didn't run into whatever it was that had moved. Instead, they walked for a while before they ran into a large group of Chinese PLA soldiers.

The two groups froze and stared at one another, and a second later, the Chinese drew their weapons and began yelling at the BOHICA team in their own language.

The six drew their weapons and leveled them at the other team. They were outnumbered three to one, but they wouldn't give up without a fight.

"Anybody speak Chinese?" Booker asked.

Lester glanced at Reen.

She bared her teeth at him. "Fuck you, asshole. I'm part Vietnamese. And that's racist to assume I'm Chinese."

He simply shrugged.

"Look, I don't see what the big deal is, we're all on the same side—the human side," Booker yelled at the Chinese, but that only made the commanders shout louder.

There was movement among the men and a lower-ranking soldier was shoved to the front. "What is your business in the Chinese quarter?" he asked. His English was slow and measured like he had to really concentrate on each word.

"We're on our way to the Russian-Japanese sector," Booker said. "There seems to be a bit of a misunderstanding happening here. There's no need for any of us to shoot each other." Booker looked over his shoulder at his team. "Stand down."

"You cannot cross through Chinese territory," the

soldier said and glanced at his superior officer. The other soldiers didn't lower their weapons.

Charles stepped forward. Several guns were immediately aimed more aggressively at him. He raised his hands. "We aren't in Chinese territory," he said.

The Brit looked at him and tried to wordlessly communicate what a big mistake he was making by glaring but his teammate ignored him.

The soldier looked at his superior officer again. "Of course this is Chinese territory!"

Roo joined Booker and Charles. "We have permission to be here from the Russians. This is their territory, after all."

The soldier was called back to his commander, who wanted to know what was going on. He began to explain in rapid-fire Chinese.

"What the hell do you think you're doing?" Booker whispered.

"Bluffing," Charles said and smiled encouragingly at the Chinese soldiers.

"Bluffing? Now is not the time to be bleddy bluffing!"

"It's like you said, they probably don't know for sure if this is still their territory or not. You thought we were close, right? So what if we fudge the distance a little?"

"Relax, Booker," Roo said. "They'll see how far that stick is up your ass and will then decide to shoot us just to put us out of the misery of being with you."

"Twat."

"Guys," Charles hissed. "Look."

The Chinese soldiers all lowered their weapons. The English-speaking man returned to the three.

"It does seem like there was a small misunderstanding. We apologize. To make it up to you, we invite you and your team to join us for a meal."

Booker shrugged. "Sure."

"Is this a good idea?" Charles asked.

"Don't know, but I figured it would probably be bad to turn down their hospitality. And considering that they significantly outnumber us, it would be too much trouble to have to fight all of them."

They watched as the Chinese PLA soldiers rapidly set up a camp and cooking fire. While they made the preparations, Booker and the others sat with the four commanders and their impromptu translator. Not much communication happened between the two groups aside from mostly smiling and nodding.

A large metal tub-looking basin was removed from their armored vehicle and set up in the center of the area the Chinese had chosen. They lit a fire in the basin. Charles admired how efficiently they worked together as a team. Most of the soldiers knew what they were doing, and he couldn't see anyone issuing orders. Ten of them walked in slow circles around the perimeter.

They ate the roasted vegetables and meat the Chinese brought with them.

"Damn, these people know how to travel in style," Roo muttered. "This is way better than MRE shit."

The highest-ranking CO and the interpreter pulled Booker to the side.

"You are going after the Russian vehicle," the soldier said.

Booker nodded. "Yes, we are." He decided there was no point in hiding it.

The CO said something and his gaze never left the Brit.

"We want to offer you a reward," the soldier said, "for turning the Russian vehicle over to us if you recover it first."

"What sort of reward?"

"The Chinese PLA is willing to pay you handsomely with technology and money for finding the vehicle and driving it to the Chinese Quarter."

"If we find it first, I will consider your offer," he said.

The Chinese commander inclined his head in acknowledgment.

He was about to ask if they had a better idea of where the Russian expedition was last seen when the peaceful camp was disturbed by a large crash and someone screamed. The three turned as a giant dinosaur-like creature burst through the trees. It snatched one of the Chinese guards and crushed him in its massive jaws. Its teeth were so large they easily went completely through the man.

The soldiers fired at the scaly creature as it made its way slowly into the impromptu encampment. It was dark-green in color, with two lines of glowing blue spots down each of its sides. Four legs with massive black claws supported the monster, and its head was diamond-shaped and almost eight feet long.

Rounds bounced off its tough hide and it blinked its glowing red eyes at the gathered humans. A low growl started in the back of its throat and vibrated the air.

Charles moved to the front of the attack and fired at the giant lizard with his flamethrower. A Chinese PLA soldier followed his lead and the twin blue and orange streams of flame forced the animal back.

It opened its maw and roared, and saliva and blood spattered as it swung its thick, spiked tail at the two men. The move forced the creature to widen its stance and exposed a strip of the lighter green scales of its belly near one of its hind legs. Reen aimed at the area and her rounds found purchase. Deep blue blood welled from the wounds. The creature screamed and turned toward her.

The flames had weakened its hide on its chest and forelegs, which made it more vulnerable. More rounds drilled into its body. It lunged toward the humans but stumbled.

The Chinese's armored vehicle smashed into its side and tipped it over.

The mutant tried to stand again, but Charles and the other soldier responded with more flames. There was one final wave of fire and the animal stilled. Its blood soaked rapidly into the ground, almost as if the Zoo was sucking it up.

Everyone watched it for a few moments, but it didn't move. A command was issued in Chinese and several soldiers moved forward and poked the beast, but it didn't stir. One of the men turned, a big smile on his face, and gave the others a thumbs-up. Cheers went up from the PLA soldiers and the BOHICA team joined in, swept up in the adrenaline of a well-fought battle.

The PLA commander produced a bottle of plum wine. He poured a splash onto the earth for the fallen soldier, then passed it around.

"*Wàn shòu wú jiāng,*" each Chinese soldier said before

taking a sip. The bottle made it around to the BOHICA team. They were encouraged to partake.

"Salud," Mick said and took a sip. The others followed his lead and each added their own version of cheers before the almost empty bottle was passed back to the CO.

The mutilated remains of the dead soldier were wrapped in a cloth and loaded into the armored vehicle.

The CO and interpreter approached the BOHICA team.

"Thank you for your help, and good luck go with you," the soldier said as the CO shook each of their hands.

"Good luck," the officer said, his accent thick.

"Same to you," Booker responded.

They watched as the Chinese expedition disappeared into the jungle again.

"Well, that was exciting," Mick said.

"What did the CO want, Booker?" Reen asked.

"He was trying to get us to turn the vehicle into the Chinese not the Russians if we found it first."

"What'd you tell him?" Roo asked.

He shrugged. "I said we'd think about it. We have to find it first." He looked at the dead body of the giant lizard. "I don't think it's on this side of the wall. We're going to have to go deeper. Not to mention, I'm sure something else is going to come avenge that monster's death at any moment so we better clear out."

"They do that?" Lester asked. "Avenge each other?"

"I think the bastards just like fighting," Roo said.

"They're all sort of connected, it seems," Charles explained. "The Zoo doesn't like to lose its own."

They walked along the ruined Wall One and searched for any sign that the Russian vehicle had passed through.

Mick stopped in front of a larger break in the wall. "This is where it went through, or at least some vehicle did."

The others stopped and looked at where he had indicated. All they saw was the ruined wall and plants.

"Where?" Charles asked.

"Through here, and based on the degradation of the tracks and the Zoo's ability to erase things, I'd say this lines up with the timeline of the Russian expedition."

They stared at him.

He pinched the bridge of his nose. "Okay, look. I know this is a stupid fucking stereotype, but in my case, it's true. I'm a great tracker. Now, most Aboriginals nowadays couldn't tell you if a kangaroo or a wombat made a track, but I can. My grandad taught me the old ways."

Roo grinned and punched him in the shoulder. "I knew it, mate."

"No. You lucked out, asshole," he retorted and rolled his eyes. "Anyway, I know something came through this way."

"Lead the way," Booker said.

They followed Mick through the wall and toward the heart of the Zoo. The foliage pressed in aggressively, but Booker warned against using machetes. They simply shoved through. The body armor they wore protected them against small cuts, but they were still cautious. It slowed the progress, but their guide didn't seem too concerned.

They moved beyond the wall for five klicks and arrived at the ruined biodomes. For a moment, they simply stood and stared at the destruction. The whole area pulsed with life and the blue of the alien goop glowed wildly. Pita plants burgeoned everywhere. The shells of the biodomes hunkered amongst the plant life. There were some jagged pieces of glass but mostly, they were exoskeletons of metal.

"Ground zero," Booker said in a hushed tone.

The plants around the biodomes seemed to grow almost in the shape of humans, like they were the shadows of the scientists who ran when things went south. It was an eerie effect that had everyone on edge.

A short distance away, something very large screamed in what sounded like fury.

"We've got to keep moving," Booker said.

Mick led them around one of the biodomes and turned back in the direction of Wall One. They were almost at the wall again when they located their prize. It was far bigger than they had expected a stealth vehicle to be. The back hatch was open, which disrupted the arrow-head shape. There were no signs of life.

They approached with caution, but it was empty. Booker and Charles looked inside and noticed all the storage hatches, control panels, and weapons stashes. It was large enough to comfortably seat ten soldiers. There was also a closed cupula.

The others walked around the outside of the vehicle. Mick kicked one of the large, heavy-tread tires. The front half was on tires, while the back half was carried by caterpillar tracks.

"I've got something here," Reen said. She held up a dented samovar.

"This was definitely the Russians," Lester said. He pulled an empty vodka bottle off a plant that tried to grow inside it.

Charles and Booker came out of the vehicle and inspected the surrounding area with the others. The American approached the wall and found signs of a fight.

"Whatever happened here, they didn't stand a chance," he said.

"What makes you say that?" Mick asked.

"You might be the tracker extraordinaire, but I know a failed fight when I see one." He pointed out the deep gouges in the wall and the brown stains of old human blood. The section of wall was covered in signs that there had been an ambush and the humans hadn't made it.

"What the fuck made them decide this was a good spot for a picnic?" Roo asked and kicked at a scrap of armor.

"I think I'd rather have ants as a picnic problem then whatever attacked them here," Reen said.

"Maybe they got cocky? Clearly, their ride was doing its job keeping them safe. It made them complacent," Booker said.

"Must've been newbies," Lester said. "No way does an experienced soldier forget he's in a warzone."

"It'll just have to stay a mystery why they thought here was as good a spot as any to have tea," Booker said.

In the near distance, they heard the sounds of animals working their way toward them.

"I think we should get inside," Reen said.

The men turned to look at her, their backs to the wall. Reen, who was closest to the vehicle, started sprinting for it. "Get inside!"

They glanced over their shoulders as six sets of claws gripped the top of the wall. They raced toward the vehicle without waiting to see exactly what those six sets of claws belonged. Roo made it barely in time for the hatch to seal them in. Something large struck the back and bounced off and rocked it on its suspension. Another animal landed on the roof. The team remained motionless and didn't dare to breathe while they heard it scratch along the top.

Reen caught a glimpse of the spiked, split tail of one of the animals as it walked past the slit of the windshield.

They were safe inside for the moment, but they were also trapped.

They waited and listened to the sounds of the animals scuffling around. Occasionally, one of the beasts would ram against the vehicle, but the armor held. Several small fights broke out between the creatures, the screams and roars loud even inside. After a few hours, though, the mutants became bored with the area and there was relative silence again.

"Do you think they're gone?" Charles asked.

Mick stood cautiously and pressed the cupula open. He climbed the short ladder and looked around. "They're gone."

They relaxed.

"What's the next move, boss?" Mick asked Booker.

"We have to decide what to do with the vehicle," he answered.

"No shit, Sherlock. That's what we're asking," Reen said.

"I think we should give it to the Chinese," Lester said. "You said they wanted to give us a big reward? Money and gear? That's a guarantee. We don't even know if these Russian bastards will give us anything."

"Why don't we just keep it for ourselves?" Roo asked. "Do the salvage rules apply to the whole Zoo?"

"It seemed like a pretty done deal for the Russians. They may not have recruited anyone specifically, but they did put out the bat signal for the return of their vehicle. I'm sure they'd pay up," Charles said. "And, since we heard about it over at the French Quarter, they must not give a crap about who brings it back."

"I don't think keeping it for ourselves is a good option," Booker said.

"Why the hell not?" Roo asked.

"I can't read Cyrillic, and you sure as hell can't read Cyrillic. We'd need to figure out everything. Also, we don't know what it runs on."

"What the hell's Cyrillic?" Lester asked.

"Russian. It's their lettering system," Booker said.

"It isn't that different than the Greek alphabet. It should be easy to figure out," Roo insisted.

"You said you're third generation. You speak Greek?" Booker asked.

"Well, no, not exactly."

"Turn it in to the Chinese," Lester repeated. "It's a guarantee."

"I think I'm with Charles in returning it to the Russians. I mean, look at this beast we're in. I'm sure they have others like it, and they seem to be someone you'd want to be on the good side of," Reen said.

"Besides, if everyone wants it, it must mean it's the best or new or something," Charles said.

"We'll return it to the Russians," Booker announced.

"Bullshit. Really? That's a mistake," Lester protested, but the others were decided.

Booker settled into the driver's seat of the vehicle and

Charles sat beside him. Mick returned to the cupula to help guide them since the thin band of triple-paned glass that served as the windshield was so small.

"I'm sure they probably have optics or something to assist," the Brit muttered.

He looked at the pedals and gears. "Seems straight forward enough." He pressed a large green button that was on the side of the steering column. The vehicle purred to life. "Perfect. Everyone ready?"

Charles looked into the back of the vehicle where Roo, Lester, and Reen were strapped into the folding chairs on the sides.

"Ready!" Mick called from his position in the cupula.

The Aboriginal directed the driver along the trail the vehicle had originally taken. It traversed the Zoo terrain with ease and the wedge shape parted the plants as it trundled forward. Surprisingly, it was quiet as it drove along.

They left the wall behind and went seven more klicks before they had to stop.

"It's too dark out there for me to see anything more," Mick said and lowered himself into the main cabin. "The night vision works, but it washes everything out too much. I can't see details like I need to be able to."

They stepped outside of the vehicle to look at the surroundings. It was rapidly growing darker, and the trees closed in. The Zoo was alive with the sounds of animals working themselves into a frenzy.

"I think our best bet is to stay the night in the vehicle," Booker said. The others agreed with him.

"Everyone take a piss now. Once that door seals it won't

be opening again. Unless you want to go out into the pitch black," Roo said, only half-joking.

Everyone but Charles was awake before dawn and waited for it to be light enough to safely leave the vehicle. Not that light meant it was actually safe. They'd merely be able to more easily locate whatever denizen from hell intended to kill them.

"Can you die from not taking a piss for so long?" Roo asked. He'd tried to find a canteen or bottle or something to use, but there hadn't been anything in the whole vehicle.

"Shut the fuck up," Reen growled. She had her eyes closed and her head pressed against the cold metal of the vehicle's side.

"Don't break the princess' concentration," Lester said, although he sounded as uncomfortable as the other two.

"If you call me princess again, Brit, I'm going to fucking kill you."

"Be my guest, sweetheart."

"Fuck you."

Charles woke and scrubbed the sleep from his eyes. He looked over his shoulder at the others. "What's going on?"

"We all have to relieve ourselves," Booker muttered. He glared at the American.

The large man shrugged. He'd slept through the night in the passenger seat. He was too tall to stretch out in the back like some of the others could, so he'd given up trying and had passed out. After he'd squinted carefully out the windshield, he retrieved his Remington from between his feet and shoved the door open.

The others gaped at him as he exited the vehicle. Reen lunged for the button that would open the hatch. Roo tried to move in front of her and she shoved him back. "Get the fuck out of my way."

They tumbled out of the vehicle into the early dawn light.

Charles waited for them with coffee when they all returned.

"Where'd you get this from?" Reen asked and cradled the cup to her chest.

He shrugged. "Found it in one of the storage compartments."

"Let's get a move on. I'm sure we can't be that far from the Russian gate. I'm ready to be out of the Zoo," Booker said.

Mick climbed into the cupula and the Brit began driving.

Their guide saw several animals from his position, and they were attacked multiple times. The assaults were mostly by the larger, scalier animals that obviously thought they could defeat an opponent as large as the vehicle. The armor held and Booker was able to maintain his speed. After several hours of driving, they arrived at the Russian gate. The wall had been painted with a word in tall red letters, but none of them understood the Cyrillic alphabet and couldn't tell what it said. They assumed it was a warning.

The top of the Russian wall bristled with heavy artillery.

"They aren't fucking around," Mick muttered.

The gate opened for them and they drove the vehicle through. On the other side of the wall, in the Russian Quarter, a large group had gathered. The team climbed out of the vehicle and stood in front of it.

"Who are you?" a man asked as he stepped forward. His accent was thick but his English was perfect and he had a large black beard and wore fatigues. He was a large man, bigger even than Charles, and he didn't look friendly.

"I'm Booker. We're with BOHICA Warriors, Inc. From the French Quarter," he said and proffered his hand.

The Russian shook firmly.

"The French Quarter, huh? You're a long way from home," the man said. "I'm Misha."

Booker shrugged. "We might be a long way from the French Quarter, but what does that matter? We brought back what you lost."

Misha commanded something in Russian and four men rushed forward to inspect the vehicle.

"The men who were with it?" he asked.

The Brit shook his head. "All gone."

"I was afraid of that. *мир праху твоему.*"

He looked at the team, his expression unreadable. One of the men returned to him and said something in Russian.

"Seems like it's still in excellent condition, and I thank you for that," Misha said. He barked another order and food and vodka was brought forward. "As a token of our thanks."

They each took a shot.

"Now, about our reward?" Roo asked.

Booker grimaced, but Misha laughed. It was a surprisingly jolly sound for such a hard-looking man.

"Smart man. Never take just vodka as payment! I will confer with my генерáл-лейтенáнт. Wait here." The Russian turned on his heel and disappeared into the crowd.

The BOHICA team waited beside the vehicle they had returned. Charles and Reen stood at parade rest while the others simply stood. The Russians soon went about their business.

"They've got some high class shit here," Roo muttered as he surveyed the base.

The buildings were more substantial and better put together than the prefabs and pole barns of the French Quarter. There seemed to be an order to the flow of traffic. Men moved with purpose in clear groups. While the French-Israeli-Indian Quarter was a collection of mercenaries and smaller companies, these seemed to all be soldiers.

Russian flags were painted on almost all the buildings in the area. A little farther away, a flagpole fluttered a Japanese flag.

"I forgot the Japs were also here. What do you think their part of this quarter is like?" Roo asked.

Booker shrugged. "Probably much of the same."

Mick straightened as if that would allow him to see over the buildings. "Looks like more of the same to me."

Lester rolled his eyes. "You can't see over the bloody buildings, you ninny."

"What if I can?"

"You can't."

"Don't see you trying to look."

The other man was about to say something when Charles elbowed him in the ribs. "Quiet. Misha's coming back."

"The loss of the men, though not your fault, has been taken into consideration. So has the condition of the vehicle. It seems most everything is where it should be. I have been authorized to offer you two million as a reward."

They stared at him and he laughed.

"You can, of course, decide if that's what you would like to accept."

Booker turned to the group. They all wore the same stunned expression. He motioned them closer.

"I mean, obviously, that's okay," Booker said. "I knew the reward was going to be large, but that's better than we could have hoped."

"Go fucking accept it," Roo hissed.

"Wait," Charles said before Booker could turn back to Misha, "before we accept, maybe we should ask if we could get a vehicle. They've got lots of them here, and if they're going to be going with that new sweet ride we recovered, well, seems to me they might have some surplus."

"What do you mean?" Lester asked. "This isn't really a negotiation. We already gave them what they wanted. If we start getting greedy, they might yank it and kick us out with nothing. Or do something worse."

Reen elbowed him. "Don't talk so loud. You want them to hear us?"

He gave her a dark look but didn't reply.

"I'm with Lester on this one," Mick said. "The odds aren't in our favor."

"I'm not saying we get the two mil *and* a vehicle. I'm

saying we should ask for a vehicle," Charles said. "One of their older ones that they're going to retire, maybe. It would still be better than anything in our quarter."

"If we get a vehicle, that's an added expense. We made a lot on our last job, but I don't know if we're making enough for the arming and upkeep an armored vehicle would most likely demand," Booker said.

"What if we asked for an older model and a million?" Roo asked. "They're already willing to give us a lot, that doesn't seem like it's that big of an ask. Besides, look around. The motherfuckers won't miss some old tank or whatever. They probably have heaps of unused armored vehicles coming out their asses."

The rest of the group agreed.

Booker turned back to Misha, who had stood nearby and ignored their conversation. "We'll take one million, if you throw in an armored vehicle like this one."

"You can't have this one. But I have something that's almost as good. It's an older generation, but I guarantee it will perform. Not to mention it's probably better than the shit you have over in the French Quarter!"

They didn't argue with him. Misha gave a few more orders and soon a BTR-90 rumbled up to them.

"It's completely fueled and fully stocked. We put a case of vodka in there as well as a further token of our appreciation."

The Russian transferred the money to the company account. Booker verified that the transfer had been successful while Charles inspected the BTR-90. It wasn't that they didn't trust the man's word, but they didn't want to be taken advantage of. The Russian didn't seem offended.

Once the Brit confirmed the transfer was complete and Charles finished his inspection, they all shook hands.

"Just follow that jeep out," Misha said and pointed to the Russian military jeep that idled in front of the BTR. "Safe travels."

They climbed into the BTR and Booker drove them through the Russian Quarter. The others opened one of the bottles of vodka and started celebrating their successful mission—and the fact that they'd return to the French Quarter with an armored vehicle and a million dollars richer.

CHAPTER SIXTEEN

French Quarter

Booker put the BTR-90 through its paces driving from the Russian Quarter along the perimeter road back to the French Quarter. He refused to give up the controls to anyone else. So, while he drove, the others drank some of the vodka and inspected the inside of the well-maintained vehicle.

The Russians had made sure the ammunition had been fully stocked and everything was in working order. They didn't fire the Shipunov or the machine gun, but Charles inspected them, and they appeared to be in perfect working order.

As they passed through the Chinese camp, Lester muttered that they could have gotten a better deal from them but he didn't seem too disappointed. It was more like he merely wanted to bitch. Charles stuck his head out of the commander's cupola and gave the Chinese who looked at them a Hollywood-worthy salute as they drove past.

The trip back was quick. It was not even an hour before

Booker announced through the intercom, "We're approaching the French Quarter."

Roo opened one of the top hatches and climbed out. Reen and Mick joined him. Lester and Charles chose to position themselves half-out the side doors.

The guard stopped them and looked surprised when he saw who it was. Charles handed him the paperwork.

"Where the hell did you get this monster?" the man asked.

He grinned. "The Russians."

They had decided before their approach that it would be all right for them to brag about where the armored vehicle came from. They wanted everyone to know that they meant serious business. The physical evidence of the Russian's appreciation was one of the best ways to do that.

"No shit. You guys recovered that vehicle, didn't you?"

Charles nodded.

"Damn. I was going to have a go at that myself if no one had. Oh, well. Carry on, gents."

Booker drove slowly into the camp. The BTR acted like a flame and the inhabitants of the French Quarter were the moths. A large group gathered and followed all the way to their converted containers.

Roo hopped off the top and gave everyone around them a shit-eating grin.

"We need to put the company name on the side of this bad boy," Charles said to Booker. "Let people know who we are."

The Brit grinned. "Seems we are generating a lot of interest."

"Where the hell did you get this thing?" a man asked.

"It was our reward for doing what none of you pussies even dared to attempt—recovering that Russian vehicle," Reen answered.

They were bombarded with questions, all roughly the same. A few personnel from some of the larger companies came to gawk, clearly impressed with the work done by the BOHICA Warriors.

Prince Akachukwu pushed his way through the crowd. He wore his usual off-mission white jeans and many-colored fringed vest. His customary team of Hollywood-ready bodyguards shadowed him.

The Nigerian walked up to Booker, Roo, and Charles with a wide smile. He patted the side of the BTR despite Roo's glare.

"Gents, looks like you've done well since we've cut ties!" Prince announced. He moved closer to the three and lowered his voice. "Listen, I've caught wind of a big job coming up. Huge. Are you interested in joining?"

"Hell no," Roo said. "We told you we were done running jobs for you. Done giving you that fucking ridiculous thirty percent cut of our winnings."

Booker frowned at his teammate. "Ignore him. We could be interested—but we wouldn't be giving you a cut. It would simply be as cooperating business entities," he added quickly when he saw Prince's frown.

"Ridiculous. I find the job and I get a finder's fee. It makes sense."

"You want us to work with you, right?" he asked.

The man nodded.

"Then no fee. You're approaching us with the offer, we

didn't seek you out. It would only work if we'd come asking for a job."

He looked like he intended to try to argue more, but Charles leaned against the BTR. The movement drew his attention back to the armored vehicle. It also seemed to remind him of the reason he had asked for the BOHICA Warrior's participation.

"Fine. Fine, no finder's fee," he said quietly and glanced around hastily to see if anyone else had heard him. He leaned in closer. "You absolutely, under no circumstances, can tell anyone that I'm waiving my fee for you. You squeal and I'll have your balls. Got it?"

They nodded.

"Great! Ah, such a wonderful feeling, getting the gang back together again," Prince said.

They didn't look as thrilled.

"What's the job?" Roo asked.

"I don't have all the details nailed down quite yet. I should have them soon, very soon. So, hold tight, gents. Keep your phone on you. I'll let you know when the mission is a go." The Nigerian looked at the armored vehicle once more. He snapped his fingers at his guards, turned on his heel, and walked away.

"Well, that was interesting," Charles said, his gaze fixed on the retreating figure.

"Who was that?" Mick asked.

"That was Prince Akachukwu," Roo said.

"A real prince? Where's he from?"

"Nigeria," Charles answered. "We don't know if he's a real prince or not."

"What do you mean, you don't know?"

Booker shrugged. "He never actually specified if it was his name or his title. We never figured it out. Everyone calls him Prince. Sometimes Prince Achoo, but it's best not to use that epithet to his face."

"Wait, aren't Nigerian princes used in Internet scams?"

"Yes."

"We still trust him?"

"He's greedy, but that's what makes him good at finding jobs. He knows where the money will be. Of course, that also means he'll get as much money out of you as he can," Charles said. "He's good people, though."

"What's the next move, then?" Reen asked and joined the conversation she'd simply listened in on.

"I think we're okay to wait for Prince to come through. We'll give him a week and then continue running missions as usual," Booker said. "For now, we'll wait and you emmets can work on customizing the vehicle."

Mick sighed. "Golly gee, I can't wait."

Charles grinned. "That's the spirit."

"I think we've had enough of this side show," Roo said. He climbed on top of the BTR. "All right, people, move the fuck on! You've had your moment to stare, now get the fuck moving before I'm forced to move you myself. Trust me, it won't be fucking pretty."

CHAPTER SEVENTEEN

The Zoo - Thor

Thor sat in the center of the small clearing he'd created and sniffed the air. He still waited in the place where Charles had last left him. He hadn't eaten in days—the smaller animals he'd killed in the beginning avoided the area, and he never ventured far. He barely held off dehydration by drinking from the cone-shaped plants that collected the humidity in little silver pools.

A slight breeze stirred the air, and he could smell Charles, although the scent was faint. He stood and wagged his tail. The man had left him there, but Thor still expected him to come back.

Teased by the scent, he trotted through the jungle to within sight of the first wall. He sat at the edge of the trees and looked out across the burned sand. From there, he could smell more than see the human guards. He could also smell the charred earth and the strong fuel used to create the marks. It made him nervous. He'd gone through the wall several times before, but that was always with the humans.

Thor huffed and uttered a small whine. His horns had grown since Charles had left him. They were a foot long and covered in a thin layer of black, velvety flesh and fur. They curved back from his skull along his back in such a way that he couldn't twist to the right angle to scratch them. Worse, they itched.

He turned away from the man-made barrier and returned to his clearing. He whimpered as the itching in his horns turned into an ache. In search of some relief, he lowered his head and rubbed them against a trunk. The tree protested a little and tried to lean away from the animal, but he ignored it and pressed harder.

Even though it hurt, he rammed his horns against the tree. The sharp tips opened gouges in the bark that snagged on the velvet and ripped through it. Thor rubbed harder and found more relief as the velvet sloughed off. His horns now gleamed black under the pulpy, bloody mess.

The tree began to splinter, but he didn't notice. After a few more hard passes, the tree groaned in protest, snapped, and toppled with a resounding crash. He looked at it and his tail wagged. His horns were now completely revealed and brought relief.

The sound attracted attention. Howls sounded close by. Thor looked in their direction. As always, the desire to run to the source was there.

He howled in response and received answering calls.

The animal looked at the clearing he'd paced out during his wait for Charles, at the broken tree, and at the tattered pieces of velvet that had encased his horns. Still drawn by his bond with the man, he turned toward the direction of the wall and smelled again for Charles, but his scent was gone.

Thor howled again, but not in reply to the cries deeper in the Zoo. He called for Charles but of course, he wasn't there to hear him.

After a long look in the direction in which the man had walked away, he loped into the jungle toward the call of his kind.

CHAPTER EIGHTEEN

Harvesters Camp

Booker, Roo, and Charles inspected the rookies' handi-work. They'd painted **BOHICA Warriors** in black letters on the side of the BTR-90.

"Not bad," Booker said.

"I've seen better," Roo said.

"Do you think we should have a symbol?" Charles asked. The other two looked at him. "You know, like a logo. Like Lampton has?"

Roo shrugged.

"I don't think a logo is necessary," Booker said. "Not at this point, anyway. Not all companies have a picture logo."

"Can you draw?" the Aussie asked.

Charles shook his head.

"Then where the fuck would we get a picture logo?"

"We can always hire someone. We don't have to design it ourselves." he shrugged. "I was just asking. No need to jump down my throat about it."

"Sorry. I'm so goddamn over this fucking waiting. It's

been five days. Do you think Prince really has a job? Or was the cocksucker trying to take out his biggest competition by making us wait for a mission that doesn't exist?"

"I asked him about it again earlier today," Booker said. "His answer was the same as it was the last bleddy time—he still has details to nail down and he'll let us know."

Roo kicked one of the tires. "I want to take this bad boy out into the Zoo and see what kind of damage we can do."

"It would be good to take it on a test run before this big job Prince wants us to do," Charles said.

They looked expectantly at Booker.

"Well," he said, "I did hear that a swamp might've sprung up about fifteen klicks in. We can take the BTR for a test drive, have a geek around, maybe pick up some two-second frogs."

"Fuck, yeah! What the hell are we waiting for? Let's get these wombats off their asses and hit the fucking road."

"We can test out the amphibious features of this bad boy," Charles said, also excited. "It'll make things a heck of a lot easier. I'd like to see one of those leeches try to bite through steel armor!"

"The fucking things would probably try," Roo said.

His teammate shrugged.

"Okay," Booker interrupted when he saw the Aussie was about to try to get a bigger reaction, "I can go get suits for the others. You two want to brief them?"

"We can do that," Charles said.

"And see if that asshole has any containers with big openings," Roo said, "it'll make things easier."

The two teammates went back to the container where the others lounged.

"All right people, it's time to get off your asses and actually do something useful, Roo said.

They looked at him expectantly, and Charles added "I think what Roo is trying to say is that we have a potential job."

"Potential?" Lester asked.

"It's not a guarantee. More of a freelance," he explained. "It's also a way to test out the BTR."

"What is it?" Mick asked.

"Asking the important questions," Roo said. "There are rumors of a swamp opening up. This happens every once in a while. This means there will be two-second frogs and people pay a shit ton for those—and they're easy pickings."

"Two-second frogs?" Reen asked.

"They're poisonous. If your skin comes into contact with the frogs', you have about two seconds to get right with God," Charles answered.

The three stared at them.

"No big deal," Roo said with a grin. "We got heaps of the things last time and we're still kicking ass today."

"Well, now," she said, "I haven't really seen you kicking ass, so that's not that much of a statement. Were you a known ass-kicker before? Maybe the frogs did affect you."

Charles clapped his hands sharply and startled everyone into looking at him before Roo had time to retaliate. "So, get your kits together. Booker is picking up some more protective gear and when he returns, it'll be time to load out."

He turned away from the group and Roo flashed the woman an obscene gesture. She rolled her eyes before she turned to follow the other man.

Charles and Roo oversaw the loading of the gear. It didn't take long since they anticipated being back by the end of the day or early the next morning at the latest.

"Put your fucking back into it," Roo said, his arms folded over his chest.

The American shook his head. "Don't think there's anything heavy being loaded on there."

"Doesn't fucking matter. It's the principle of the thing. They can put their metaphysical backs into it."

"I think you mean metaphorical," Mick said as he walked past with his arms full of sample containers.

"I know what I fucking said," Roo retorted. Mick laughed and ducked in the side doors of the BTR.

"How long are we expecting to be gone?" Lester asked.

"Pack rations for three days," Charles said. "We're aiming for a quick in and out, I think. The swamp isn't supposed to be deep into the Zoo. But it's always good to be prepared."

"You heard the paranoid boy scout, now move!"

Lester raised an eyebrow and continued about his business.

"Were you ever a drill instructor?" Charles asked.

"What? No. What makes you say that?"

"You just standing here, barking nonsense orders. I'm having flashbacks to boot camp."

Roo shrugged. "Nah, I was too hot-headed for that shit. Besides, I wanted to be in the action, not training some bogan how to make his bed and shine his fucking shoes."

Booker returned when everything was stowed.

"We'll have to make do with what containers we have," he said.

"Why?" Roo asked.

He shrugged. "Dan had a few wide mouth sample containers, but he wanted an insane price for them."

"We can afford it."

"I don't give a fuck if we can afford it or not," he responded, "I'm not going to be swindled."

"Jesus, Booker, we're worth at least a million and you're still a penny-pinching asswipe."

"We can't go crazy with the spending. We might be bleddy flush now, but things are too unpredictable here."

"Booker's right," Charles said before the other man could continue to argue. "How about we go make some more money so Booker here will loosen up and you'll stop complaining?"

He walked past them and climbed into the BTR. Lester, Reen, and Mick followed him in.

"Are you going to continue throwing a fit, or are you going to get in the bleddy vehicle?"

Roo scowled and climbed through the side doors.

The armored vehicle drew plenty of attention again as it rumbled through the Harvesters Camp toward the gate. The procedure of driving through the walls to the Zoo was much the same as when they walked through on foot.

"Tell me again how many rounds we have for the Shipunov?" Booker asked through the intercom system.

Mick's voice crackled back at him. "Ten."

The Brit halted after the last wall. The vehicle ticked in the heat as they idled in the sandy area between the wall and the Zoo.

"Yo, Booker, what are we waiting for?" Charles asked.

He sat beside the driver in what would have been the commander's seat.

"Everyone holding onto something?" the Brit asked. "I have a feeling it's about to get a little rough."

He pressed the accelerator and they rumbled into the Zoo.

Smaller trees bent and snapped beneath the BTR. It was a bumpy ride, but he didn't really care. He laughed as they bounced over another tree and glanced at the gyroscopic navigator the Russians had installed. It was supposed to be oriented to the direction of the gate. He flicked it and frowned. They were barely in the Zoo and the thing was already acting up.

Booker maneuvered around a particularly large tree. The BTR was a beast, but he wasn't stupid enough to try to ram the biggest ones.

"How many klicks in was the swamp?" Charles asked.

"Fifteen."

"Think we'll make good time?"

"In this thing? Sure." He frowned and immediately braked sharply to avoid a particularly large tree.

"Can I have eyes at my six?" he asked over the intercom.

"I got it," Reen said. She looked through one of the periscopes and directed him as he backed up.

He moved forward again. Something struck the right side of the vehicle with a dull thud.

"What was that?" Charles asked.

"Looks like we have one of those Komodo dragon-like things trying to get a piece of us," Roo announced. "Should I take it out or see what the BTR can take?"

"Let's see what we can take," Booker said, "for now."

He continued to push the vehicle forward and the creature kept pace. Occasionally, it pounded its scaly shoulder into them. It hissed and roared in frustration and tried to bite and claw at the armor but didn't make a scratch.

Soon, the solitary animal was joined by three others. The mutants flung themselves at the vehicle. The sound of their bodies colliding with the armor grated on Booker's nerves, but he could barely feel the impacts of the animals against the BTR's bulk. He squinted through the small windshield, his brow furrowed in concentration as he swerved to avoid the larger trees.

"Okay," he said, "I'm over this bullshit. Roo, do something about these bleddy nuisances."

"You got it, boss." He flipped one of the gun ports open and stuck the barrel of his AK-47 through it. Lester did the same with his M5 on the opposite side. They opened fire. The animals screamed but the rounds merely angered them rather than doing much damage.

"Fuck," He said and drew the weapon back inside. "This isn't going to work. We don't have a good angle on them."

Lester shut the gun port he was using. "What do you want to do?"

Before Roo could answer, Reen flung one of the top hatches open. She scrambled upward and tossed a grenade toward the right side of the vehicle where the Komodo dragon-like creatures were gathered, ducked, and slammed the hatch shut. The grenade exploded to blow two of the animals into big chunks. It also snapped a tree which fell in front of the BTR.

Booker cranked the wheel in an attempt to miss the

new obstacle. The right-side wheels rolled over the tree and rocked the vehicle.

"What the bleddy hell was that?" he asked.

"Sorry," she said, completely unapologetic.

The remaining animals retreated.

The Brit glanced at the gyroscope again. "What a piece of shit," he muttered.

"Not working?" Charles asked.

He shook his head. "Not really."

"How far have we gone?"

"About ten klicks."

"We should be hitting it soon, then."

"Yeah."

As they proceeded, there were periodic clanking noises on the roof. "Okay. What the fuck is that?" Booker asked.

Charles shrugged.

"Anyone know what that sound is?" the Brit asked. "If this thing falls to fucking pieces, I'm going to go back and rip that Russian a new asshole."

Lester flung the roof hatch open. He was about to swing himself up and out when a rock hurtled into the compartment and he jerked back to avoid it.

The rock bounced and rolled to a stop against Roo's foot. He looked at it, then at the canopy moving past ahead of them. A large troop of monkeys kept pace with the vehicle. Their strong prehensile tails ferried them easily through the trees. Their yellow eyes glowed against the dark green leaves and they glared angrily at the humans.

"It's those goddamn monkeys," he announced. He gave them the middle finger and closed the hatch again. Another rock bounced off.

"Where are they even getting rocks from?" Reen asked.

"Who fucking cares?" Lester asked. She scowled at him.

Mick laughed. "Oh, my God, I've always wanted a monkey to throw something at me."

Roo, Lester, and Reen stared at him. He shrugged.

"What? Haven't you thought it would be hilarious? It's my favorite thing they do in movies—when a monkey throws something at people."

Roo clapped him on the shoulder. "That is an example of things you should keep to your fucking self, mate."

"It's comedy gold," the man protested.

Reen shook her head. "You're ruining it. I was just starting to think you were smart."

"We need more eyes," Charles said. "Someone get in the gunner's position and see if you can locate the swamp."

Mick scrambled into position before the others could. "It only makes sense," he said over his shoulder. "I'm the best at finding things."

They all glowered at him and he grinned.

"I'm not seeing anything yet," he said. There was nothing but jungle in front of them. Nothing unusual or remotely close to being a swamp.

Booker drove around a large copse of trees. As he maneuvered around them and plowed through the thick underbrush, the space in front of the BTR opened.

Mick saw a large patch of mud. Before he could say anything, the vehicle lurched forward. Watery mud sprayed up around them before the front tires sank deep and the vehicle came to a jarring halt.

"I think we found the swamp," he said. "Or what's left of it."

"Why didn't you say anything?" Booker asked.

The engine whined as he tried to reverse. The tires spun but couldn't gain traction.

"I saw it the same time you drove us right into it!" he protested. "You could see just about as much as I could!"

The Brit decided reversing out of the mud wasn't an option. He attempted to drive forward to turn and move back into the jungle. The heavy vehicle plowed forward and sunk deeper.

He cut the engine. "Fuck."

"Way to go," Charles said.

"Didn't see you volunteering to bleddy drive, asshole," he pointed out belligerently

"You wouldn't let anyone else drive, Booker."

He started to say something but didn't have a comeback. Instead, he simply shut his mouth. They climbed into BTR's crew compartment with the rest of the team.

"What's the next move?" Reen asked.

"We should see if there's anything left out there. We hit the last swamp right before it was swallowed up, and that was the best time for the two-second frogs," Roo said.

"We might as well have a geek around," Booker said. "We can also check out how deep we've sunk into the mud."

"I thought this thing was amphibious," Mick said.

"You see any water around here?" Lester asked and threw the side doors open. He jumped out and sank calf-deep. It smelled like sulfur and shit.

The others climbed out behind him.

"This doesn't look promising," Charles said.

There was nothing but mud and vines. A few bright

green seedlings dotted the ground here and there, but there were no remaining swamp animals.

"Fucking hell," Booker said. He walked around the BTR, his mouth set in a grim line. The tires were firmly embedded and the weight dragged it deeper into the mud.

"How the bloody hell are we going to get the vehicle out?" Lester asked.

"There's no fucking way we can push it," Roo said.

Charles raised an eyebrow at him.

"Come on, Yank, you know for damn sure we would just be wasting our time. The thing weighs a fuck-ton. We can't do it."

"Twenty," Booker grumbled.

"What?"

"It weighs right about twenty tons."

They stared at the stuck vehicle.

"Anyone got any ideas?" Roo asked.

Charles walked to the front of it and then a little farther ahead. He watched his feet as he walked.

"Charles, what the fuck are you doing?" the Aussie asked.

He ignored him and paced deliberately in front of the BTR. He dug his heel into the mud and carved a line.

"The mud isn't as deep here. This is the end. We go any farther in, we'll only sink. If we can get the vehicle to turn and make its way up here, we can be on more solid ground and will hopefully be able to get traction."

Booker climbed back in and started the engine. He tried to turn, but the wheels only created deeper ruts. After a couple of attempts, he returned to the others.

"We obviously need something to catch on the tread," Lester said.

Reen nodded. "What if we cut some branches or saplings and made a ramp toward the shallower mud?"

"That could work," Charles said.

"Of course it'll work," Reen said and seemed to warm to the idea. "I've done it before when I've been mudding with my cousins in the woods. You get in too deep you've got to give yourself something to grab onto."

"All right, Reen," Booker said, "since you've done it before, tell us what you need us to do."

"Right. Roo, you and Mick bring back a few thick branches. We need them to be about wrist thickness. Booker, you and Lester get some more leafy branches or bushes that seem to have durable stems," she said.

"What about you and Charles?" Roo asked, clearly not thrilled with the idea of cutting branches from the trees and not being paired up with her.

"We'll get vines and other odds and ends. If we do this quickly, we should be out of here in no time," Reen said.

They separated and gathered what they needed. Roo and Mick cursed as they cut branches from the nearby trees.

"These motherfuckers won't stay still," Mick growled. He held tightly to the end of a trembling branch as his teammate hacked through it as fast as he could. Another branch from the tree whipped down and smacked the Aboriginal on the side of the head. "Ouch! You fucking bastard. I'm going to get all the branches from you, just to spite you, asshole."

"You know they can't actually understand you, right?"

He frowned and ducked another swinging branch. "You don't know that. These wankers sure are smart enough to try to fight us off, what makes you think they can't fucking understand us?"

Roo halted his sawing. "Huh. I guess you could be right. Who knows what all the alien shit does to them? Maybe they're not just cranky-ass trees but super-human trees."

Mick groaned. "Whatever, Roo. Just hurry the fuck up. And I'm cutting the next branch."

"It was your theory," he muttered and finally separated the branch from the trunk. The tree shuddered and swung at them, but the men ducked out of the way.

"You two should stop complaining," Booker said, "it's bleddy annoying." He pulled up a few strands of the ground cover plant that was everywhere in the Zoo.

Roo dodged another branch. "Fuck you. You got one of the easy jobs."

"We've got company," Lester announced, dropped what he'd gathered, and raised his weapon.

Three of the panther-like animals slunk out of the nearby trees and rumbled low growls. Lester fired a few rounds at one of them and killed it, but the fatality angered the other two. With matching screams, they leapt toward the humans.

More howls and roars erupted from the jungle. The panthers had company.

"Everyone back to the BTR!" Booker yelled.

They took shelter and Charles eliminated another of the panthers on the way. They sealed themselves inside. For several moments, they simply listened while the animals screamed in fury and tried to gain access.

"Well, this puts a damper on things," Reen grumbled.

"We'll just wait them out. They should lose interest soon," Booker said.

Charles glanced at him and he shrugged.

An hour passed, and then two.

"Doesn't seem like they're losing fucking interest," Roo said.

Booker threw his arms up in exasperation. "What am I? A fucking crystal ball? It was just a guess. They normally don't stick around so bleddy long."

"Even if they leave soon, it'll be too dark to do anything safely," Charles said.

"So, looks like we're stuck here for the night," the Brit retorted.

"Fucking brilliant," Lester muttered. He slumped and leaned back against the wall.

They arranged themselves in the BTR and prepared to sleep through the night. Booker assigned watches, even though they seemed to be safe inside the vehicle.

Mick said as much.

The Brit shrugged. "We are safe, for now. But who knows when something bigger will come along and if we're all asleep, we'd be fucked."

No one argued.

"I need out of this goddamn vehicle," Roo said. All through the night, a steady stream of Zoo traffic had kept them confined. Now that it was morning, there seemed to be something of a lull.

They all stumbled out of the BTR and stretched their stiff muscles.

"If we have to keep spending the night in those confined spaces, we might want to think of investing in bunks or hammocks or some shit like that," Reen said.

Booker inspected the vehicle once again. "Well," he said, "the good news is, I don't think we sank any deeper."

Charles tried to get it moving forward but the wheels simply spun.

"The bad news is we're still fucking stuck," Roo said.

Reen dragged up a portion of the material they'd gathered the day before. Some of it had already been swallowed by the Zoo again, but a few branches and vines remained. She began to arrange them in front of the first set of tires.

"Should we put them in front of the rear set, too?" Booker asked.

She shook her head. "You can, but I think we should focus all our efforts on this front set. We get this moving and it should be able to haul itself out."

"Should?" Lester asked.

"It's not an exact science."

He folded his arms, his expression unimpressed. "So you aren't even sure it will work?"

"Of course I'm not fucking sure, but I didn't see you offering up any suggestions. Shut the fuck up and help spread the branches out or figure out a better way."

He looked like he wanted to argue with her but said nothing.

Between them all, they made quick work of positioning the vegetation.

Reen gave Charles a thumbs-up through the small windshield. "Let 'er rip, Tillman!" she yelled.

He revved the engine and pressed the accelerator slowly. The tires spun once, then twice, sucked up some of the smaller branches, and shot them out the other side. Reen frowned. On the third rotation, the front two tires caught.

"Easy!" she yelled.

Charles kept the BTR in the lowest gear and at a crawl, the vehicle edged forward. The front set turned and caught traction in the shallower mud, exactly like he had said they would.

With a whine and a wet, sucking sound, the BTR freed itself from the mud. The sudden traction mixed with the release of the pressure that had held it back, made the vehicle lunge forward. The others dodged out of the way to prevent being crushed.

The American didn't stop when he was free of the mud. He drove forward slowly and the team clambered inside.

Booker dropped into the commander's chair. "Not too shabby driving for someone who normally drives on the wrong side of the road."

Charles grinned.

"We going to try anything else?" Roo asked through the intercom system.

"No," the Brit answered. "I think it's better that we return to base. We don't have enough information at this time to be successful."

"Isn't something better than nothing?" Reen argued.

"We'll keep an eye out, but don't get your hopes up."

"What a fucking waste," Lester said. "This bloody

vehicle is turning out to be more trouble than it's fucking worth. We should've just taken the two mil from the fucking Russians. This was all a bloody stupid idea."

"You're still on the intercom," Booker said.

"I know."

The Brit flicked the gyroscope again. "Bleddy thing doesn't work properly."

Charles glanced at it. "You think it's very far off?"

"No. But it isn't very accurate. If we were any farther in, we'd be in deep shit if we thought we could rely on it. Since we aren't, we should be okay following its course."

As they drove back to the gate, more animals tried to attack the vehicle. Several more of the dragon-like creatures attempted to breach the armor. Charles noticed that only the larger predators actually attacked them physically. Smaller creatures merely screamed their annoyance, and— if they could—threw things at them like the monkeys had.

"No wonder the Russians didn't mind giving us this thing," he said.

"What makes you say that?"

"It's like a freaking magnet. All the animals just want to attack us."

He rammed into a bright green, giant lizard before it had time to spit acid at them. He was fairly sure the steel would hold, but he didn't want to take any chances.

Booker grimaced. "I think you're right."

Charles nodded.

"Fuck! This really throws a wrench into things, doesn't it?"

He slowed when the trees vanished, and they crossed the sand. No animals followed them.

"We can't tell anyone," Booker said.

"What?"

"We can't mention that this thing is a critter magnet. It's better to keep that knowledge amongst ourselves."

"You're probably right."

"I am right."

"Okay. We won't tell," he agreed. He shifted in his seat as the darkness of the first wall enveloped them. "I don't like keeping so many secrets. It's never a good thing. You get too caught up in trying not to tell people things that they all spill out and bite you in the butt at once."

"I don't understand your analogies," Booker said.

He grunted. "You get what I'm trying to say, though."

"Sure, and you know what I have to say to that?"

"What?"

"Fucking suck it up."

CHAPTER NINETEEN

Harvesters Camp

Booker stood outside Franco's door with the other team leaders where they waited for the dispatchers to arrive. He didn't like standing around like that. It made him feel useless or like he was begging for a hand-out. By nature, he didn't beg and craved the day when people would seek them out for jobs instead of the other way around.

"Did you hear what happened to Cyrus' team?" one of the leaders said.

He didn't normally engage in the small talk that took place there, but that didn't mean he didn't pay attention.

"No," another man said. "What happened?"

"Wiped out."

"No shit. The whole team?"

The first man nodded.

"Jesus. You know how?"

"Fuck no. Does anyone know how people get butchered

in there? They went in. They didn't come back out. End of story."

There was a pause. "You know what's happening with their spot?"

"What spot?"

"You know, that building they had? That big two-story out by the registration building?"

"I don't know. But now that you mention it, I might try for it."

"It'll be fucking expensive, I bet. It's a great crib."

"Sure. I mean, I've seen better."

"Of course you've fucking seen better. But this is the goddamn French Quarter. Everything here is shit anyway. It's better than most of the shit housing, though."

"Well, it doesn't matter. It's probably been snapped up."

"The contract, at least, probably has been."

"When do you think these assholes will show up? You'd think that they'd be a little more prompt. It's not like they work hard."

Booker eased away from them. He thought about what they'd said. The BOHICA Warriors needed a better situation than renting converted containers from Prince. If he could determine what had happened to that building, he could try to get it for them.

He knew exactly who to talk to about the now-empty house. As casually as he could, he turned away from Franco's and walked toward the armory.

"Booker!" The supplier grinned when he walked in. "What can I do for you today?"

The Brit noted the slightly crazed look in Dan's eyes.

He only got that look when he'd acquired something particularly grand or expensive.

He thought about making small talk until the subject of housing came up but decided to cut to the chase. "You heard about a building opening up?"

Dan's grin widened. "Ah, so you come seeking information about Cyrus' old place, huh?"

"You know about it or not? I can go ask someone else." He turned to leave.

"No! Don't go, don't go. Of course, I know about the building."

Booker turned back toward him.

He leaned over his table. "Rumor has it one of the companies is trying to snap it up and turn it into a covert command center."

"They're already losing out on the covert part if you know about it."

"It's my business to know things. Besides," he said and leaned even closer, "I know who has the contract for it."

Booker groaned inwardly. He already guessed the answer, but he asked anyway. "Who?"

"I do."

"Of course you do."

Dan laughed. "Damn. Am I getting predictable?"

"How seriously are you taking the offer?"

"Depends."

"On what?"

"Are you offering something?"

Booker pursed his lips. He knew he shouldn't make an executive decision and purchase a building, but he also knew he needed to strike while the iron was hot.

"I might be. What's it look like?"

"How about we take a stroll and I'll show you?"

He followed the supplier through the Harvesters Camp to a two-story concrete and wooden structure. It wasn't the most appealing building he'd ever seen but it was utilitarian and would serve their purposes nicely. He made sure to keep his expression neutral as they approached.

Dan nodded at one of the armed guards at the door.

"What's with the guards?" he asked.

The man laughed and unlocked the door. "I've got to protect what's mine. Everyone will know soon that this place is up for grabs. If I don't keep a guard over it until it's been sold, I risk losing it to some asshole squatter."

Most of the previous inhabitants' things had been removed. Booker didn't doubt that a lot of the items now sat on Dan's shelves, waiting for a buyer.

The first floor of the building was mostly open. There was a back stairwell that led to the quarters on the second floor. Without a doubt, the first floor could be converted into an office for their company.

He followed the supplier up the stairs. There were four bedrooms, a rec room, dining area, another bathroom, and a small kitchen.

"All this shit works," Dan said with a wave of his hand.

"Where'd all the furniture go?"

"Did you think I'd stage it for you? I told you, I'm not some goddamn realtor. This ain't HGTV."

Booker wanted the building. It was perfect for the team. He could feel anticipation in his fingertips and was ready for the negotiation.

Dan led him outside and re-locked the door.

"What company is asking for it?" Booker asked.

"It might or might not be a company starting with L, and you might or might not know some of their higher-ups. Some of you know her biblically, as they say."

"You're a real man of mystery, Dan."

He shrugged and glanced at Booker out of the corner of his eye. "You interested, Brit?"

"I might be."

Dan turned fully toward him.

"How much?" Booker asked.

He frowned a little. "That's no fun, Booker. You're supposed to hem and haw more."

The Brit simply regarded him in silence.

"Fine," Dan said and sighed. "Those bastards are offering me two-fifty for it."

Booker looked at the plain building again. The offer was lower than he'd expected. They'd have to get furniture for it, and then there was the upkeep of water and electricity to consider. With the money from the Russians, they could definitely afford the building.

"Two-fifty, huh?"

"Yep. They're fucking low-balling me."

He raised an eyebrow. "Are you feeling all right, Dan? You off your game?"

"No. Like I've told you assholes before, you're some of my favorite customers. I don't lie."

"What's the favorite customer price for taking this piece of shit off your hands?"

"Calling it names isn't going to lower the price, Booker. You make an offer. I'll let you know if you need to go higher."

Booker studied the building again. There was room between it and the other buildings, meaning it would be relatively easy to add onto it. A lean-to had been constructed already and was big enough that the BTR and probably the Mule could fit.

They wouldn't have to pay rent to Prince anymore. He was sure everyone would be on board with that idea.

He wondered again if he should consult with the others first because they were a team. While he had a full partnership with Charles and Roo, he also knew he needed to act fast.

"Three hundred."

Dan snorted. "Come on, Booker. I said I liked you. I'm not fucking in-love with you. Be reasonable."

"Three-fifty."

"Eh."

"It's not furnished."

"And for three-fifty, it still won't be furnished."

"Four."

"Four-fifty."

"You're pushing it. This isn't a fucking palace."

"You're not the queen of England. Four-fifty and I'll bring the furniture back."

Booker raised an eyebrow. "What's wrong with it?"

"Nothing. That's the liking you part kicking in. Besides, I told you, I'm not a realtor."

He looked at the building again, then at Dan, who watched him carefully.

Another guard came around the corner, and the Brit watched him for a moment. There were four guards and he knew the supplier was probably paying a pretty penny for them. He was right—he wasn't a realtor and wasn't set up to operate a land business. Dan was best in his warehouse with all his goods lined up. The building was too far away for him to be able to properly care for and guard it.

"Four-fifty and you bring the furniture back?"

"Down to the stepping stool."

"You've got yourself a deal," he said and extended his hand.

Dan shook it and grinned. "Excellent! I'll have the guys bring everything back and set it up the way it was. I'll give you the paperwork for the building. But I'll take my payment now."

Booker transferred the funds.

The supplier handed him the key. "Now, if you'll excuse me, I get to go tell someone she can shove her offer up her ass."

The Brit walked back toward the converted containers. For a moment, he was worried he'd been too hasty in making the decision on his own, but he soon pushed that thought aside. He was sure the others would appreciate not renting from Prince anymore—not to mention they'd have more space.

When he walked up to the container, the team was engaged in what had become their usual between mission activities. Charles did push-ups. Mick tried to master cat's cradle with his parachute cord. Roo attempted to flirt with Reen and was shot down, and Lester sat brooding in the shade.

"I've an announcement," he said.

They all looked at him.

"We're moving."

"What the fuck are you talking about?" Roo asked.

"We're moving. I just bought us a building."

"You bought a building?" Charles asked and frowned.

"I thought you were looking for a mission, not house hunting," Reen said.

"Do you want to continue living in these converted containers and paying rent to Prince?" he asked. They didn't say anything. "I didn't think so. Look, under normal circumstances, I would've consulted you, but the opportunity was there. The time was ripe, as they say, so I took advantage."

"Let's go see it," Charles said.

Booker gave them the grand tour, which didn't take long.

"Where'd all the furniture go?" Roo asked.

"It's coming back," he assured them. "Anyway, I think the first floor can be the company office. We can set it up to look professional and maybe even hire someone to field calls."

"I think you're jumping ahead a few steps," Reen said.

"Or we could put a pool table down there," Roo suggested.

"Didn't you hear what I said? We're trying to look professional here, not like a bleddy pub."

The other man shrugged.

"How much did you pay for it?" Charles asked.

"Four-fifty."

"For this POS?" Roo demanded.

"I thought it was going to be more expensive," the American said.

Booker shrugged. "There was another offer, but it was very low."

"Who was the offer from?" Charles asked.

"Roo's favorite one-hit wonder."

The Aussie rolled his eyes and gestured rudely. "It wasn't a one-hit wonder, asshole. And really? What did Lampton want with this?"

"Who gives a shit? It's ours now."

"Does this mean I get to have a room to myself now?" Reen asked.

The men looked at her.

"What?"

"I thought you weren't going to play the special-treatment-because-I'm-a-woman card?" Lester asked and he smirked.

She scowled at him. "Look, asshole, that was on-mission. But I'm not asking for a room to myself just because I'm a different gender than you are. I like men as much as the next girl, but when it comes to sleeping arrangements, I definitely prefer women. You all snore."

"You snore too!" Mick protested.

"Perfect! Now you won't have to listen to my snoring. It's a win-win."

"Fine," Booker said. "You can have your own room."

Reen grinned.

"Hey, wait just one minute, mate. If she gets one, I want one," Mick said.

"Do I look like I give a fuck?" Booker asked. "You room with Lester."

"So, you're saying you prefer to sleep with women?" Roo asked her.

She winked at him.

"I think she's saying she doesn't want to sleep with any of us," Lester said.

"I wasn't bunked up with you to begin with," Roo said.

Reen rolled her eyes. "And you're still not, Aussie. Now get your head out from down under and stop acting like a pussy."

Charles snickered.

"Where does one find a rutting partner 'round here?" Mick asked.

Booker pinched the bridge of his nose. "Is that all you Australians think about? Sex?"

"Isn't that what everyone thinks about?"

"There aren't that many birds around here, and most of them have been around the quarter a few times."

"You're one to talk," Charles said. "You weren't so high-and-mighty when you were getting your dick wet with Shira."

Roo stared insolently at him but managed to not respond.

"Can we move on from these juvenile matters and discuss something important?" Lester asked in a long-suffering voice.

They all glared at him. He didn't seem to mind.

There was a knock on the door. "Special delivery!" Dan called from the other side.

Mick opened it. Dan stepped inside then out of the way as several men entered, carrying furniture.

In less than half an hour, the furniture was returned to where it had originally been when the supplier had cleared the building. Two simple wooden tables were put on the first floor, obviously for use as desks. Iron bunks were set up in three of the rooms upstairs. A long wooden table with eight chairs went into the dining room.

The furniture was bare-bones, but Booker decided it was a good start.

"You got any safes?" Charles asked before Dan could leave.

"Sure do. I've got any kind of safe you want. What are you looking for?"

"Nothing too fancy. But nothing small either."

"What'll you put in it?"

"Guns, valuables—that sort of thing."

"I think I have something perfect for you."

"We won't pay more than fifty for it," Booker said.

The man looked like he wanted to argue but surprisingly, he didn't. "Sure. Okay. I'll have the guys drop off a safe today."

It arrived shortly after he left. They hauled it up the stairs and put it in the fourth bedroom they'd decided to turn into the armory.

Mick, as it turned out, was good at fabrication and woodworking. He fixed the safe to the wall and Charles helped him mount a gun rack. They padlocked the door with the intention of reinforcing it at a later date.

Lester made dinner for everyone—over-cooked spaghetti with bland sauce.

"Next time, warn us that you're a god-awful cook," Roo said but he ate anyway.

"I didn't choose to cook for you," Lester said and glowered at Reen.

"What? Oh, 'cause I'm the woman I should be in the

kitchen, cooking for you? Dick. Trust me, I'm the last person you want preparing your food."

"Whatever. Food is food. Just shut the fuck up and eat."

Everyone at the table stared daggers at Lester. He ignored them.

"Should we call this place something?" Mick asked.

"What do you mean? Like HQ?" Roo asked.

Mick shrugged. "Maybe not HQ, but something along those lines."

"Why does it need to be called anything?" Lester asked.

"It's always easier to have a name for something," Roo said. "Gets rid of confusion."

"What about Fiddler's Green?" Charles asked.

"That's seaman's shit," Booker said.

Roo and Mick laughed. The Brit looked at the ceiling with a long-suffering sigh.

"What's wrong with Fiddler's Green?" Reen asked.

"Of course you'd take Charles' side," Roo said.

"We Marines don't leave any man behind."

"Anybody got any better ideas besides Fiddler's Green?" Charles asked.

Roo made to say something but Reen said, "Don't you dare fucking suggest HQ," before he could open his mouth.

"Well," Booker said with a sigh, "I guess Fiddler's Green will have to do…for now."

Charles and Reen high-fived.

CHAPTER TWENTY

Harvesters Camp; Fiddler's Green

Charles dropped from the pull-up bar he'd installed and wiped the sweat off his face with his shirt. "I've got an idea."

"Oh, look, the big guy can think," Lester said.

He ignored the man. It had been three days since they'd had a mission and they were all getting antsy. The break had been purposeful—Booker thought they could use the time to improve Fiddler's Green. There wasn't much that needed improving, and none of the team had any strong desire to rearrange furniture. The result was everyone sitting around waiting for the next mission.

"I'm just trying to figure out the animal attack patterns. They don't always attack. And when they do attack, it isn't always right away. What if something was triggering them?"

"Like what?" Reen asked, humoring him.

"Like the plants."

"What?" Booker asked. "What do you mean?"

"You know how sometimes, when we walk through, the plants give off a smell. Or how the trees fight back when we're trying to cut branches off of them. After that happens, we're generally attacked. What if the plants are releasing some sort of pheromone distress signal that triggers the other animals in the Zoo?"

"That actually makes a lot of sense," Booker said.

"Gee, thanks."

"You know what I mean. Even if the plants were a contributing factor, it'd be damn near impossible to avoid crushing them underfoot."

Charles shrugged. "Nearly impossible isn't impossible." He looked at the others and noted their unconvinced expressions. "Look, what harm would it do to test it out? Huh? No harm. Booker, why don't you go to Franco's and get us something easy. We can test it out."

"Fine," Booker said. He stood from where he'd played chess with Lester. "I'll go see what I can find."

He returned a half hour later with a bark harvesting mission.

"Perfect!" Charles said. His eagerness spread to the others and soon, their kits were put together and they were ready to load out.

"No BTR today?" the guard asked when they reached the gate.

"We can't always dazzle the shit out of you," Mick said. "We don't want you to get bored, mate."

The man laughed and waved them through.

At the edge of the jungle, Charles stopped them. "Remember. We're avoiding the plants. That means brushing against them too if at all possible. But the important bit is not crushing or breaking." He entered the Zoo and did his best to avoid the flora.

Booker and Mick followed him.

"Fuck, this is going to take forever," Lester said between his gritted teeth.

"It's not like you were doing anything important," Reen said and pushed past him and into the Zoo.

After an hour, they'd only made it about three klicks in —but nothing had attacked. They found that brushing against the plants did nothing, so they were able to move with more freedom. The dense plants made it extremely difficult to move without touching anything.

"I think it's working!" Charles said.

"Don't get ahead of yourself," Roo said. "We're barely in."

"What are we looking for, Booker?" Lester asked.

"A tree with leaves that are red on the bottom."

"Is there a particular spot this tree'll be?" Reen asked.

"I don't think so," Booker said. "They're usually spotted about five klicks in."

They walked on, weaving in and out of the plants. Still nothing attacked. When they reached five klicks in, they spaced themselves apart to cover a larger area to find their objective.

"I got it!" Mick called and they gathered around the large tree.

It was tall and so wide Charles' arms wouldn't have been able to wrap around it. The leaves were deep-green with blood-red undersides that shimmered in the light. The bark of the tree seemed thin and was the color of melted milk chocolate.

Booker produced long cork-harvesting knives. He gave one to Mick and one to Lester and kept the last for himself.

"The moment of truth," he said and carved a section out of the trunk of the tree.

Crimson sap welled up, oozed from the cut, and dripped like blood. The tree shuddered. He deposited the strip of bark in his sample container with a wet thump.

They looked at the surrounding jungle but nothing appeared.

"Maybe it's just an off-day?" Mick suggested. He made a cut similar to Booker's, put his piece in the sample container, and a howl sounded in the near distance. It was soon joined by others.

Booker glanced at Charles, who looked smug. "This doesn't necessarily mean anything."

"Sure it doesn't."

"Keep harvesting. We'll keep these fuckers at bay," Reen said.

Four giant wolf-like creatures burst from the trees and snarled. Their obsidian horns gleamed sharply. Reen and Charles opened fire. The wolves narrowed their glowing red eyes and growled.

Roo stood on the opposite side of the tree and he fired as three more slunk toward them. There were more howls. One of the wolves opened its mouth and gave an answering cry, and the sound made the hairs rise on the humans' necks.

Reen sighted down her M492 and fired. Her round found its mark in one of the oncoming wolves' eye sockets. The beast fell and its companions renewed their snarls as their hackles rose.

Lester put the final sample in his container as Roo killed a second animal. The other wolves hesitated and looked at the dead.

With angry snarls and barks, they retreated into the trees.

"We have all the samples we need," Booker said. "Let's get out of here."

On the way back to the Harvesters Camp, they weren't as careful of the plants. Charles didn't remind them to be more cautious as much. He assumed their caution would be cancelled out by the fact that they held four sample containers full of chunks of Zoo tree. Even though the synthetic chambers had a tight seal, it wasn't foolproof—or even top-of-the-line. He was sure some of the scent could get through, even if he couldn't smell anything.

A six-legged panther crossed paths with them. It hissed at them and its yellow eyes gleamed. In a blur of movement, it launched at Booker. Reen fired her Beretta. The panther's lifeless body collided with the man and hurled him down.

Charles heaved the big cat off him and pulled him to his feet. "You good?"

"I'm fine," he said, dusted himself off, and tried to wipe the animal's blood away. "Keep moving."

They marched on and increased speed. It was getting darker and their caution upon entering the Zoo had eaten a lot of time.

"I'm not convinced the plant theory has anything to do with them attacking or not," Lester announced.

Reen rolled her eyes. "Of course you aren't."

"And you are?" he retorted acidly.

"Sure."

"You always going to take his side?"

"Until I don't agree with him, yeah."

"Bloody Americans," he muttered.

She smiled at him.

"There might be something to it," Mick said. "I mean, we made it all the way to the tree without any incident. That doesn't happen that much, right? If at all?"

"Right," Booker said.

"You're still not convinced?" Charles asked. "We weren't attacked until you started cutting away at that tree. Then you were attacked, and you're the one carrying the samples."

"Could be a coincidence," the Brit said with a wave of his hand.

"I don't think so," Charles said.

Lester stumbled for a moment when the toe of his boot caught under one of the creeping vines. The plant's thin roots popped out of the earth and he kicked them away.

"Nothing's happening," he said. "I ripped that thing out of the ground and nothing bad has happened to me."

One of the snake-like vines snaked from the canopy, its round mouth open to take a bite out of the man. Roo lunged forward and slashed with his Ari B'Lilah. He lopped the vine off before it could attach itself to Lester's face.

"You were saying?" Charles said with a grin.

He gave Charles a withering look. "Doesn't fucking prove anything."

The American shrugged.

"It doesn't," he insisted.

Roo laughed at the man as he wiped his knife on his

pant leg. "It's no good arguing with him, mate. Not when he goes all strong-silent-type on you. The fucker won't give you the time of day."

"As thrilling as this conversation is," Booker said, "we should keep moving."

Lester jogged alongside Roo. "Hey, what kind of knife was that?"

"An Ari B'Lilah."

"I've never seen one quite like that before."

"Of course you haven't. It's specially made. Commissioned. Usually only elite Israeli soldiers get one of these. The YAMAM and shit like that."

"Why do you have one?"

Roo's eyes narrowed in suspicion. "Why all the fucking questions? You a Chatty Cathy all of a sudden? What gives?"

"Just trying to be friendly."

"Well, fuck off."

"Roo," Booker warned.

"And you can go fuck yourself too," he retorted.

Booker kept up a fast pace, even though they were close to the wall. The shadows grew darker around them and pooled in the spaces between the trees. The foliage thinned and they were able to smell the scent of freshly burned sand.

They crossed the space between the jungle and the wall and noticed a few new scorched patches had appeared.

"Do you think it was a plant or an animal?" Reen asked.

"What?" Booker asked.

"The reason there are more burns."

"Looks like an animal," Mick said. "The sand in that area is too churned up for it to have been vegetation."

"Have you ever seen an animal attacking the wall?" Lester asked as they slipped through the first gate.

Booker shrugged in the eerie blue glow. "Not since we've been here. I mean, I'm sure it has happened. We just haven't witnessed it."

"That'd be a sight to see," the man said, "all those Ma Deuces in action."

For once, they were all in agreement.

CHAPTER TWENTY-ONE

The Zoo - Thor

Thor stalked through the jungle. He followed on the heels of a pack of fourteen adult wolf-like animals. They were like him. Of that, he was certain. His horns had grown larger and sloped along his back. They had stopped itching after he'd shed the velvet that covered them.

He kept his distance from the pack. For now, he didn't feel ready to approach the other animals, whether they were like him or not. There was still a tug in his stomach. He knew it wasn't food as he'd eaten since the feeling had started.

It was, of course, the idea that Charles might call him back. The life he could remember up until the moment when the man left him in the Zoo had been as a pet. He struggled as his feelings for the human and those toward the pack conflicted. Instinctively, he knew he would find acceptance amongst the animals. Charles, Booker, and Roo had been his first pack, and his loyalty to them still remained at a basic level.

Thor lagged behind as the wolves surged forward and howled. His hackles rose and a tingle of excitement zipped through him. They were on the hunt. He felt a buzzing in his veins and a pull in the back of his mind and raced to catch up with the others.

There was a commotion of gunfire and snarls ahead. He slowed again and slunk forward. From cover, he peeked through the ferns and watched as Charles, Booker, and Roo fought against his brethren. The two groups were pitched against each other.

He noticed that not all the pack attacked at once. If they had, surely they would've overwhelmed the humans. Instead, half moved in while the others circled immediately beyond the humans' sight.

Thor wanted to run to Charles, but there was another feeling there as well. Deep in the back of his mind, he felt a tug and anger filled him. He bared his teeth, but he wasn't sure why.

One of the wolves fell, then a second. The others retreated into the jungle and left the humans behind.

He remained and watched the group as they walked away from the murdered wolves. Instinctively, he growled. His muscles twitched and bunched, ready to pounce—but he held back.

The animal moved deeper into the undergrowth as the humans passed him. He watched Charles go. The man didn't look back. He realized Charles couldn't sense he was there.

Thor sagged for a moment as the small parade of humans was swallowed by the jungle.

He stood and walked toward the fallen wolves. The

earth sucked in their black blood greedily. The voracious vines wove through the thick fur and wound around the lifeless limbs. They pressed the bodies into the moist ground.

The creature drew a deep lungful of air. He smelled the death, the lingering scent of gun smoke, and the distinct smell that was Charles. Still conflicted, he stood and looked toward where the pack had disappeared and then to where the humans had walked away. They were in opposite directions.

Thor ran into the jungle again and followed the trail the pack had left.

CHAPTER TWENTY-TWO

Harvesters Camp; Fiddler's Green

They returned to their quarters and Booker unlocked the door. He remained in the office area while the others—except Charles—went upstairs. The American stayed behind to check the vehicles they had stored in their lean-to. He didn't think anything would've happened, but it was always good to check.

The Brit looked around the office space. It was pathetic, really. He wanted something that said, "Look at me, I'm confident and will get shit done." At that moment, the office said, "Please don't give me a second thought. I really can't do this." He merely wasn't sure how to achieve his goal.

Charles strolled in. "Everything's in order."

"Good. Were you worried it wouldn't be?"

"Not really. It seems that, for the most part, people will leave your shit alone in camp. Besides, it's not like anyone would steal the BTR. It's the only one in this quarter. We'd track down whoever did it and skin them, and it would be all too easy."

"You worried about sabotage or something?"

"No. The engine compartment is too hard to get into. Too much of a risk. Just wanted to satisfy my curiosity."

"Hey, I've been meaning to ask you something," Charles said as if it has popped into his mind and wasn't something he'd thought about ever since he'd released Thor into the Zoo. "What do you think would happen if a Zoo critter was taken out—you know, out there?"

"Like to the labs? They've done that."

"No, I mean, out there to live."

"A zoo? Not our Zoo, but like the London Zoo?" Booker asked. "It would cause a lot of commotion, that's for sure. But the governments aren't going to let that happen. Too many questions."

"And if it wasn't in a zoo, but like, taken on home."

Booker laughed out loud and then said, "Right. Someone's going to take a six-legged dinosaur that spits acid home with him. Sorry Mr. Customs Agent, don't mind my pet. Charles, I love you, but sometimes, you ask the stupidest questions."

"Oh, yeah, right. I didn't mean it would actually happen. Just imagining what would happen if it did. You know, for fun."

"You have a weird idea of fun."

A large crash echoed from upstairs before Charles could respond. The two men looked at each other and raced up the stairs.

They arrived in time to see Mick haul Roo off Lester and Reen hold the Englishman back. Lester's lip was split and bleeding, but still he sneered at his struggling opponent.

"I know it was you, motherfucker!" Roo yelled.

"It wasn't me!" Lester shouted in response.

"What's going on here?" Charles asked, his voice raised.

The men stopped struggling and turned to look at him.

Roo pointed a finger at Lester's chest. "This motherfucker stole my knife."

The man bared his teeth in rage. "I didn't do it!"

"Bullshit!"

"Someone want to give us a better explanation?" Booker asked.

"I was in the shower, so I put my Ari B'Lilah in my locker until I was done. I got out, went to strap it on, and it was gone. So, I came out here and asked nicely if anyone knew what had happened to it."

Charles snorted. "I'm sure you asked nicely."

"Of course, I fucking asked nicely! I wasn't born under a rock. I have manners. If it was all some prank, I'd get over it. But now they're all saying they don't have it...but I know. I know it was Lester. That motherfucker was asking all sorts of questions about it in the Zoo. He wanted it, saw the opportunity, and took it."

Lester scoffed. "That's rich. You? Manners? I've met koalas who had better manners than you, and they were STD ridden, obnoxious little animals."

"Leave the goddamn koalas out of it!" Roo tried to lunge at him again. "Where's my fucking knife?"

Charles grabbed him by the scruff of the neck and hauled him back. "Relax, Roo. You can't just go around beating up people on our team."

"I'm sure there's a logical explanation for where the knife is," Booker said. "Maybe you only thought you put it in your locker? Is it possible it's in the armory?"

"Yeah. He fucking took it. That's the logical explanation," the Aussie said. "Why the fuck would I put my knife in the armory? I always have it on me."

"I don't have to put up with this shit!" Lester said. He threw his hands up, stormed out of the room, and slammed the door on his way out.

"Look what you did," Booker said and shook his head.

Roo shrugged out of the big man's grip. He glared at him. "Who gives a fuck about that asshole's feelings? I know it was him."

"You can't just go around accusing people of stealing," Charles said.

"Like hell, I can't. I can, and I just did. I trust that asswipe about as far as I can throw him. I don't know why you aren't taking this more seriously." He marched up to his locker, flung it open, and rooted through his things in search of the knife and sheath. "It's not fucking here. Unless there was some master thief who snuck past all of you in the five minutes I was in the shower, it was that goddamn bastard."

"We do take it seriously, Roo," Booker said. "You still can't go around accusing people without evidence. It causes rifts and tension."

"I'd like to cause that fucker a few rifts." His growl of rage said he meant it. He slammed the locker shut and stared angrily at it.

Reen opened the locker again and ran her finger along

the locking mechanism. "This wasn't tampered with. I don't see any signs of forced entry."

"That's what I'm saying! It was an inside job!"

They looked at Roo.

"I know he did it!"

"There's no proof, mate," Mick said in an effort to calm him.

"He might be an asshole, but you can't just accuse him of shit like that," Booker said. "I'm going to find him and bring him back. Then you're going to apologize."

"No fucking way am I apologizing to that arrogant piece of shit!"

"I'm bringing him back and you *will* apologize. You need to calm the fuck down, got it? You don't have to be best friends with the man, but you have to be civil. Can you at least be civil? We'll keep looking for your knife. I'm sure it'll turn up. If it doesn't…well, we'll cross that bridge when we come to it."

Roo started to flip him off out of habit, then shrugged instead and said, "Fine. I can be civil. I still know the wanker did it, but I won't accuse him of it again until there is proof."

Booker groaned. "That is beside the point."

"I think that's as good as it's going to get, Booker," Mick said. "Roo doesn't give up. He's like a fucking bulldog, lock jaw and all that shit."

The Brit shook his head. "Don't I know it. Okay. I'll be back in a bit."

He found Lester in the Wateringhole, staring into a whiskey. The man looked up and glowered at him as he approached.

"You here to accuse me, too?"

Booker shook his head. He sat on the stool next to Lester and ordered a beer. "Nope. I'm here to bring you back."

"Fuck that."

"Thought you might say that."

"Look, Booker, I know no one likes me. That doesn't fucking bother me. I know they got my back when it counts and I have theirs, but I'm not going to just stand there and be falsely accused for something I didn't bloody do."

"Yeah, I get it. But look, you've gotta come back. Roo said he'd apologize."

"Bullshit."

"He did."

Lester gulped the rest of his whiskey. "Ah, fuck it. That's something I'd like to see."

The two men returned to the building. They found the others seated around the dining room table. Roo sat with his arms folded belligerently, and he watched them with distrust.

"I hear you've got something to say to me," Lester said.

Booker elbowed him.

A blotchy redness rose up Roo's neck and he curled his hands into fists. Charles nudged his chair with his foot.

"I apologize," he said through his teeth.

"For what?" Lester asked and made no attempt to hide his smile.

A muscle in the Aussie's jaw pulsed and his eyebrows drew together. "For accusing you of stealing without having any proof."

The man frowned. "Not much of an apology."

"Listen asshole—" Roo started and rose from his chair. The American grabbed him by the shoulder and shoved him down.

"Well, now that that's out of the way. Should we plan our next move?" Charles asked brightly.

Lester and Booker sat. Roo still glared daggers, but Charles released him.

"What's the next move?" Mick asked, pulled out his parachute cord, and wove his fingers through it.

"That's what we should plan," Charles said. "Booker, any news from Prince?"

"Not yet," he said. "And that last mission was pretty worthless. I think we should go out again. Maybe killing some more Zoo animals will calm everyone down. Tensions are too bleddy high. We're a team."

"Sounds like a good plan to me," Reen said. "I'll go catch some Zs while we wait, then. I'll see you fellas tomorrow. Though if Roo decides to try to kill Lester again, someone come get me. I want to watch that happen."

Roo scowled at her retreating back.

CHAPTER TWENTY-THREE

Harvesters Camp

The next morning, Booker ran into Prince on his way to Franco's.

"Hey, Prince, any word yet on that mission?"

The Nigerian smiled. "Booker, you're relentless."

"Well, the longer we wait around here, the more I don't believe you had a job to begin with."

"That hurts, Booker—and after all the ways I've helped you out!" He laughed.

Booker folded his arms over his chest.

"Look. This is a...delicate matter. Certain things have to line up in order for this to work. I'm monitoring the situation. I have a feeling it will happen soon. I'm as anxious as you to get on with it, believe you me. It'll be worth the wait, though, I promise you that."

"All right. We'll keep waiting, but the natives are getting restless," he said. "Don't forget, Prince, you aren't taking a commission from us."

A brief frown flashed across the man's face but he

quickly plastered his usual grin on. "I won't forget, Booker."

"Yeah, not if I keep reminding you."

"Wait for my call. I'm sure it'll happen soon," he said and walked away.

"What a bleddy tosser," Booker grumbled at the man's retreating back.

Prince glanced back at him and waved. He smiled and waved in response.

He continued toward Franco's. The conversation with Prince made him late, and the dispatchers were already assigning missions. He wasn't too concerned as he was looking for a simple and quick mission to help re-establish a team connection.

Franco spotted him and waved him over.

"Got anything for me this morning, Franco?"

"How do you feel about harvesting some vines?"

"What sort of vines?"

"Smart man. You always ask the good questions. I've got a request in for some of those vines with the mouths. You know the ones I'm talking about, I'm sure."

He grimaced. "Yeah, I know what you're talking about. Please tell me you don't need the whole plant."

"I don't need the whole plant."

"Wait, really? Or is that a bleddy joke?"

"No joke. They just need a few heads and maybe some non-mouthed vines from the same plant. Easy."

"Nothing is ever easy."

Franco shrugged. "Not really my problem. You want it?"

"No one else wanted it?" Booker asked and eyes narrowed.

"I haven't offered it up yet. I was hoping you'd show up. It's a bit of a fast turnaround. I needed a team that I knew would get the job done."

He straightened. "Well, we'll get the job done for you."

"Excellent. I'll send you the details."

"When do you need them?"

"Tonight."

"Sure thing. I'll be back with the specimens."

"And I'll be here with the money."

"Everyone gear up and get ready to move out," Booker announced. "We've got another job. It's got a fast turn-around so we need to get out there."

"What sort of job did you get?" Charles asked. He bolted up from where he'd been doing push-ups.

"Vine collecting. So, everyone grab your knives." The Brit immediately cringed. "Er, I mean…"

Roo flipped him off and sneered at Lester. He stomped out of the room and muttered curses as he went.

"Real smooth. And here I was under the impression that you Englishmen were supposed to be good with your words," Reen said.

Booker shook his head but said nothing. He honestly didn't want to get into it with her, too.

"Vine collecting? That seems too easy," Mick said.

"We need the ones with the teeth."

"Of course we do," Charles said.

"Enough sitting around. We really do have to get going," Booker said. "Oh, and Lester and Mick, don't bring any packs. You two have the honor of carrying out the vines."

"Deadly," Mick said.

"Can't fucking wait."

Booker decided it would be easier to stop at Dan's on their way to the Zoo.

The supplier sat outside his building smoking and looking absently out past the camp and into the Sahara.

"You ever get tired of it being so hot?" he asked when they were within earshot.

"All the fucking time," Roo said.

Dan snuffed his cigarette out on the side of the building. "What can I do for you?"

"We need larger sample containers," Booker said. "I'm looking for something about twelve inches wide and twenty-four inches long. If they can be easily strapped to someone's back, that's what I want."

"Sure thing. Give me a minute. I've got exactly what you want."

He soon returned with two back-pack-like contraptions. Dual synthetic sample containers were held in a cradle of wide nylon straps that could be loosened or tightened to release or secure the containers.

"This what you're looking for?" he asked.

"Actually, yes. That's exactly what I had in mind."

Dan nodded. "Great. That'll be fifty K."

Mick and Lester shrugged the container harnesses on.

"Thirty," Booker said.

"Does it look like I'm running a goddamn charity? Fifty."

"Forty?"

"Fifty."

"You know, this isn't how a negotiation works."

"I don't give a fuck. This isn't the Wild West, Booker. I'm not a tradesman, I'm a businessman. Fifty."

"Fine."

"I thought you were some big negotiator," Reen said when they left.

"Fuck off."

Booker led them through the first two walls. The guard at the third wall turned to punch in the code to open the door when a blaring alarm sounded. The Ma Deuces at the top of the wall thundered to life. The rapid-fire rat-tat-tat sound drowned out the alarm.

"What's going on?" the Brit asked.

An animal's screams reached them from over the inner wall.

"Looks like there's an attempt at a perimeter breach," the guard said. He fired his weapon up. It wasn't a rifle any of them had ever seen. Two chambers on each side of the sleek weapon glowed a deadly blue.

"I want one of those," Reen said and nudged Charles with her elbow.

"What is it?"

"Who gives a shit? It looks fucking killer, and I want one."

The guards at the top of the wall converged on a section not far from the gate. Two of them started their flamethrowers and the whoosh of the flames joined the machine guns.

More roars reached their ears and then the distinct sound of something large crunching into concrete.

They drew their weapons.

"Whatever it is, it shouldn't make it over," the guard said, although he tightened his hold on his weapon and looked nervous. "I hope. If it does, remember to stay where you are and don't leave the path. We've got mines and other surprises out there."

The barrage continued for too long a time, and the six, along with the guard, strained their necks to see the top of the inner wall. At last, after a final scream, the weapons ceased firing. A few moments later, the alarm deactivated. The guard wiped his brow in obvious relief and powered down his weapon. He waited a few more minutes before he turned and punched in the code to open the gate.

"You've got the go-ahead."

"We haven't been here when a Zoo animal has tried to attack," Booker said.

The man shrugged. "It's been happening more frequently. No one really knows why. Though none of the bastards have made it over, and we plan to keep it that way. Have fun out there."

The door slid open and the Brit led them through.

"You think we should continue with the mission?" Mick asked.

"You chickenshit?" Roo asked.

"Fuck, no. Just wondering how wise it is to go out there right now for a mission we don't really need if the Zoo's all riled up."

"Pussy," Reen said and shouldered past him.

"Aw, get the hell over yourselves."

"We'll still complete the mission," Booker said. He pressed the button and the door slid open.

They were momentarily blinded by the sunlight after the darkness and blue light of the passageway.

To their right was a patch of freshly burned sand. Five fresh gashes had been gouged out of the concrete wall.

Roo whistled. "Whatever the fuck that was, it sure isn't anything anymore."

"Yeah, I wouldn't want to be on the receiving end of a Ma Deuce," Mick said.

A swirl of green blood seeped into the sand. Chunks of body parts were scattered around the burned area.

"What do you think it was?" Charles asked.

"Who gives a shit? It's dead now," Booker said.

They moved quickly over the hot sand into the humid shade of the jungle.

"It seems too quiet," Reen said as the canopy closed in above them.

"I'd have to agree," Lester said, "especially after an attack on the wall."

"Good thing this'll be just a quick in and out then," Booker said.

"Got any feelings about this, Roo?" Mick asked.

The Aussie shrugged. "Not having my knife blocks my psychic abilities," he said and gave Lester a withering look.

The man rolled his eyes. "I told you, I didn't take your goddamn knife."

"Roo," Booker said, "this isn't the time for your bullshit. Keep bleddy moving."

"How deep do we have to go?" Charles asked.

"Probably only about six klicks."

"So, we're just going to go in, behead a couple vines, and get out, right?" Reen asked.

"Something like that."

They marched deeper into the Zoo. The only animals that crossed their path were small and avoided the humans.

"I don't like this," Roo said after they'd gone four klicks with no contact with anything determined to kill them.

"What?" Mick asked.

"It's too fucking quiet. We should've been attacked or something by now."

"We have had missions where we weren't attacked before," Charles said. "Or at least close to it."

Roo grunted.

"Is it really the knife that's bothering you?" Reen asked and jogged up beside him.

He shrugged.

"Leave the silent stuff to Charles, bunj," Mick said.

"Can't you get another one made?" Charles asked.

"Sure. But it won't be the same."

"Why not?" Reen asked.

"Because my daughter helped pick out that one."

"Cassie helped you?" Mick asked. "I didn't know that."

"It's not something I advertise, all right? She was with me at this knife show. I was mad at the ex for something and took Cassie with me even though her mom didn't want her to go. I said fuck it and brought her. She picked the knife out for me because she liked the name. Lion by night. She thought the name was kickass and I thought having a specially designed counter terrorism knife was killer. It was a win-win."

"Did she really use the term 'kickass'?" Mick asked.

"No, you fucking moron. She's just a little kid. She's not allowed to swear."

"Just checking."

"Not to be that person," Booker said, "but everyone needs to shut the fuck up. We're on a mission here, not out for a bleddy picnic in the jungle."

They fell into a column formation with Booker leading followed by Mick and Reen. Roo and Lester followed, and Charles brought up the rear. They all were on edge after the attempted breach of the walls, but nothing rushed out of the jungle to attack as they marched on.

"Okay," Booker finally said over his shoulder, "we've gone about five klicks. Everyone keep a look out for these bastard vines."

Roo looked toward the right and searched the canopy. His head was turned, and he didn't see the panther until it was already in motion. The six-legged animal pounded into his side and the two rolled in a flurry of limbs. The impact hurled his AK-47 out of his hands.

He shoved at the panther's neck and tried to prevent it from biting him.

Lester aimed his SIG and fired. His round struck the mutant in the temple. The animal's skull caved in and it went limp.

Roo shoved the dead creature aside.

Lester offered his hand to him.

The Aussie stared angrily at the proffered hand and stood on his own. He attempted to wipe some of the panther's blood off but wasn't very successful.

"You all right?" Charles asked.

"I'm fine."

"You sure?"

"I said I was fucking fine."

"Okay." Charles held his hands up. "I believe you."

They all looked at the dead panther.

Reen glanced around. "Do you think that's the only one? Don't they usually travel in packs?"

"I'm not sure there's a definite pattern to any of these things most of the time," Booker said.

Mick looked into the canopy that was high above their heads. Vines twined and swayed through the trees, creeping along. Some of them began to trail down toward the humans. "Bingo. Looks like we found ourselves some vines."

"Do we just wait for them to come down to us?" Reen asked.

"They sure are taking their goddamn time," Roo said.

Charles ejected the slugs he had in his Remington and loaded buckshot. He raised the shotgun. "Okay. I'll shoot at them and that'll make them drop faster. Everyone ready?"

They unsheathed their knives. Roo gripped a machete.

"On my count," the American said. "Three...two...one."

The buckshot peppered some of the lowest creepers and the plant reacted in fury. Vines rocketed toward them. The mouthless tendrils tried to wind around the humans. The mouthed ones attempted to rip chunks of flesh.

"Booker, how many of these do we need?" Reen asked as she lopped off a mouth section that tried to bite her face. The vine segment writhed and a sludgy, bright green substance oozed from the cut. The mouth continued to open and close. She stomped on it to keep it from biting her ankle.

"Just enough to fill the containers," Booker said.

More vines dropped from the canopy and it became harder to fight them off.

"Charles, want to thin the herd a little?" Lester yelled.

The Remington thundered and shredded more of them.

Mick and Lester began to shove the vines into the sample containers.

"Jesus," Mick said and snapped a lid shut, "these things are vicious. Why aren't they dying?"

They retreated from beneath the tree where the vines seemed to be concentrated. Charles fired into the canopy again. The creepers jerked up and writhed in the air above their heads but didn't attack.

Booker stared as the round mouths of the vines tried to chew through the synthetic containers. The teeth looked substantial but they didn't even scratch the clear container walls. The antifreeze-green blood-like substance pooled in the bottoms of the chambers. Steam rose from the chunks of vine and fogged the inside.

"That shit's nasty," Roo said. "Glad I don't have those fuckers strapped to my back."

Lester and Mick glared at him.

"Okay, people. Let's move out," the Brit said. He began to lead them back the way they'd come.

They had traveled two klicks when he held a hand up to stop them.

"What is it?" Mick asked quietly.

He pointed wordlessly.

Ahead of them were three large bear-like animals that snuffled around in the undergrowth. One of them raised its head and let out an eerie cry that sounded like a woman wailing.

Booker turned and waved them back the way they'd come.

"Why aren't we fighting them?" Roo asked when they had moved to a safe distance from the monsters.

"I don't think it's worth the trouble at this point," he explained. "It would take too much time and ammunition. Besides, those things are big enough that if we killed them, we'd probably draw more unwanted attention to ourselves."

"Don't be such a pussy, Booker."

Charles shook his head. "Booker's probably right."

Roo sighed dramatically.

"We go around," Booker said firmly.

Lester looked at the ferns and other smaller foliage while the two men argued. "Hey," he said, "look. There's one of those flower things." He pointed at a Pita plant that was nestled under a fern.

He stepped toward it. "Why can't we get this thing, again?"

"Leave it where it is," Booker said. "We're moving out."

Lester fell reluctantly into position.

"Pitas are dangerous to collect," Charles said and stepped beside the man as they marched. "They apparently release some sort of pheromone if you remove a plant that triggers blood lust in the Zoo. It's like a siren call for everything in here. They try to rip apart anything that has stolen the Pitas. It's the alien goop. It's what created the Zoo—what's still creating the Zoo. Since the plant itself is so vulnerable, it's like a failsafe to keep it protected so it can continue creating. At least that's the theory I'm hearing."

"Would it really be so bad?" Lester asked. "I mean, it's not like there can be that many animals in one area at the same time. Look at this trip in. We saw one panther and those three bear things. Other than that, it was all small-time shit."

Charles shrugged. "As I said before, there are teams who harvest the flowers, but we're not willing to risk it. As far as I'm concerned, if you go for Pita, you better be prepared for the freaking worst fight of your life. We won't mess with something that might decide to change the so-called rules and decide to go ape shit even when we only pick the flowers, not the whole plant. The pay day is great, but it is barely worth the price you'd pay to gather it."

Silence descended over the group as they focused on getting out of the Zoo. They didn't encounter any other obstacles on the short march back.

The bodies that had scattered the sand when they first entered the jungle were long gone, but they had been replaced with fresh kills. The sand was churned and freshly burned in a different area. Two new gouges were half-way up the wall, but whatever it had been was driven back.

It was clear for the moment, and the guards at the top of the wall gave the go-ahead and their counterpart at the gate opened it and let them through.

CHAPTER TWENTY-FOUR

Fiddler's Green; Harvesters Camp

Roo seemed quiet as they cleaned and put away their gear after the mission. Booker had left to drop the vines with Franco and collect the payment.

"What's wrong?" Charles asked him.

He looked up from where he was sharpening the edge of his machete. He shrugged.

"Come on, man. I know something's wrong. You aren't usually this quiet."

"Not that he's complaining," Reen said. "Sometimes you're fucking obnoxious. I swear you can talk more than some women."

Roo flashed her a baleful look but didn't retaliate. "Nothing's wrong. Maybe I'm just tired."

"You need to take a nap? Should we have Charles read you a bedtime story?" Mick asked.

"Fuck all of you. Nothing's wrong, wankers. Can't a man be contemplative?"

"Well, there's a ten-dollar word if I've ever heard one," Lester said with a grin. The others laughed.

"Laugh it up, assholes. See if I care."

"Aw. We didn't mean to upset you, ginger," Reen said. She looped her arm around his neck and gave him a shake.

He pushed her off. "I'm fine!"

"Sure, sweetheart," she said.

"Let's find some food," Mick suggested. "I'm fucking starved."

Roo lingered near the lockers while the others went to scrounge something to eat. Lester walked back in and dropped some of his gear in his locker.

"Hey, Lester," the Aussie said and stopped the man from walking out of the room.

"What?" he asked and narrowed his eyes.

"I didn't thank you. For earlier."

"What are you talking about?"

He dragged in a deep breath like it was physically taxing to get the words out. "I wanted to thank you. For saving my life with that bloody panther-thing."

Lester shrugged. "Don't mention it."

"No, mate, I'm serious. Thank you. Things can go bad so fast out there, you know? We have to have each other's backs out there. So, thanks for that. You prevented me from becoming another casualty and made sure my daughter still has a father." He held his hand out.

The man looked at it, hesitated, then reached out and shook it. "No problem. We're on the same team. When we're out there, we fight for one another."

The sound of a phone ringing broke the semi-awkward silence that fell over the two men.

"For fuck's sake, someone answer the goddamn phone!" Roo bellowed.

"Sounds like you're back to your usual sunshiny self," Reen yelled in return.

"I got it," Charles said. He ran down the stairs to where Booker had left the device.

"Do we have anything to eat?" the Aussie asked as he walked into the kitchen and dining room area.

"There's never anything to eat," Reen said. "Not with the way you assholes eat."

"How is this our fault?" Mick asked. "You eat just as much—no, probably more—than all of us."

"What bullshit."

"Strewth," he said. "No need to be ashamed, doll. We appreciate a woman who can eat."

She threw an MRE packet at his head. He dodged, laughing.

"You know what I miss? Spring rolls," she said. "I had this girlfriend who made the best spring rolls. She had these delicate fingers that could roll them so tightly. It was amazing, really."

"Is that girlfriend, one word? Or girl friend as in girl who is a friend?" Roo asked.

"Wouldn't you like to know."

"He really would," Mick interjected. "I think we all would."

Reen merely grinned.

"I miss bangers and mash," Lester said.

"I think you mean sausage and mash, mate," the Aboriginal corrected.

"No. I mean bangers and mash. Also, spotted dick."

Roo popped a beer open. "You should get that looked at, mate."

Lester frowned. "I know you Aussies have it too."

"Hey, it's rude to assume that of someone," Mick protested. "We might rut more than you Brits, but it doesn't mean we have more STDs."

"Good on you," Roo said. He and Mick high-fived.

"Fuck the both of you. You know I'm talking about the pudding."

"Sure, bunj. Whatever y'say." Mick laughed.

"Oh, my God, you are all infants," Reen stated disbelievingly.

"That's why they keep us around," Roo said.

"And here I was thinking it was because of your superior intelligence."

"Just 'cause you're a woman doesn't mean I won't punch you."

She grinned. "Bring it on, Aussie. I can whip your ass with one hand tied behind my back."

"I'd like to see that," Mick said.

"Me too," Lester agreed. "My money'd be on the American."

Roo glowered at the two men. "Fuck you, dickwads."

Booker walked in as Charles hung up the phone.

"Who was that?" he asked.

"It was Prince," the American said. "He said the mission is a go."

"Great. We can go tell the others."

The Brit started up the stairs but stopped and returned to the first floor, looking pensive.

Charles folded his arms with a sigh. "What's wrong?"

"What do you think happened to Roo's knife?"

"That's what you're worrying about?"

"'Worrying' is a strong word. I'm merely...curious."

"Sure."

"So, what do you think happened to it?"

"How the heck should I know? I think he might've misplaced it."

Booker snorted. "Bollocks. He loves that fucking knife. He wouldn't just misplace the bleddy thing. You can't really think he misplaced it."

"You're probably right."

"I know I am. Did someone really steal it?"

"At this point, that's looking like the best possibility."

"Fuck."

"Yeah."

"You think Lester did it?"

Charles didn't respond.

His teammate groaned. "Look, I know I brought the dud. Sorry about that, but my options turned out to be more limited than I anticipated."

"No one would blame you for Lester's actions—if he did actually take the knife. He's just a dud personality-wise. He's a good fighter, calm under pressure. I wouldn't beat yourself up about it."

"I guess you're right," Booker said.

"I know I'm right. Now, let's tell the others that we're finally getting that mission from Prince."

CHAPTER TWENTY-FIVE

The Wateringhole; Harvesters Camp

Prince's connections allowed him to empty the bar and fill it with the large team he'd created for the mission. There were at least thirty people in the room. Booker noted that some were teams of Indians and Israelis—the other two countries who shared the quarter with the French.

The Nigerian stood in front of the crowd, flanked by his guards. He wore fatigues instead of his usual off-mission outfit. Another guard set up a large flip chart.

"Now that you're all here," he began, "let's get down to business. This is time-sensitive as we don't know how long our window of opportunity is going to be." He flipped to the first page, which was a map of the Zoo and the sectors. "Another new species has been discovered, and it's quite the motherfucker. They're calling it a gorgorex. These things are like a cross between a T-rex and...well, a bunch of other stuff. The point is, they're giant, scaly, killing machines. The pack was first discovered in the UK-

German Quarter," he said and indicated the section on the map, "right near Wall One. They wiped out a twelve-man team. Then the pack moved through the Sahara Coalition. They tried to intercept them, but both teams were wiped out."

He looked at the team he'd put together and grinned at the fact that he had their full attention. "Now, I've been keeping track of these things. They've now arrived in this quarter. The gorgorex pack consists of two adults and five adolescents. From what I've gathered, the adults are each around nine meters long. The adolescents aren't far behind." He paused again.

"So, we're going to kill one of these things and bring it back?" a man from the crowd asked.

"Killing it would be difficult enough, but we're doing something even more challenging—we're bringing one in alive."

A murmur went through the gathered team. "I hate to point this out," someone said, "but the other two quarters have better technology and equipment and they weren't able to stop these things. What makes you think we can bring one in alive?"

"I have confidence in our abilities. Those other teams are a bunch of pussies. We go into the Zoo as often as they do with, as you put it, lesser equipment, and still we keep coming out alive and keeping pace."

Prince flipped the chart again to show a drawing of what one of the gorgorexes looked like.

It had a large head with jagged teeth like a T-rex. A forest of spikes started on its forehead and ran all the way down its spine to the tip of its tail. It seemed to stand bipedally, with heavily muscled hindlegs and slightly smaller forelegs. Its hindlegs ended in five long claws. There was a wicked-looking spur near each of its knees like a rooster's. Instead of the short arms of a T-rex, though, the gorgorex had longer forelegs and five clawed toes that looked like they could grab onto something.

"Of course," he said, "this isn't exact. We've tried to photograph it, but it's surprisingly difficult. It has pretty decent camouflage for something so large. We do think that each of the animals has four goop bags, which is another reason to bring one in alive. We pull this off, and there'll be quite the payout."

"If we don't pull it off?" someone asked.

"If we don't pull it off, you'd be happy if the outcome was not getting paid. We leave at oh-five-hundred tomorrow, so get your gear together and be ready by the gate at that time." Prince gave a dismissive wave and the team began to filter out. "Oh, Booker, I wanted to speak to you," he called as if it was an afterthought.

Booker and the others made their way through the men to him.

"Obviously, this is going to be difficult to work out," he said before they had reached him. "That's why we need the BTR. Your team's job will be to draw as much critter action as you can. Hopefully, that will make it easier on the team and we can make it smoother."

"Do you think he knows?" the Brit asked Charles under his breath as they walked toward Prince.

"Knows what?" he asked, matching the volume level.

"That the BTR is an animal magnet?"

Charles shrugged. "Doubtful."

They stopped in front of Prince and watched him turn the chart. He drew a smiley face with dollar signs for eyes.

"Are you expecting to haul one of those things out with the BTR?" Booker asked.

The Nigerian shook his head. "Hopefully not. We'll have a lowboy we can strap it to."

"So, you just need us to run interference?" Charles asked.

"For the most part, yes."

"We don't even get to be in the thick of the action?" Roo asked.

Prince grinned. "I don't think that's something you'll have to worry about, friend." He sobered. "We'll all be tested on this."

They left the Wateringhole to get their gear together.

"Is that wanker always so dramatic?" Mick asked.

"Yes," Roo, Charles, and Booker answered.

"I think we should get some more shells for the Shipunov," Roo said. "It sounds like ten might not be enough."

"What about the AGS-Seventeen?" Reen asked.

"What about it?"

"We should get grenades for it."

"Of course, we want to be prepared for Armageddon, but we can't really afford it all. We've got to be careful. Sure, this could be a big bleddy payday or it could be a lot of medical bills and the expense to fix broken or lost equipment." Booker was quiet for a moment. "Okay. Charles, let's go get the mule and we can load up supplies."

A large group waited for Dan to assist them. Many of

the men waiting around were from the team Prince had put together. Everyone was stocking up.

The supplier noticed Booker and Charles when they strolled in. He yelled over his shoulder for an assistant to come help the man he was with and walked toward them.

"You guys going on the mission too?" he asked when he was within earshot.

"What mission?" Booker asked. He wasn't sure how much information Prince wanted floating around.

Dan laughed. "Real coy. Cut the bullshit. Everyone knows. You're going after the gorgorex with Prince's crew."

"Bingo," Charles said.

"What can I get you?" he asked.

They bought ten more shells for the Shipunov, two drums of 30mm grenades, and two boxes of ammo—one of regular and one of armor-piercing rounds—per weapon for the team. They also filled up four tanks of propane for Charles' flamethrower.

"Need anything else?"

"Nothing comes to mind," Booker said.

"You got any harpoons and launchers?" Charles asked.

The Brit raised an eyebrow and even Dan looked taken aback. "Interesting request, but yeah, I think I have a set laying around here somewhere. Let me go check."

"What do we need a harpoon for?" Booker asked.

Charles shrugged. "Depending on what he wants for it, it might be good to have around for fauna capture. Like extreme spear fishing."

"Except we aren't underwater and these things aren't fish."

"That's the extreme part."

Dan returned with a primitive-looking weapon with a thick barrel and shotgun stock. He carried three long, barbed harpoons. "What do you think of this?"

The American inspected the gun. The harpoon slid into the barrel only about half-way. The projectiles were designed to have a rope attached in the center. It would do the job, but he decided he'd have to be up close to whatever he attempted to harpoon.

"How much you want for this?"

Dan looked at the large stack of ammunition and pursed his lips. "Give me one-twenty for everything and I'll throw in the harpoons and launcher."

Charles looked at Booker.

"Fine," the Brit said.

The supplier grinned. "As always, it's a pleasure doing business with you gents. Now go kick some ass and keep coming back." He saluted them as they loaded the Mule down with the ammunition and fuel.

The gathered crew buzzed with anticipation as they waited to file through the gate and into the Zoo.

"Prince said these things travel close to Wall One," Booker said, "that means we've got about forty klicks to go. I think he wants to go straight in and then figure it out from there."

The majority of the team was on foot. A team of four rode in the Oshkosh M1070 tractor-trailer that hauled the lowboy. Charles had winced when he saw the trailer. It would be slow going and would certainly rip up all the plants, which in turn would cause chaos. The BTR was the only other vehicle.

Booker drove a short distance away from those who were on-foot. It was their job to draw the attention of the animals but also to create a semi-clear path for the lowboy to follow. Prince had hoped this method of moving would be the fastest and most efficient way to travel through the Zoo with the large vehicle and trailer.

The team made it a few klicks in when the Zoo animals began to attack. The plan to draw most of the aggression to them seemed to be working.

"Fuck, those guys behind us are going to need some help. We can take it, but it looks like they're going to be struggling," Roo said.

The other team fought off the attacking green lizards and did their best to avoid the acid spit.

Reen heaved the top hatch open so she had a better visual on the creatures and opened fire with her M492.

"Aim for the sacs when they're expanded," Roo said as he hung out the side hatch and fired his VZ.58V.

The creature he aimed at whipped its head toward him. The bright-blue venom sacs under its chin and between its shoulder blades expanded and glowed as it prepped to spit. His rounds found the thinning skin and the sacs exploded. The creature's own venom melted through its hide and killed it.

"Fuck, yeah!" he yelled and dropped another.

The animals that attacked the M1070 abandoned it and converged on the BTR. They managed to kill six of the enemy before the creatures gave up and melted into the jungle.

The other mercenaries waved their thanks for the assist.

They drove deeper into the Zoo. The men on foot avoided much of the fighting as the animals seemed to direct their fury at the two vehicles. After traveling twenty klicks in, they halted for the night. Although they worked together, most of the teams remained separate. Prince walked around to each group, checking in.

"We should reach our goal tomorrow," he said. "You guys…and, uh, lady, ready?"

"Bring it on," Roo said.

"We have any casualties?" Booker asked.

The Nigerian shook his head. "A few close calls but the creatures really were concentrated on the vehicles. So, my plan is working."

"Where exactly are you expecting to find these things?" Charles asked.

"I'm hoping they maintain their pattern of sticking close to Wall One. They might be big fuckers, but they're surprisingly stealthy and hard to get a bead on."

"Think we'll actually make it?" Mick asked.

"You're new, so I'll cut you some slack. I'm not in the habit of failing, and I have no intention to start now." Prince walked away to the next group.

"I've got a good feeling about tomorrow," Roo said.

Lester rolled his eyes and Reen smirked.

"Really?" Mick asked.

"Sure. We're going to get through this and come out on top."

"Don't get too cocky," Booker warned.

"I'm not cocky, just confident."

No one bothered to correct him.

The next day had a quiet start and they made good time. The larger animals stayed away, so the run-ins were brief and non-threatening. Several packs of panthers attempted to attack but were no match for either vehicle and gave up quickly.

They were within three klicks of the Wall One when Booker halted the vehicle and killed the engine. A man stood in their way, waving his arms.

"What is it?" Roo asked through the side door.

"Prince wanted you to know that you should hang tight here. He thinks we're close enough and the gorgorexes should be in the area. The lowboy will join us, but Prince wants you to hang back until you're needed."

"Is he going to send someone to get us?" the Aussie asked.

The man shrugged. "Don't know. He sort of just said you'd know when to join the party. You know how Prince is. He likes to keep his cards close to his chest."

"Right. Well, thanks, mate. We'll camp out here."

The man nodded and jogged to the M1070. After speaking to the driver, he climbed onto the trailer and they drove into the jungle in the direction of the main group.

"I've always hated all the hurry-up-and-wait shit," Reen said and settled herself into a comfortable position.

"We're really going to just sit here and then supposedly be able to figure out when we should join the fight?" Lester said. "How the bloody hell are we supposed to know?"

Mick shrugged. "They're not far off. I imagine we'd be able to hear them."

"It's such bullshit that radio communications don't work in here," Lester said.

"Just how hard do you think this is going to be?" Reen asked.

Charles appeared in the main chamber of the BTR. "It'll be hard but it's not impossible." He attempted to stretch but was too tall for the space, then opened the upper hatch and climbed on top.

"The three of us managed to catch a three-headed beast —twice. So, with this many men and this much firepower, we should be able to do it."

"Three-headed?" Mick asked.

"It was a baby," the American said through the hatch.

Roo gestured rudely. "It still had three heads."

"Was it easy?"

"Well…no."

"The first one died on us," Charles clarified. "Quite literally, actually. It was some real nasty shit. All this puss and blood. We all got a wicked rash and had to stay out of the Zoo for ten days."

"No shit?"

"It wasn't fun," Charles said.

"Hopefully, this thing just has its size, claws, and teeth." Roo actually sounded a little optimistic.

"That isn't bad enough for you?" Lester asked.

The Aussie waved dismissively.

"What else do you think they could have?" Mick asked.

"Who knows? We still haven't run into a fire-breathing

animal, and I feel like it's just a matter of time. That would be pretty ball-busting, actually."

"Roo, stop borrowing trouble from the future," Charles cautioned.

"What? You scared, boy scout? What did I say yesterday, huh? I've got a good feeling about this."

His teammate shook his head and looked around. He didn't see any movement, which made him nervous. Even the plants seemed to have stopped moving. Dread washed over him. Something wasn't right.

He spun in a slow circle and studied the jungle that surrounded them. Every once in a while, in the distance, he could hear the other members of the team moving around.

Charles whipped his head to the right when he thought he saw movement. He caught a brief flash of black and brown in the underbrush, but in the next moment, it was gone. Nothing leapt from the trees or made a sound. For a brief second, he wondered if it was Thor. He really hoped the animal was still alive. Although, when he really thought about it, he knew it wasn't such a good idea. Wild animals who had lost their fear of men became the most dangerous maneaters. It was hard to think of Thor that way, but he had to be realistic.

He stretched and cracked his neck, itching to get the show on the road. His worry made him want to get the business over with. If he was going to die, he didn't want to put it off any longer than was necessary.

A huge roar, followed by the sound of rending metal, broke the silence. He readied his Remington and aimed it in the direction of the noise. Gunfire erupted, interspersed with men's screams.

More roars thundered so loudly they made his ears hurt. He didn't feel a strong desire to meet whatever made that rage-filled sound.

He dropped into the vehicle. "It's almost showtime."

"You think that's the gorgorex?" Roo asked.

Charles shrugged. "Whatever it is, it's not small. Don't think they'd complain if we swooped in and helped."

He sat in the commander's chair.

Mick climbed into the gunner's position, ready to put the Shipunov to good use. Roo positioned himself on the left-side of the vehicle, where the AGS-17 grenade launcher was affixed. He put the new barrel on and fed one of the drums of grenades into the weapon.

Booker started the engine and drove slowly toward the sound of the battle, while Lester and Reen kept a lookout.

The eardrum-splitting roars were once again followed by more crunching metal.

The Brit grimaced. "Something tells me the Oshkosh and lowboy are out of commission."

The ground beneath them trembled and the vehicle shuddered. Suddenly, a large, scaly beast raced past them and thumped into them as it ran. It was an iridescent black color with crimson spines all the way down its back.

"Holy shit," Charles said as the animal cut in front of them. "Gorgorex."

The mutant paused and looked at the BTR. It narrowed all six of its glowing orange eyes at them. Two rows of sharp teeth lined its massive jaws. The canines were easily eight inches long and milky-blue saliva dripped from its mouth.

"You think that's poisonous?" he asked.

"Most likely."

"Fun times."

It bellowed at them and spittle flew while its muscles coiled. The noise was deafening even in the BTR.

Charles thought it would charge them, but there was an answering roar and the creature ran ahead. Its massive hindlegs carried it at a startling speed.

A red flare rose above the canopy. "I think that's our cue," Booker said. He rammed the BTR into gear and they lurched toward the sound of the firefight.

They bulldozed through the trees and burst onto the scene. The M1070 lay in two pieces and the lowboy was twisted and cracked down the middle. Bodies littered the ground, and the survivors fired desperately at five gorgorexes.

The two adults were easily thirty feet long from head to tail. The adolescents weren't much smaller—each appeared to be between fifteen and twenty feet long. Their scales shimmered in the sunlight, which made it seem like waves of green and purple rippled through them. Their orange eyes glowed with menace.

The smallest of the monsters was the target. It had been wounded and one of its forelegs dangled by a few tendons. Blue blood dripped down its chest and pooled at its feet. Several men attempted to cast nets over it, but the creature dodged constantly and screamed all the while.

One of the adults lumbered forward, its head lowered, intent on skewering the attacking men. Rounds ricocheted off its skin.

"Mick!" Booker yelled.

The Aboriginal aimed the Shipunov and fired. The gun

roared and the shell burst from the barrel and struck the charging mutant on its side. It exploded and the animal toppled and shrieked in anger. Blood gushed from the wound where a chunk of flesh had been gouged out. The injury was deep enough that it seemed to have exploded one of the goop sacks inside. The bright blue, glowing goop oozed out with the blood.

The other adolescent monsters attacked. Their tails whipped menacingly and a man was unable to evade one fast enough. A spike from a gorgorex's tail pierced his body and his attacker simply snapped its tail out and his body catapulted into the jungle. The creatures didn't hesitate. They slashed through the mercenaries that tried to stand in their way. Their claws cut through flesh like the proverbial hot knife through butter.

Roo fired a few grenades. The explosions slowed the animals somewhat but they continued their assault while they dodged and wove to present more difficult targets. One stopped to bite onto an escaping human and its large teeth pierced his torso top and bottom. It shook its head viciously and the motion ripped the man in half.

Mick fired again at the adult he had wounded. Its scream was cut short when the shell struck its head and almost removed the lower half of its jaw. The mutant stood in shock with its lower jaw hanging from its head. Then, its glowing eyes rolled back into its skull and it collapsed with an earth-shaking thud.

The rest of Prince's team struggled to subdue the targeted gorgorex. It clawed and snapped at them. The bodies of a few men who had been cut by the creature's claws lay crumpled on the ground at odd angles. Their limbs were skewed like they'd convulsed, and blueish-green foam still bubbled from their open mouths.

Booker drove the BTR directly toward one of the aggressive mutants. "Come on, asshole, show me what you got." Neither yielded as the moment of impact hurtled closer.

"Brace!" Charles yelled.

Roo fired the grenade launcher and struck the animal a second before they collided. The explosion knocked it back a little before the BTR pounded into its chest. It screamed and closed its jaws on the barrel of the Shipunov.

The Brit shifted into a lower gear and pressed the accelerator to the floor. The engine whined and the wheels spun before the heavy vehicle lurched forward.

He stopped after they rolled over the gorgorex, aware that he needed to keep the adults within range of the Shipunov.

Charles launched himself from the commander's seat and snatched up the harpoon launcher. He looped the projectile's rope over his shoulder.

"Charles, what the fuck are you doing?" Reen yelled as he scrambled out.

He raced toward the struggle and fired his Remington at a six-legged panther that sprinted toward him. The buckshot shredded the beast and it fell.

Smaller Zoo animals had come to join the fight. He was sure there would be more soon, although he hoped they'd be able to put some distance between them and the gorgorexes by the time that happened.

Prince saw him coming and waved him over frantically. "We need to take this thing down!"

"Tie this to something heavy!" he yelled, loaded a harpoon into the launcher, and threw the end of the rope to him.

The Nigerian hastily secured it around the broken axle of the M1070.

Charles moved as close as he dared to the struggling gorgorex, planted his feet shoulder-width apart, and fired the weapon. The harpoon rocketed forward and the barbed end buried into the monster's shoulder. The animal jerked and shrieked and the rope went taught. The axle was yanked forward.

The American and several other men lunged at the rope and caught hold of it. They held the line taut while the beast struggled to free itself. Their combined efforts managed to anchor it a little and allowed the others to push closely enough to throw Prince's electrified nets over their quarry.

The Shipunov blasted again and struck the other adult who attempted to rescue the captured adolescent.

The shock of the electricity in the net brought the trapped gorgorex to the ground. Men rushed forward to secure it further. They taped its jaws shut and wound tape around its sharp claws, careful not to cut themselves.

Booker drove the BTR closer and forced the adult back. It roared defiance and Roo launched a grenade at it. The mutant swerved out of the way in time to avoid serious injury aside from a seared flank.

The adolescent the BTR had run over dragged itself up on wobbly legs. Reen grabbed one of the AK-47s and fired round after round to force it back. The gorgorex squealed plaintively and the adult responded with a scream. It whipped around and raced into the trees.

"Fuck! Where'd it go?" Mick yelled.

"I don't see it." Roo squinted into the vegetation in search of any sign of the monstrous creature.

"Eight o'clock!" Lester yelled and fired at the attacking gorgorex.

"It's going to ram into the side," Reen said. She slammed the side door Charles had left open.

The mutant swerved at the last second and turned toward the adolescent. The BTR rocked in its wake. The adult nudged the younger creature forward and they raced into the jungle and vanished quickly amongst the trees.

"Holy shit." Reen breathed raggedly. Then, she laughed. "That was fucking awesome."

They exited the BTR and surveyed the damage. Fifteen of the team remained alive, most of them barely injured. They looked haggard and avoided looking at the mutilated bodies that littered the ground.

Mick and Reen approached the dead adult. Its blood began to foam and hiss and blue-gray steam rolled off it. They didn't get too close since they didn't have protective masks and the steam was most likely poisonous.

"That is one nasty motherfucker," he said.

Roo joined them. "Nice shot, Mick."

The Aboriginal bowed. "Hold your applause."

Booker and Lester joined Charles and Prince, who examined the restrained gorgorex. It was injured but mostly intact. While it struggled continuously against the restraints, it couldn't free itself.

"Is that duct tape?" Lester asked and indicated the silver tape around the animal's jaws.

Prince nodded. "The stuff works wonders. These things have one nasty bite, but it seems their jaws work just like an alligator's. It can't open its mouth."

They turned and looked at the ruined lowboy. "How are we getting this thing back?" Charles asked.

Prince walked around the twisted trailer. He kicked one of the tires and it rolled away. "Huh." He turned to Booker. "Think the BTR has enough power to haul that thing?" He gestured toward the captive.

Booker shrugged. "Yeah. No problem."

"Okay. Here's what we're going to do. We're going to take pieces of this lowboy and make a sled. We can strap the gorgorex to it and then attach it to the BTR."

The men standing around looked blankly at him. "Get to it!" he yelled. "We don't want to stick around here for much longer."

The survivors made quick work of prying apart the badly damaged lowboy. Charles advised them on the best way to attach the cobbled-together sled to the BTR. Finally, they dragged the struggling creature onto it.

Although they were tired from the fight, they worked quickly, knowing the wrath of the Zoo would soon descend upon them.

"Why doesn't everyone climb onto the BTR?" Booker suggested. "It can handle it. And we'd make better time. We'd also have an advantage from up there to fend off an attack."

Prince climbed inside and sat in the commander's seat beside the Brit who drove down the path they'd bulldozed through the jungle. The foliage hadn't had time to recover completely so it was relatively easy, but dragging the gorgorex did slow them somewhat, even if the way was clear. The animal writhed and fought constantly and they had to stop every klick or so to retighten the bindings.

The first attack came five klicks away from Wall One. A pack of panthers and the wolf-like creatures attacked as a team. Machine guns coughed and the animals screamed.

"I think they're trying to break the ropes," Reen said and shot a panther in the head. The animals did seem to converge on the ropes that secured their prize to the sled. They bit and clawed at them when they passed.

Roo used the grenade launcher to clear a path forward, but he couldn't risk hitting the gorgorex or the ropes behind them. The others used their position from on top of the BTR to eliminate the attackers that tried to attack from the rear.

After six panthers and five wolves were dead and several more injured, the animals retreated.

The vines overhead snaked down and snatched at the men on top of the vehicle. One of them wound around a man's neck and yanked him into the canopy.

"Stop!" Roo yelled.

Booker braked so abruptly a couple of the passengers up top almost toppled off.

"What the fuck? Why are we stopping?" Prince yelled through the intercom.

"Someone was just taken into the canopy," Charles answered.

"We don't have fucking time for this!" he responded. "We have to keep going."

"We have to try to get him back," the American said.

They could hear the man's screams from the treetops but they couldn't see him.

"There's no time!" Prince repeated. "We're fucking moving on. He's a casualty. It's shitty, but it's how it's got to be." He turned toward Booker. "Move."

"But—"

"I said fucking move!"

The man's screams cut off abruptly and he bounced off branches during his descent and landed with a sickening thud.

"It's too late," Charles said. He jumped off the BTR, grasped the broken body by the belt, and with one arm, heaved it to the top of the BTR before he clambered after it.

"Okay, now you can go," he yelled and scowled at the Nigerian as if daring him to say something

Booker put the BTR into gear and the armored vehicle lurched forward.

"Can this go any faster?" Prince asked through gritted teeth, taking his anger at Charles out on the driver.

The Brit's fingers white-knuckled on the steering wheel. "I'm going as fast as I can hauling something. You nervous?"

His anger at Charles ignoring his orders turned off like a switch and he laughed. "I don't get nervous. Just thinking about getting the gorgorex back in one piece. If the worst-case scenario happens, we should be safe inside the BTR. At least long enough for the animals to calm the fuck down."

"What do you think will happen?"

"At the very least, we could lose the gorgorex. That would be a major pain in the ass and better not fucking happen. Worst case? We run out of ammo."

Booker drove faster. They couldn't afford to run out of ammo. If they did, they'd all be dead. The BTR could only offer shelter to a certain point.

Another wolf-mutant pack attacked. Charles killed two of them. At the back of the pack, amongst the frothing, giant beasts, he thought he saw black and brown fur. He tried to see if Thor really was amongst the attacking beasts, but they moved too fast.

Reen killed another of the wolves and the pack reeled away and vanished into the jungle. He looked for Thor's distinctive fur, but he didn't see him.

Even with the added weight and strain of dragging the large animal, the BTR made good time. With the fifteen extra fighters, the attacks were warded off, although ammunition among them was close to low levels.

"I'm out," a man said and strapped his AK-47 to his back. He moved into the belly of the BTR so those with firepower had better access and joined the other two who had run out.

"Booker, how much farther do we have?" Charles asked.

"Hold on for five klicks more, then we'll be in the clear."

Three blue Komodo dragons attacked. Lester dispatched one of them and another merc annihilated the other. The last dragon dropped back but didn't leave. It bit down onto the end of the sled and held on.

"Shit, we've gotta get this thing off our tail!" Roo said.

Charles moved to jump off but his teammate pulled him back. "Don't think so, cowboy. You've had your turn."

He leapt off and landed with a roll. By the time he was on his feet, the dragon was almost parallel to him.

Roo began to run. He aimed his Smith & Wesson .500 at the monster's head and fired.

It released the sled with a hiss and lunged toward him. The two collided and he slid his arm around the dragon's neck and hauled back. The beast's body bowed slightly before it rolled and forced him to release it. It pounced on him and he struggled under it while he tried to avoid being raked by its long claws. He pulled his knee up and managed to kick upward. The dragon twisted its body with a hiss and lunged to bring its teeth to bear. The movement was enough to allow him to press the barrel of his handgun into its scaly flesh. He fired twice and the animal slumped. With a muttered oath, he shoved it off and pushed to his feet.

The distance between him and the BTR widened and he sprinted after it.

Charles leaned off the back, caught hold of his team-mate's arm, and heaved his friend onto the relative safety of the BTR.

"You satisfied now?" he asked.

Roo grinned and pumped his fist. "Fuck, yeah. I'm killer-bad."

The American laughed.

They made it to the wall without losing another man. The gate opened and Booker drove slowly through.

"I have a vehicle waiting on the other side," Prince said, "to take the gorgorex to a buyer. When we get through, my people will unhook the sled from your vehicle. I'll meet up with you again when I've secured the payment."

"Remember, you don't get thirty percent from us," Booker reminded him.

He grimaced. "Right. I was hoping you'd forget about that."

"I don't forget things like that."

"No, you wouldn't."

The Nigerian's team set to work to drag the gorgorex onto a waiting lowboy the moment they were safely inside the Harvesters Camp. The weary survivors slid off the BTR.

"Congrats, gentlemen, the mission was successful!" Prince announced. "I'll be back in a few hours with the payment. Just think, you won't have to split it so many ways now." He laughed but no one joined him.

"Too soon, man," Mick muttered.

The man shrugged, saluted, and stepped into his waiting vehicle. They drove the captive away.

"I won't complain if that's the last time I see one of those things," a man said.

"That was a total shit show. I hope it's fucking worth all the lives we gave for it."

The group was quiet for a long moment.

"Hey," another of the remaining men said and broke the somber mood. "Meet up at the Wateringhole after we get paid? We can drink to the fallen."

"And if we get shit-faced, that won't be too bad either. We can drink to forget."

Everyone agreed.

CHAPTER TWENTY-SIX

The Zoo - Thor

Everything smelled like blood and sulfur. Thor watched the tail of the gorgorex as it struggled against being dragged behind the armored vehicle. The humans retreated and the animals gave chase, but he remained in the war-torn clearing.

Only half the gorgorex carcass remained. The Zoo was already reabsorbing its creation. It gave off the scent of rot and something else, something sweet and exciting. The smells made him angry. He was swamped by the urge to pursue the humans again and wanted to rip them apart.

But that was Charles out there, and the warring emotions confused him. Thor whined and sat.

He'd seen it all happen and he hadn't done anything. The humans came roaring in with their guns and grenades and had killed the animals. He had darted through the fighting and always avoided joining a side.

The truth was that he had wanted—still wanted—to join the fight against the humans, but he'd held back.

Charles was there, and he was still loyal to him. He recognized the man as his alpha. For some reason, he was testing him by leaving him behind. It was the only explanation. He had to remain strong.

But it was a little harder each day.

Thor watched vines twine around the black scaled body. He heard the popping of joints and cracking of bones as the body was compressed downward. The trapped gas and air burbled out of the collapsing corpse. The earth seemed to slurp the blood and goop that pooled around it.

The smell of the goop sparked something in his blood. The sweet scent promised so much. It wound around him and filled his senses until all he knew was its siren call.

Thor didn't notice the eight adult wolf-creatures that crept into the clearing. They approached him in a half-circle. Their fur was matted and the color of starless night. Their red eyes glowed. Their horns gleamed obsidian and twisted down their backs.

When he saw them, he stared as they crept forward. He wasn't sure what to do, but something in the back of his mind urged him to get closer to the ground. He tucked his tail between his legs and whined.

The largest of the wolves stepped forward, his head up and tail held high. He bared his teeth at Thor.

He dropped closer to the earth.

The other wolves yapped at him, their tails high.

The alpha stepped closer. His cold, wet snout poked at him. He breathed him in. Thor remained still.

The larger wolf moved away, sat, and looked expectantly at him.

Thor stood slowly, his tail still tucked. The other wolves sat and stared.

The alpha huffed out a breath and turned. He trotted into the jungle and the other seven followed him. Before he disappeared totally into the trees, the large mutant wolf turned and barked at Thor.

He could feel Charles sliding farther away from him, like only a thin tether held them together. Tentatively he sniffed the air but he could no longer smell Charles. The tether snapped.

Thor bounded toward the adult wolves and followed them into the jungle.

CHAPTER TWENTY-SEVEN

Harvesters Camp; The Wateringhole

The BOHICA team arrived at the bar, freshly showered and in clean clothing. They joined the remaining fourteen who had cleared the back quarter of the bar and shoved tables together so all of them could fit. There were already pitchers of beer on the table.

They walked up to the group and cheers erupted. Pints of frothing beer were shoved into their hands.

"Well, if it isn't the Black Cavalry," a man said as he pushed Charles into an empty chair.

"The Black Cavalry?" he asked and raised an eyebrow.

The man grinned and nodded so hard he spilled beer on his shirt. He didn't notice. "Yeah, that's what we've all decided to call you."

"What's your name?" he asked and still regarded the man with skepticism, wondering if he should be offended or not.

"I'm Liam, and your harpoon move saved my fucking

life." Liam stood again and raised his pint glass. "To the Black Cavalry!"

Cheers and whistles erupted down the length of the table.

Roo glowered at his teammate. "If you think I'm going to call you that, you've got another fucking thing coming to you, mate."

"I like it," Mick said and snort-laughed into his beer. "It fits you, Yank."

Charles groaned. "Please don't start calling me that."

"Has the party already started? And without me? For shame," Prince said as he breezed into the bar. He grinned at the table of mercenaries.

"Tell us what we got!" a man yelled.

"Yeah, let us know it wasn't all a waste."

"Gentlemen, please. When I promise a big payday, I deliver a big fucking payday. You know that. The capture of the gorgorex and delivery of its live body was a two-point-five-mil endeavor."

More cheers issued from around the table. Beer sloshed across the floor and the tabletop.

Roo, who had managed to chug two beers, was fired up by the atmosphere. He stood and brandished his glass. "To us, the fucking gods of the Zoo!"

The waitress brought fresh pitchers of beer, and glasses were quickly drained and re-filled. Reen bet Julio, the man who sat beside her, that she could chug more Jäger bombs in ten minutes than he could.

"You're on, princess."

"I wouldn't have called me that. Let's say we make it interesting. I win and you give me a hundred grand—and that nice little piece you're carrying," she said and nodded to the Colt Python he had strapped to his hip like an old-timey cowboy.

Julio narrowed his eyes at her. "And if I win?"

"If you win—which you won't—you'll get the satisfaction of knowing you're the only man to ever drink me under the table. And, of course, the hundred grand."

He grinned and put his hand out for her to shake, "You've got a deal, princess."

She frowned and tightened her grip on his hand. "Again, I don't think it's in your best interest to call me that." She released him and he shook the blood back into his fingers.

"Hey, babe," Reen said to the waitress, "how's about we get a few bottles of Jägermeister and some more beer. We're about to have ourselves a healthy competition."

The waitress winked at her. "You've got it."

"Oh," she said and stopped her from turning away, "and bring a bucket. Julio here is about to puke his guts up like a teenage girl drunk on wine coolers."

"Let me in on this," Roo said and squared his shoulders.

"Ah, the boy from down under wants to try to drink in the big leagues. Listen, Roo, maybe next time around. This competition here is for Julio. After I've beaten his ass, I can beat yours."

He glared. "Ah, bite me."

"Is that an invitation?" Reen asked with a wicked smile.

Roo sputtered into his beer.

Mick elbowed him. "Close your mouth, you bogan."

The group split into two camps—the Reen supporters and the Julio supporters. The other patrons gathered to see what the commotion was about. A waitress stood on each side, prepping the drinks.

"You ready, Julio?"

He jutted his chin out and reached for his first glass. "Fuck yeah."

"Booker, you mind timing us?"

The Brit grinned. "It'd be my honor. Now, on the count of three...three, two, one, drink!"

Reen chugged her drink and was onto her second by the time Julio finished his.

Someone wolf whistled. "Man, that chick can swallow!"

She gave him the finger and continued to drink.

Roo found the speaker and punched him in the face. No one bothered to help the other man as he toppled. The Aussie stood over him and said, "Watch your fucking trap, asshole. Didn't your mum teach you better?"

Mick started collecting bets on who would win.

Charles stood back and watched it all, his arms folded over his chest, and nursed his second beer. His thoughts drifted to Thor. He was certain he'd been there in the heart of the Zoo. He hoped so.

"What's wrong, Charles?" Booker asked, his words starting to slur.

"Nothing! I guess I'm just tired."

"Yeah, that mission was a fucking shit-show. But we made it out all right and got a bleddy fine chunk of change."

He nodded.

"This isn't about Thor, is it?" his teammate asked in a whisper—or what he thought was a whisper.

Charles sighed and gave him a long-suffering look.

"Shut up, Booker. You're drunk. Why don't you go make sure Roo doesn't knock all that guy's teeth out, yeah?"

The Brit looked over to where Roo sat on the chest of the man he'd punched. The merc struggled beneath him and he merely grinned, cocked his fist back, and prepared to hit the man again.

"Aw, shit." Booker stumbled over and hauled him off. "Calm the fuck down, Roo. This isn't a bleddy brawling party. God, you bleddy fucking gingers. A real pain in the arse."

Julio began to sweat and went a little cross-eyed. The men who'd placed bets on him looked a little nervous.

Reen simply laughed.

Charles worked his way around the crowd toward the door.

"Where d'ya think you're going?" Lester asked and stepped in his way.

"I'm going to turn in. This isn't my scene right now. I'm tired."

"You're just an uptight asshole, aren't you? Everyone thinks you're the fucking best, but you're bloody not. You're a grade-a twat."

He pushed the man out of the way and walked on.

"Yeah, walk away, you fucking pussy."

Charles pivoted, squared his shoulders, and drew himself up to his full height. His adversary took a step back.

"Think you've made a mistake?" he asked quietly.

Lester nodded. "Yeah. A mistake. Sweet dreams."

The American slipped out of the Wateringhole. A roar

of cheers followed him out and he assumed—correctly—that Julio had passed out and Reen was the winner.

He walked through the dark camp and welcomed the cold desert night. Perhaps it would help him to clear his head. He couldn't be so hung up on Thor. It would take him off his game and he knew he couldn't afford that. Distractions got a man killed.

In Fiddler's Green, he walked past the lockers they'd installed and noticed that Lester's was partially open.

"He must've forgotten to lock it in the rush," Charles said. "And now I'm talking to myself like a crazy person."

He went to close the locker but before he did so, he caught sight of something. After a hasty glance over his shoulder, he opened the door wider.

Nestled amongst Lester's folded shirts was Roo's Ari B'Lilah.

Charles grabbed the knife and inspected it. "Ah, fudge, this is definitely Roo's."

He thought about taking it but decided against it. Regretfully, he put it back where he'd found it, then closed and secured the locker.

"Looks like Lester's got to go."

CHAPTER TWENTY-EIGHT

Harvesters Camp; Fiddler's Green

It was midmorning and everyone but Charles was hungover. They slumped over the table and the mugs of extra-strong coffee he passed around.

Someone pounded on the door.

Roo groaned. "What the fuck is that? Is that someone knocking on the door, or is that really just my pounding headache?"

"You know what I've just decided? Australian accents are the fucking worst when you're hungover and it's the crack of dawn," Reen snarked.

For once, he actually chose to ignore the slight.

The person knocked again.

"Charles, answer the bleddy door already! Tell the wanker to go away and come back when it no longer tastes like I've had someone's gym sock in my mouth."

"Gross," Mick said. He cracked an egg into a tall glass of milk.

Lester wrinkled his nose.

"Works like a charm every time," the Aboriginal said with a shrug. He pinched his nose and chugged the milk, then gagged.

Charles opened the front door and a man in all black fatigues stood in front of him. The logo of a man holding the world was embroidered on his left shoulder. He scrutinized the American from under the brim of his black ballcap. The same logo was in the center of the cap with an "AC" in the globe the figure held.

"Can I help you?" Charles asked.

The man removed his cap to reveal his high-and-tight buzzcut. "Is this the BOHICA Company?" he asked. He looked around with cold, calculating eyes. The corner of his mouth twitched.

He didn't like how high and mighty the messenger was. "What can we do for you?" he asked, folded his arms, and drew himself to his full height.

"I'm from the Atlas Corp. In case you haven't heard of us, we're a multinational company that operates mostly in the US and UK-German Quarters. We've started a satellite office here." The man paused in his speech and looked at him expectantly.

He merely waited in silence.

The messenger cleared his throat. "Right. Well, some of the higher-ups caught wind of what your company has been doing. They were especially interested in your involvement in the retrieval of the Russian stealth machine, and the successful capture of the gorgorex. I've been sent here to see if your company was interested in contracting with Atlas."

Charles stepped back from blocking the doorway.

"Come on in. You can go ahead and wait right there." He pointed to the row of high-back wooden chairs they'd lined one side of the room with. "Let me get my guy who usually does all the job negotiations. I'll be back in two shakes."

The man stood beside the chair but he didn't sit.

The American took the stairs three at a time. "Booker!" he yelled.

Everyone groaned and winced.

"Now the giant decides to be loud," Mick mumbled.

"Where's the fucking fire? What the hell is it?" Booker asked, pinched the bridge of his nose, and squeezed his eyes shut.

"There's a messenger downstairs."

"A messenger? Well, what does he want? Why does he need me to deliver a message?"

"He's from the Atlas Corp."

Booker raised an eyebrow. "Atlas?"

"Some big-time company in the US and UK, or something like that. They've heard about us and are interested in maybe hiring us as private contractors."

The Brit stood so hastily his chair shot out from behind him. Then, he swayed and squeezed his eyes shut again as he drew deep breaths through his nose. "Jesus H. Christ. Why did this happen today?"

"You want me to go with him?" Charles asked.

"No, no. I'll go. I'm fine." He gulped down the rest of his coffee. "I'll be fine. You get the rest of them sobered up and ready."

Booker disappeared down the stairs.

"Ready for what?" Mick asked and jerked upright from where he'd been slumped, half-asleep on the table.

"Some big-time company might want to do business with us," Roo said. "I don't see the sense in getting ready right the fuck now. I mean, they might not have anything for us for a while."

"It's always good to be prepared," Charles said and poured more coffee. "Hey, Roo, can I…talk to you for a minute?"

His teammate scowled at him. "What do you want?"

"Can I…uh, speak with you…alone?"

"Are you two going to go make out in the corner? Can I watch?" Reen asked.

Roo threw her a scathing look. "Fuck off. Charles, why can't you just talk to me here?"

"It's important. Please."

"Fine."

He followed the big man into the room they'd converted into their armory.

"What is it?"

Charles looked at him and pursed his lips. He opened his mouth and closed it again. The plan had been to tell him about finding the knife in Lester's locker, but now that he was about to speak to him, he was chickening out.

"What the fuck is it, mate? Just spit it the hell out!"

"Do you think we should clean the weapons?" he blurted.

Roo stared at him. "Excuse me?"

"The weapons," he said, "do you think we should clean them? We were in such a rush last night that not everyone cleaned their weapons adequately."

"Is that a proposition, Charles? I know I'm devilishly handsome, but, Christ, you know I don't swing that way."

"What? No! That wasn't a euphemism."

"What the fuck, man? You drag me in here with all your fucking secrecy just to ask if I think the weapons should be goddamn cleaned? The hell, Charles? You couldn't've said that in front of everyone else?"

Charles shrugged. He decided he'd tell Booker first and they'd ease Roo into the news. He knew the Aussie would lose his shit when he found out Lester had definitely stolen his knife. Backup would be needed when that happened.

"Unbe-fucking-lievable." Roo jerked the gun cabinet open. He yanked weapons out while he muttered curses and shoved the rifles at his teammate. "Here. Fucking take these and have the others start on them if you're so concerned that they be cleaned. Jesus."

The American took the weapons into the other room and put them on the table.

"What is this?" Lester asked.

"They're AK-47s," Roo answered and dropped brushes, rags, and gun oil onto the table.

Lester thumped his palm on his leg. "No shit, dynamo. I mean, why are they on the table?"

"We're cleaning them," Charles said.

"We did it last night after we got back."

He picked up Lester's rifle, opened the breach, stuck his finger inside, and brought it out covered with dirt.

Reen sighed and reached for hers.

Almost an hour had passed before they were finished the task.

"Where the fuck is the wanker?" Mick asked. "How long does it take to say 'Hey, we're available for missions?'"

"He likes to think he's some big negotiator," Roo said. "The asshole's full of hot air and likes the sound of his stupid fucking Cornish accent."

"He'll be back soon," Charles said.

"How do you know?" Lester asked.

He shrugged.

Booker barreled up the stairs. "Everyone, get your shit together. We've gotta move."

"Why the fuck is everyone in such a hurry today?" Mick asked and rubbed his temples.

"I thought your hangover cure worked every time," Lester said.

Mick ignored him.

"Hey, Booker, can I talk to you a second?" Charles asked and grabbed his elbow before he could walk out of the room.

Booker shook him off. "Not now, Charles. We've got to go."

Reen gave Charles an odd look as she walked out of the room to gather her gear. "You good, Tillman?"

He gave her a half-smile and nodded. From the corner of his eye, he watched Lester open his locker and shut it quickly before anyone could see inside.

"Doesn't feel right not having my fucking knife," Roo muttered as he pushed past to grab the weapons that were still on the table. "I've got a bad feeling without it."

His friend grimaced but didn't say anything.

"Charles, what the hell? Why aren't you getting ready? We have to move out!" Booker yelled.

They arrived at the gate and the messenger was waiting for them, along with another man. The newcomer was older with defined lines in his leathery skin. He had three stripes on his sleeve and was clearly of higher rank.

He stared at them through his dark Oakley sunglasses. "This your team?" he asked. His accent gave him away as an American.

Booker nodded. "This is the BOHICA Warriors Company."

They stood in a loose line behind him. Reen and Charles waited at parade rest.

"You two Marines?" the man asked.

She nodded. "We were, sir."

He grunted. "That's all right. You ready for the mission? Heard you fellas were out late last night having a good time."

No one bothered to ask him how he knew that.

"We're ready, Carlton," Booker said.

The man frowned at the use of his name. "Very well. This is a simple fauna capture mission. We don't need the thing alive, but it has to be recently dead. No more than four hours. I've given your team leader the details but thought I'd stick around to size up the rest of you." He nudged the messenger. "Sam, give them the tablets."

Sam rushed forward and handed each of the team a small, thin tablet that looked more like a phone. They were sleek and black and no longer than six inches.

"What's this for?" Roo asked.

"The dissemination of information," Carlton said. "I

know you have a team leader, but this is the easiest way to ensure all members of a team have access to the information they need at any time. That's how we operate at Atlas. We make sure every cog on the machine knows what it's supposed to be doing."

He tapped the screen and the spinning Atlas logo appeared. Then, the image of a bird-like creature filled the screen. It was bright blue and black and resembled a cross between a marabou stork and a cassowary and had a long, thick beak that turned into a wicked looking casque. The body was a mass of bladed quills that masqueraded as feathers. It had two scaly legs that ended in a wide, three-toed foot, each toe tipped with a thick talon.

"That is the Carabou, and it's your objective. Bring us back one of those by the end of the day and we'll see what the next steps are," Carlton said.

"I thought caribou were those bloody great reindeer in Canada," Mick whispered to Reen.

"Those are two different animals, fuckwit," Reen said out of the corner of her mouth. "And he said Carabou not caribou."

"Sounds the same to me."

Sam handed Booker a shiny black disk, also with the Atlas logo on it. It was roughly the size of a coaster.

"You'll use that to capture the asset. Place the disk on any part of the animal and press the center of the logo to deploy," Carlton said.

"They sure like to put their logo on stuff. Is it a brag or a dibs thing?" Roo muttered to Charles.

His teammate elbowed him in the side.

The Atlas man pretended not to hear what he had said. Sam didn't try to hide his dirty look.

"We'll be waiting for you at sixteen-hundred hours," Carlton stated before he and his subordinate walked away.

Roo scanned through the details on the Carabou. "Well, it's omnivorous, but at least the wanker seems to only eat bugs and plants. Though, it's not comforting that it can crush your skull in its beak."

"Oh, look," Mick said, "it can kick you into next Wednesday and rip your stomach open with its talons. Sounds like a fucking good time."

"Charles, do you think you could rig the harpoon launcher to shoot a net, or should we make a quick stop at Dan's before we go in?" Booker asked.

Charles shrugged. "Don't see why it'd be a problem. It doesn't have to be exact, not if we're harpooning the thing. No need to spend more money. We're good to go."

"You're a regular black MacGyver," Reen said.

"I think I preferred the Black Cavalry."

"They're both shit," Roo said.

She smiled. "Ah, is someone jealous?"

"Get stuffed."

"Okay. We're wasting time. We want to instill confidence that we're the best, and we aren't doing that standing around arguing about nicknames," Booker said.

"Waiting on you now, mate," Mick said.

He turned to lead them through the walls. Charles brought up the rear and glanced from Roo to Lester. He wasn't sure he could hold onto the information for much longer. One of the reasons why he had stayed away from home for so long was because he had never been good at keeping secrets.

They were walking into the jungle when he grabbed Roo by the shoulder and hauled him back onto the sand.

"What the fuck, Charles?"

"I have to tell you something."

He looked warily at his teammate. "If this is one of those 'cleaning the rifles' situations again, I'm going to knee you in the bollocks."

"It's not," he said and moved away from Roo's reach. "You have to promise you won't blow a gasket."

"What the fuck? I can't promise anything, but now you sure as fuck have to tell me what's going on."

"I know where your knife is."

The Aussie grasped the front of Charles' shirt and twisted it bring him closer so they were face to face—or at least as close as they could be with the height difference. "What the ever-loving fuck, Charles? You have my knife?"

He shoved the shorter man away. "No. I don't have your knife, Roo. Fudge, you think I'd do that to you?"

"Then where is it?"

"You can't freak out."

"No promises."

"Maybe I should tell you after the mission. We need to focus. This is obviously a test."

"No shit. And there's no way on this fucked up earth I'm waiting for you to tell me after we get back out of this shithole. You're going to tell me where it is. Right. Fucking. Now."

"Lester has it," Charles said. He studied Roo, but the other man seemed frozen in place.

Blotchy redness crept up the back of his neck and he balled his hands into fists.

"That goddamn fucking wanker! I knew that fucking asswipe stole it!"

He launched himself into the jungle before his friend could stop him.

"I said don't freak out!" He ran after him.

Roo tackled Lester and the two men pounded into the ground. The Aussie landed a few solid punches to the man's jaw and nose before he was hauled off by Charles.

The big man held him in a full nelson. Using his height, he lifted him off the ground.

Lester struggled to his feet and shoved Booker's offered hand away. He wiped his mouth and spat a stream of blood to the ground. "What the actual fuck, man? What did I do?"

"You know what you fucking did," Roo growled and fought against Charles' hold but with little success. "You took my knife, you goddamn son of a bitch."

"I didn't take your bloody knife!"

"Yes, you did! Charles saw you with it."

Lester glared accusingly at Charles who stared back, unapologetic.

Booker pinched the bridge of his nose. "Fuck! We can't bleddy do this right now. It's a goddamn test and we're failing. I presented us as a well-oiled machine, and this here is a shit show. Roo, Charles is going to put you down and you absolutely will *not* attack Lester. Do you understand? You are going to put aside your differences and carry out the mission. We will deal with everything when the asset is secure and has been passed over to Atlas. Do I make myself clear?"

Roo spat at Lester and struggled harder. His teammate applied more pressure and he went slack.

"Do we understand one another?" the Brit asked and fixed the Aussie with a hard gaze.

"I can't believe you're siding with that asshole."

"I'm not siding with anybody. I'm trying to keep things together. We have a mission to complete. We'll get your knife back when we return to camp. Lester, can you be civil?"

"I'm always bloody civil."

"You know what I mean."

"Yes. Though I don't like being falsely accused of thievery."

"Lester!"

"God, okay. Yes. I'll be civil."

"Roo?"

He leveled a black look at Lester, then at Booker. "Fine. Now put me the fuck down, Charles."

Charles dropped him and he turned and shoved the big man away.

"Sorry," the American said. He ran his fingers through his short hair, then gripped the back of his neck.

"If anyone should be apologizing, it's that ugly bitch," Roo said.

"Roo! What the fuck did I just say?" Booker yelled.

"I'll be civil!"

The Brit stared at each of them in turn. "Are we going to be okay for the rest of the mission? We all need to be sharp. It's life or death in here, as you all know. We can't have contention. We all have to rely on each other when we're in here. That's the only way this works. Got it?"

They all nodded.

"Good. Now move the fuck out. No more bleddy stalling. We've got to find ourselves a fucking Carabou."

The map that Atlas uploaded onto the tablets was more detailed than anything Booker had seen to date.

"Of course, the technology is bleddy brilliant," he grumbled. According to the map, the Carabou territory was ten klicks in. It was an easy distance to cover and gave them time to maneuver if obtaining the creature was a struggle.

There was just enough information to describe it but there were details missing. He assumed they were intentionally removed to see how the team did with a limited amount of information.

"They're definitely holding out on us," Reen said from her position directly behind him.

"Yeah, I think so too. There's no way they don't know more about this animal."

"Exactly. Why wouldn't they tell us if it was solitary or a flocking animal? And I'm sure they know if it prefers to be on the ground or in the canopy."

"It's obviously a test."

"No shit, Sherlock. I'm just saying, what's the point in throttling info? This still seems like more than what we've had on previous missions."

"They're a mega company. Bigger than anything we've worked for or with before. They might not realize that missions are being run on far less intel."

She fell silent.

Booker increased the pace, driven by the need he felt to complete the mission as quickly and efficiently as possible. He needed Atlas to know why BOHICA had made a name for itself in the French Quarter. It was the opening they'd waited for, and he was ready for it.

The jungle around them grew denser and forced the team to slow. The canopy blocked out the sunlight.

Charles walked between Roo and Lester and used his body as a barrier between the two. The Aussie grumbled constantly and he periodically poked him in the back to remind him to be quiet.

"Stop fucking poking me, Charles." He hissed his aggravation.

"Then stop complaining to yourself."

Roo flipped him off.

Booker held his hand up in a fist and they halted and looked around to see why they had stopped.

"According to this map," he said, "we should be in the middle of the Carabou's territory. Charles, I think now is a good time to rig up the net."

Charles nodded and set to work weighting the ends of one of the nets they had with rocks.

Mick stood over him and watched. "How are you going to get it to close around the thing?"

"I'm not worried about that so much as getting it to generally fan out. It's obviously far from perfect. It'll do in a pinch, though. Can I see your parachute cord?"

He frowned. "What for?"

"I'm going to use it to pull the net shut."

"I don't have enough for that."

Charles raised an eyebrow.

Mick sighed and dug around in one of his pockets. He withdrew four long sections of parachute cord. "You're getting me new lengths when we get back, bunj."

"Of course."

"So," Reen said, "how do we find ourselves a Carabou?"

"Looks like they're making our job pretty easy. They have a soundbite of a Carabou mating call. We use this and one of the buggers will come to us."

"In theory," Lester said.

"Yeah, in theory. Everything's in bleddy theory in here."

Booker played the soundbite. A strange, low pulsing sound emitted from the tablet.

"I'll stay here with Charles and the net," Booker said. "Everyone else fan out and see if you can find anything."

"First person to spot the fucker gets to drive the BTR," Reen said.

The Brit pursed his lips. "I don't think so."

"Come on, Booker. You can't keep hogging the BTR."

"Watch me."

"I think that's a good idea," Charles said. "Last person to the showdown buys everyone beer."

"Fine," Booker said.

Reen and Mick high-fived.

Charles and Booker remained where they were but hid themselves next to a tree covered in vines. The others vanished into the jungle in search of their objective.

"Think anything nasty's going to climb out of here?" the American asked and cast a wary glance at the vines.

"It looks pretty benign right now."

"Let's hope it stays that way. I don't want to be hunting

some killer bird and worried about a vine trying to choke me out at the same time."

They hunkered down to wait. The soundbite droned on and the repetitive sound grated on their nerves. Half an hour passed before suddenly, a new sound answered from the thick vegetation.

The two men looked at one another.

Booker paused the mating call. After a few seconds, a low cry issued from the jungle. It was deeper and louder than the recorded call.

"Bingo," Charles whispered.

The Brit pressed play and the Carabou answered and moved closer to investigate. A few soft thuds confused the men for a moment before the large bird rushed forward. It stood at about a meter and a half tall and shivered, which made its quills rattle together.

Booker ended the mating call and the avian paused and cocked its head to the side. A bright pink tongue flicked out to taste the air. It clacked its bills together, the clicking sound surprisingly loud. It called out again and waited, then rattled its quills once more.

He was about to play the soundbite again when another Carabou answered. Charles' eyebrows rose.

The creature in front of them reacted to the other call with hostility. It spread its black wings and shook them violently. The sound of the quills grating together was tremendous and it screeched a warning.

The unseen mutant responded, its call filled with equal animosity.

The Brit played the mating call again. The Carabou's head whipped in their direction and it lowered its long neck until it was parallel to the ground. It clacked its beak and stalked forward.

The avian made it two steps before the second creature lurched out of the jungle. The sound of its quills was almost deafening, and its beak clacked in irritation. It barreled into the first bird and its talons swiped at the other's quills.

The first swung its long neck back and drove the sharp edge of its casque into the attacker. The two giant birds shrieked at one another as they grappled and fought.

They could tell the two birds apart only because the second had more blue on it than the first. The original Carabou was larger than the other, although not by much.

Their quills battered together in an endless series of piercing clatter. Their casques pounded together and the bone-on-bone noise made the hairs on the back of Booker's neck rise.

Charles prepared to shoot the harpoon gun at the warring creatures. The others used the fighting as a distraction to move in closer and surround the two combatants. They waited for the right moment to step in and capture one of the birds.

The larger mutant leapt on top of the other and managed to close its beak around its rival's neck. The neck snapped with a violent crunch from the force of its beak closing.

The winner shook the lifeless body, then dropped it and dug its talons into the corpse. It uttered a triumphant call.

Charles fired the harpoon. The barbed end of the projectile buried itself immediately under the bird's right wing. The net spread and the rocks prevented the edges from bunching. The Carabou screeched, stumbled back, and tried to claw at the harpoon and rip the net off at the same time.

The ungainly attempt gave Mick enough time to dart forward and grasp the end of the parachute cord Charles had woven through the ends of the net. He yanked hard and the mesh pressed in around the top half of the bird's body. Yellow blood bubbled from around the harpoon and dripped down its black quills.

"Watch out for its talons!" he warned and leaned out of the bird's reach while he maintained his hold on the end of the cord. Charles kept the net taut by tugging on the rope he'd attached to the harpoon.

The mutant clawed uselessly at the air and squawked in fury.

The BOHICA team moved in with their weapons aimed at the struggling bird.

"Someone, keep watch," Booker said.

Reen and Roo pulled back and turned toward the surrounding jungle.

"Should we kill it?" Mick asked. "They said it could be dead, right?"

"Yeah," the Brit said.

Lester fired his M5 at the bird's head. The round buried itself harmlessly in the dirt. "Shit."

Booker tried next, and his round cut into the Carabou's neck. Yellow blood gushed and it gurgled and twitched. Its struggles lessened a little, which allowed the humans to move in closer. Lester fired the kill shot into the head just below its casque and it slumped and stopped moving.

Charles moved forward while the others held their

guns trained on the bird in case it was simply playing dead. He yanked the harpoon from its chest.

"Well, there we go," he said. "Should we take the other one, too, or just the one?"

The Brit shook his head. "I don't know if we can carry both out. Besides, we only have the one disc thing." He retrieved the disc Carlton gave them, pressed it to the Carabou's body, and depressed the logo. A thin, black, net-like substance erupted from the center of it and wound itself around the shape of the creature before it contracted and sealed the bird in completely.

"Perfect," Booker said. "Now, let's bring this thing back and show Atlas what we're made of."

"How, exactly, do you propose we do that?" Reen asked. "It's not exactly small."

He looked at Charles.

The big man sighed. "I suppose you want to strap that thing to my back. I'm not a freaking mule, you know. Other people are perfectly capable of carrying stuff."

"Right. I know that. But it's big," he said. "We can't use Roo. The Carabou is taller than him."

"Fuck you."

"Fine," Charles said. "I'll carry the stupid thing back."

"Atta boy." Booker grinned at him.

He glowered and gave him the finger.

Atlas' containment net prevented the Carabou's blood from seeping out. It also prevented the quills from cutting through. They tied a rope through their net with the Carabou inside and strapped it to Charles' back. The rope secured it around his shoulders and middle like a ruck-sack's straps.

They set off in the direction of the gate. Lester constantly tried to bring up the rear, but the American wouldn't let him.

The Englishman knew they'd go back to the camp and find Roo's Ari B'Lilah in his locker. He knew he was about to be fired and needed a backup plan.

He studied the jungle around them as they marched back to the French Quarter. The American made no secret of the fact that he kept an eye on him, so he tried to be discreet. Then, he thought of the perfect solution and stopped.

Charles stopped too. "What is it?"

"I dropped my bloody knife."

"Your knife?"

"Yes! I accidentally dropped it," he said and patted his pockets. "It must've slipped out. Just let me drop back and get it. I'll only be gone a second."

The big man frowned. The others had stopped too and watched the interaction.

"You can't go back by yourself," Booker said.

Lester scowled. "Why not?"

"It's not safe. Besides, we can just get you another one."

"It would be so much work to get a new one. I had that throwing knife weighted perfectly. It's hard to find a good throwing knife anymore. I'll just be back in two shakes."

"Well, at least take Charles with you," Booker said.

"No!" he said, then cleared his throat. "No. That's okay. I can get it myself. I'm a grown-ass man. I don't need a babysitter. If you're so intent on waiting, just sit tight here and I'll be back." He turned and jogged back the way they had come before anyone could protest.

Once he thought he was out of sight, Lester stopped and turned sharp right. He ran in a crouched position and tried to be silent. After only a few moments, he found what he'd been looking for—a Pita plant, and a small one, at that. He had caught a glimpse of it moments before, although he hadn't been sure that it was one without getting closer.

He glanced furtively around to make sure no one had followed him, leaned down, and eased the small shrub from the soil. Carefully, he wrapped it in a handkerchief and tucked it into his pack. He looked around again.

"Zoo will go crazy my ass," he muttered. "What a bunch of twats."

He drew his throwing knife from the sheath at his ankle and rubbed it in the dirt.

Lester turned and jogged toward the others, who stood in the same place, waiting for him.

"Found it!" he said and held up the slightly dirty knife.

"Great," Booker said and resumed the march again. "Let's get back—"

A horrible roar rent the air. The canopy came alive with the shrieks of animals. The trees around them shuddered, bent toward the group, and attempted to attack them.

"What the fuck?" the Brit yelled.

"Go, go, go!" Charles said and pushed into a run, even with the added weight of the dead bird.

Two panthers leapt toward the group and yowled in anger. Their yellow eyes glowed brightly. More mutants appeared out of the jungle—a bear creature, two of the acid-spitting lizards, and another Carabou.

"Tighten up!" Booker yelled. "Back to back!"

"What the fuck happened?" Reen yelled and fired round after round at the oncoming animals.

The crazed creatures didn't care that they were wounded and simply continued the onslaught.

"We can't stay here! We've got to find a way to move," Charles yelled. His Remington roared and removed the head from the charging Carabou. Its body twitched at his feet and he could've sworn it looked like the corpse still tried to attack him.

They held a tight arrow formation, Booker spearheading them, as they pushed forward toward the gate. The plants wound around their ankles and tried to trip them and drag them down. Animals poured out of the underbrush amidst screams, howls, and roars.

They made slow progress. Roo went through one clip on his AK-47 and had almost finished his second. He paused to throw a grenade. It exploded and maimed a few panthers but the limbless animals still struggled forward and clawed their way along the ground.

"Jesus, it's like they're fucking possessed!"

"This was not how I wanted to fucking die!" Mick yelled and lobbed a grenade of his own. "I wanted to die in my sleep next to a woman half my age with big tits and a nice ass, not ripped to shreds by goddamn aliens!"

"You're not dead yet, Mick," Booker shouted.

Roo stumbled over the fallen body of a lizard. He caught himself before he landed in some of its acid and was still bent over when a six-legged panther leapt over him and sank its claws into Lester.

The man screamed as the monster's jaws closed over his shoulder and ripped his arm off. Roo fired and killed it, then took a step toward the wide-eyed Englishman. Another feline launched out of the foliage behind the man and the force of the impact hurled him to the jungle floor. Its teeth sank into his back and its claws raked his sides.

Roo fired at the creature, but his rounds didn't slow it at all. The other animals refocused and now channeled their ferocity toward Lester.

The team couldn't keep the mass of creatures away and they surged forward to drive a wedge between him and the others.

Charles dropped the Carabou from his back to focus on the fight at hand and to free himself to move better. His Remington thundered but barely made a dent in the frenzied animals.

Lester's screams were muffled but they could still hear him being ripped apart. Through the snarls and roars, there was the distinct crunch and snap of bone and the wet squidge of flesh being flayed.

"Don't hit Lester!" Booker yelled.

"Does anybody see him?" Charles asked and edged closer to the struggle.

"Help!" the man screamed. It was a distorted sound, muffled by bodies and his own blood.

They circled the surging creatures and kept others from joining the fray.

"Fuck! There are too many!" Reen yelled as she felled a Komodo dragon-like animal that tried to climb onto the heaving pile.

"We have to do something!"

"Do you think we could use a grenade?" Mick asked.

"Are there enough bodies on top of him to keep him mostly shielded?"

Charles loaded more shells into his shotgun. "I don't think so. We need to get eyes on him!"

"I see him!" Roo yelled. "He's on this side!" He was on the opposite side of the heap to Charles and Mick. Booker and Reen worked their way toward him.

Lester's head made a brief appearance. He looked at Roo with his one remaining eye and half his face had been torn off. "Kill me!" he pleaded. "Kill me!"

"We're going to get you out." The Aussie's expression was pale and grim.

Lester writhed and was dragged out of sight. He screamed louder than before. Several fights broke out amongst the monsters. Two panthers rolled from the pile and battled each other for a length of intestine. The tidbit snapped in half and the creatures left it in the dirt and attempted to push back into the battle. Booker killed them both.

A monkey shrieked in triumph and struggled from beneath the larger animals. Reen shot at it as it scampered up a tree. It had Lester's pack gripped tightly in its prehensile tail. The pack split open and she could see the contents. She caught a glimpse of the Pita plant Lester had pulled before the monkey disappeared into the canopy.

It was like a switch was flipped. The animals instantly darted away and dissolved into the jungle. The team fired at the retreating monsters.

"Hold your fire!" Booker yelled. "They're not attacking. We have to conserve ammunition."

A quiet settled on them as the tail of the last panther vanished.

"Jesus," the Brit whispered.

Lester's broken body lay in a large pool of blood. Both his arms and one of his legs were missing. His stomach was clawed open and entrails spilled out. He was twisted at an odd angle as if he'd tried to curl into the fetal position in the end. His flesh was scored by deep gouges and punctures from claws and teeth.

"Holy fuck," Roo said. "Holy shit. I didn't like the guy, but no one deserves that."

Charles stepped forward and leaned closer. He pressed two fingers to what remained of Lester's neck. He closed the man's remaining eye.

"There's no way he survived that," Mick said.

He shook his head. "Had to check. Just in case."

They stared at the dead man. Roo suddenly turned away and threw up.

"What the fuck was that?" Mick whispered.

"Should we try to bring him back?" the Aussie asked.

"We have to," Booker said. "I'm just not sure…how."

Charles returned to the dead Carabou and disengaged Atlas' net. He redeployed it around Lester's remains.

"Are we still taking this thing back to Atlas?" Charles asked.

Booker grimaced. "I think I have to. Lester died, maybe not for this exactly, but we can't let his death be in vain. We can give the money to his people or something."

"Did Lester have people?" Reen asked.

"Everybody has somebody."

The man's body was secured on Roo's back. They re-strapped the Carabou to Charles.

"I want out of this goddamn jungle," Mick said. He started toward the gate. The others trailed after him.

Reen grabbed Booker's arm. He glanced at her. "What?"

"In Lester's pack," she said, "he had a Pita plant. I saw it when the monkey took to the trees."

"Jesus," he muttered. "That's what happened. We fucking told him not to mess with them."

"Why do you think he did it?" Charles asked.

The Brit shook his head. "He knew we were going to have to fire him. He probably thought it was a good way to make enough money not to worry about going back to the UK."

They stumbled forward in a numb silence, Mick leading the way. A few howls sounded close by.

"Are you fucking kidding me?" The Aboriginal growled a protest and pushed into a jog. "Not today. I'm not going to fucking die today."

A lone wolf leapt out of the trees toward them. Charles put a slug in its head.

Booker surged to the front with Mick, then stopped the group. "How much ammo does everyone have?"

The American grimaced. "Not enough."

"Fuck."

"We've got to get out of here ASAP," Reen said.

"I think we're only three klicks from the gate. Can everyone run for that long?"

They all nodded.

"I can't fucking hear nodding," Booker snapped.

"Yes, sir!" they answered.

"Good. Now, we're going to make it out of the bleddy Zoo. Lester was an unfortunate casualty, but it was his own goddamn stupidity. We did what we could and that's what we have to live with. We're going to keep going and we're going to make it out."

"Yes, sir," they chorused again.

Booker nodded, his mouth pressed into a grim line. "Charles, you take up the rear. Now, move out. Weapons at the ready."

Charles saluted. He chambered more slugs and slid a new magazine into his AK-47.

They ran into the jungle toward the gate and scanned the foliage as they passed, ready for any attack.

CHAPTER TWENTY-NINE

The Zoo - Thor

Thor felt nothing but driving rage as he sprinted through the jungle alongside his pack. They snarled and howled as they ran. The fight called to them. The Pita plants called to them.

Faintly, under the Pita's distress signal, he smelled something familiar, but it was easy to shove that aside in the growing rage that had built within him.

They reached the scene of the fight. Dead bodies were already being covered by vines. The desperate need to tear something to pieces began to wear off. He smelled human blood and for a moment, fear flooded him. It was human blood, and he thought it was Charles'. His scent was thick in the area, but another sniff of the blood reassured him. It wasn't his human alpha's. The blood belonged to one of the others.

Thor smelled the air and picked up the trail the other people had taken. The pack smelled them too.

While the other animals had given up the fight, the

alpha howled and raced again through the trees after the humans.

As they pursued the group, excitement stirred in the pit of Thor's stomach. The smell of Charles grew stronger and he recognized Booker and Roo's scent too.

He sprinted after his pack, anxious for his two families to meet.

The pack came abreast of their prey but remained in the thick underbrush and ran past. They were intelligent and when they saw the dead animals, they knew the humans were dangerous. The alpha wanted to select where they would attack. Thor slowed, tempted to rush to Charles, but his leader howled and spurred them onward until they were positioned ahead of the humans' position. They lay in wait.

He sniffed again. Along with the smell of humans, there was something else. He didn't recognize the smell, but whatever it was made the hair on the nape of his neck rise. He looked around for the source until he found it.

The alpha chose the spot for a reason, and he wasn't the only one who recognized a good place for an ambush. There was an unnatural patch immediately ahead of where the pack crouched—a slight rise of the earth. Thor smelled danger and crept forward. The rest of his pack watched him but didn't prevent him from moving. The alpha growled a warning but that was all.

He approached the area. Suddenly, the patch of earth heaved upward, and a giant spider-like creature leapt forward, its iridescent fangs dripping with poison and ready to strike. Only his reflexes saved him, and barely. He yelped and dodged the assault. The creature stopped as if afraid to get too far from its hole, then darted back. A moment later, the door closed and left the ground as it was before.

In the distance, Thor could hear the humans approach. The alpha—and the spider-thing—had chosen wisely. The humans would pass through and be easy prey.

Thor was a creature of the pack, the social imperatives embedded in his psyche. His first alpha was Charles, and that would never change. He knew that the man was in danger.

He darted to the side, then circled the trap. The door was hinged to give the monster about three hundred degrees of access. He approached quietly from the masked sixty degrees.

While he could move quietly, he still massed a hundred kilos, and the ground trembled enough for the spider-thing to sense him. It darted out of the hole, but away from Thor. That split second before it could fully emerge and turn was the edge he needed. He pounced and sank his fangs in behind its head.

The monster tried to twist and its red-and-black legs scrambled for purchase to pull itself—and Thor—into its hole. He attempted to plant his feet, but his adversary was too big and too strong. Slowly but surely, step by step, the spider pulled and yanked its way back into the hole while he held on for dear life. Its fangs dripped with poison and clacked when it tried to bite him. It came close to one paw, which he barely managed to yank out of the way, but in doing so, he lost more purchase. With a final heave, the spider managed to pull his head into the hole. Now, eighteen legs dug into the side of the tunnel, while his four legs struggled against the larger creature.

He knew this was a losing proposition. This was the spider's home, and it had the advantage. He had to do something. Instead of pulling back, he released his hold long enough to push forward and sank his canines into the connection between the creature's cephalothorax and abdomen. Putrid blood filled his mouth.

The spider squealed and six of the forelegs tried to push him off. But Thor did not intend to give up. The more the legs pushed, the more the creature's body tore.

Whether in confusion or in fear, the monster reversed its direction and instead of trying to sink farther into the hole, it pushed its way out. He was taken by surprise and couldn't stop it. The two, still locked in a deadly embrace, tumbled out onto the jungle floor.

The spider began to shoot silk in all directions, but Thor was too close and the spinarets couldn't find their target. With a last heave, it broke free and tried to skitter away. That was its mistake. It outweighed its attacker by three hundred kilos, and now that he had lost his grip, it could have immobilized him with its silk for the kill.

A smart Thor would have broken the fight and scrambled for freedom, but his fighting rage was in full force and all he could think of was Charles heading into a trap. He launched at the spider and thrust through the tangle of legs to land on its cephalothorax and flatten it for a moment. As it struggled to stand, he bit down. His canines cracked the exoskeleton and severed the connection between its head and the rest of its body.

The mutant convulsed twice and died and the legs slowly curled in. Thor held on, afraid to let go.

The pack had silently watched the fight. Now, the alpha gave a single yelp, and Thor realized the humans were almost upon them. The wolf mutants began to spread out, ready for them.

They ghosted through the trees and he watched them for a moment. He hadn't fought the spider only to watch his new pack attack his old one. With a low growl, he marched stiff-legged to the alpha, ready to challenge the larger animal.

The leader paused and turned to look at him.

He continued his approach, still growling. His hackles rose and his eyes glowed bright crimson.

The leader snarled, lunged, and brought his horns down toward Thor. The younger wolf scrambled away and tilted his head down so his own horns met his adversary's. The impact was bone-rattling and he collapsed under the larger wolf's attack. The alpha growled and bared his teeth but didn't attack further. He didn't have to and had easily proved he was still the alpha.

That didn't mean he wanted to kill the young pup. He stood over Thor for a long moment, then spun and left him there. His sharp bark was one of command before he vanished into the jungle. The rest of the pack followed him.

Thor stood trembling in the clearing. He waited for the pack to return, but they didn't.

The sounds of the humans moved closer and he glanced in their direction. He limped out of sight and hid himself under a fern.

CHAPTER THIRTY

The Zoo

"What the fuck is that noise?" Roo asked. Horrible howls drifted through the jungle ahead of them.

"Sounds like a fight," Mick said.

Booker slowed the pace.

The sounds quieted, but the team still proceeded with caution until they reached a small clearing. A giant spider curled in the center of it, its yellow blood soaking into the ground. The hole it had come from gaped black and empty at them.

"Aw, fuck no. Nope. What did I tell you? I said no giant spiders. What the fuck is that thing?" Mick hissed in horror and recoiled.

"Relax, you pussy," Reen said. "It's dead."

"I don't give a fuck if it's dead or not. Christ! There are probably more of the buggers lying in wait around here." He turned in a circle and inspected the ground for any more trapdoors.

"Relax, Mick. The big, bad spider can't hurt you," Roo said.

"Fuck you."

"Can you tell what killed it?" Booker asked.

Mick swallowed and shook his head. He set his jaw and looked around at the surrounding jungle.

The Brit moved closer to the dead creature. He studied its large, green fangs and the blue poison that still dripped from them.

"Reen?"

"Yeah?"

"You got any sample containers in your pack?"

"Sure," she said. "What do you need them for?"

"See if you can get some of that poison or whatever it is into a sample container."

"I'm on it." She shrugged her pack off and retrieved a receptacle. Careful not to touch the poison, she held it below one of the spider's fangs and let the poison drip into it.

"Looks like dingo tracks," Mick said and toed a paw print in the soft earth. "A big fucking dingo." He frowned and looked at the body of the spider. "Though it couldn't have been that big. Look, the spider must've been three times the size of whatever killed it. Those puncture wounds aren't that deep. Must've been a fucking determined little bugger."

He walked around the dead mutant and dared to get a little closer.

Roo and Charles kept a watch on the perimeter.

Mick leaned in and grabbed a tuft of black and brown

fur that had been snagged on one of the spider's claws. He shrugged and tossed it aside.

Charles looked at the fur and his stomach lurched. His heart rate accelerated. He recognized the fur—it had to be Thor.

Reen stood and snapped the container shut. "I think that's all I can get without touching it—which I'm not going to do."

"Wasn't going to ask you to," Booker said. "All right. Let's keep moving we're nearly there."

The others followed him out of the clearing. Charles was about to follow too when he spotted something. He turned and saw a pair of glowing red eyes staring at him from beneath a fern.

"Thor?" he whispered.

The eyes blinked.

He glanced around and could barely see Reen's retreating back before he looked at the dead spider again. He knew, then, that Thor was the one who killed it. And he was sure he'd done it to save them.

Charles stumbled and searched the undergrowth for him. And there he was. Two red eyes stared at him from under a giant fern.

He opened his mouth to call him but shut it. No matter how much he wanted to reunite with Thor, no matter how much he missed him, nothing had changed, and he couldn't take him back to camp with him. He might've saved their lives—or at the very least prevented serious injury. That still didn't change the fact that he'd killed a human being in the Harvesters Camp, and no one else would forgive that.

It was pure selfishness for him to even consider it. Thor

was a wild animal, a Zoo animal, and he'd be happiest—
and safest—in the jungle with his own kind. Still, maybe he
could manage to spend time inside the Zoo with him, even
for only a short while?

His heart plummeted and his stomach churned. He
knew what was best for Thor, no matter how much it hurt.
Charles whispered, "Thanks, Thor. I don't know how, but
I'll figure out something," before he turned and ran to
catch up with the BOHICA team.

EPILOGUE

The Zoo - Thor

Thor stared at the place where Charles ran into the woods and whimpered. He didn't understand what had happened. The man had seen him. He was sure of it. They'd made eye contact. He'd said his name, and he'd expected him to call him. Thor was ready to spring into Charles' arms. He was ready to go back to the land of the humans. He wanted to sleep on his cot and play fetch with the old tire.

But Charles hadn't called for him. The man had left him and run after his team.

Thor sat and waited. Maybe he would return. There was still a chance he'd come back.

His side ached. The spider's carcass melted into the Zoo. Still, Charles didn't return.

Not far off, he heard the familiar sound of the alpha's call. The larger wolf should have killed him, but he was still alive.

Charles wasn't coming back. Thor stood, cocked his head, and listened for the call.

It came again.

He turned and raced into the jungle to join his pack.

My first author notes! I'm ex-Army, ex-Marine, ex-married, now living my retirement in Thailand.

I'm a proud whale reader, constantly in a book, and I wanted to see if I could write a novel. They say write what you know, so I wrote BECOMING A MAN IN THAILAND. The book contains some adult nightlife scenes, and the Thai government doesn't always take kindly to that, so to protect my retirement visa, I chose a pen name.

I'm also a beta reader for several other authors including for Jonathon who I met in the VFW. That opened up the chance for me to write with Michael Anderle and Jonathon in THE BOHICA CHRONICLES. It's been heaps of fun, and I want to thank Michael and Jonathon for the opportunity.

C. J. Fawcett

I'm Jonathan Brazee, a retired Marine infantry colonel and full-time writer. *Degenerates* is the second book in the BOHICA Chronicles is Michael Anderle's Zoo Universe. Michael is a good friend of mine, and while eating tacos at Sabor in North Las Vegas one afternoon, he invited me aboard the Zoo. It sounded like a lot of fun, and after another dinner a few months later, we put together *Reprobates.*

We hashed out a Zoo story with emphasis on military characters. Michael and I came up with the concept, I wrote the beats, and C. J. Fawcett did most of the heavy lifting with me editing and rewriting some passages.

I write military, military science fiction, and military paranormal, and these two books, along with the third that will be soon released, were a fun departure for me. I hope you had just as good a time reading in as I had in the writing of it.

If you liked *Reprobates* and *Degenerates*, I invite you to try out some of my other works. My best-selling Recruit is the first book in an eight-book series in my United Federation Marine Corps series, and there are three follow-on series in the same universe. You can find Recruit here: http://mybook.to/recruit .

For more about me, my family (my wife and I just had twin girls in January), and my books, you can find my website at http://jonathanbrazee.com.

Or, you can see my author FB page at https://www.facebook.com/jonathanbrazeeauthor/ .

If you'd like to join my mailing list, you can sign up at http://eepurl.com/bnFSHH .

Thanks for giving *Degenerates* read.

Jonathan
North Las Vegas, 2019

CONNECT WITH THE AUTHORS

Jonathan Brazee Social
Website:
http://jonathanbrazee.com/

Email List:
http://eepurl.com/bnFSHH

Facebook Here:
https://www.facebook.com/jonathanbrazeeauthor/

Michael Anderle Social
Website:
http://lmbpn.com

Email List:
http://lmbpn.com/email/
Facebook Here:
https://www.facebook.com/OriceranUniverse/
https://www.
facebook.com/TheKurtherianGambitBooks/
https://www.facebook.com/groups/
320172985053521/ (Protected by the Damned Facebook
Group)